New Beginnings

by

Olivia Claire High

New Beginnings
Olivia Claire High

Fireside Publications
Oxford, FL 34484
www.firesidepubs.com

Printed in the United States of America

Copyright © 2016 by Olivia Claire High

ISBN: 978-1-935517-37-5

For additional copies of this book, please visit:
http://firesidepubs.com or
www.amazon.com

OR
Contact the author at:
Joeclaire2424@comcast.net

Prologue

A summer storm blew in during the night echoing down the mountainside slamming against the gray stone mansion and blanketing the ground with pelting rain. Flashes of lightening forked across the sky slicing through thick black clouds momentarily illuminating the darkness.

The unmistakable sound of human wailing inside the house blended eerily with the harsh noise of thunder. Voices called out. Running feet raced through hallways. A woman rushed headlong, stumbling in her haste to flee until she reached a large window. Her hands pulled frantically at the iron bars that blocked her way to freedom. She dared an anxious glance over her shoulder and screamed at the sight of the frightening apparition coming toward her.

Collapsing to her knees, she lay there trembling in terror awaiting her fate.

Dedication

To my husband, Joe,
The best in all the world,'
I Love You,
Always!

Chapter One

Holland Wallace surveyed the mansion in front of her and wrinkled her nose in distaste. Partially shrouded within the shadows of several towering trees, the gray stone walls looked cold and gloomy despite the bright sunny day. The place was larger than she'd imagined with its seemingly endless additions. Was it a haven of peace or a house of horror? Town gossips called it the Devil's Domain and claimed the matriarch Marguerite Howard was kept prisoner here by her three grown sons since her husband's death years ago.

Holland recently arrived to help care for her aunt, May Tyler after hip surgery. This small town tucked away in the mountains of northern California was a direct antithesis from the large urban area where she lived further south. Her Uncle Leo encouraged her to take a drive today while May napped. He gave Holland directions when she mentioned being curious to see this house, especially after he said the inhabitants used golf carts to get around inside.

The mansion dominated the area literally dwarfing every other residence. But size didn't necessarily equal beauty in her mind. She decided not to spend any more time staring at this pile of stones when there was prettier scenery to explore.

Holland was about to walk back to her car when a large black SUV drove up and stopped. The tinted window on the driver's side rolled down just enough to reveal a thick thatch of bronze colored hair and sharp looking dark eyes.

"Why are you standing out here?" a man's deep voice asked from within.

"Excuse me?"

"I asked why you were out here. Didn't you ring the buzzer next to the gate?"

"Buzzer?" Holland looked around, confused at this unexpected greeting.

"Yes, unless you plan on scaling the fence," he quipped before pressing a remote inside the car causing the heavy wrought iron gate to rumble open.

"Follow me. I'm sure they're waiting for you inside."

"You've made a . . ." she didn't get to explain his error before he drove through the opening.

He'd obviously mistaken her for someone else. Holland decided she'd better tell him. She ran to her small sedan and drove up the long asphalt driveway. She watched the man climb out of his car and stride quickly to the house. Inches over six feet, he was built like an athlete and moved just as one might expect of a man in peak physical condition. His features were rugged enough to save him from being what Holland would've called pretty boy handsome.

She scrambled out of her car when she realized he was waiting.

"Listen, I'm not . . ."

New Beginnings
Olivia Claire High

"We'll talk inside," he said and opened the massive front door, motioning for her to enter.

Holland couldn't think of what else to do, short of shouting for him to stop, so she stepped inside the wide foyer. Candle wax, furniture polish, and the scent of fresh roses in a vase on a nearby table mingled with the telltale stale air of a house closed up for too long.

He shut the door.

"I assume my brother hired you. What is your name?"

"Holland Wallace," she mumbled, suddenly distracted by the elegant chandelier. "That chandelier is absolutely gorgeous. Is it an antique Murano?"

"Yes. You know antiques?"

"Kind of."

"Did you say your name is Holland, as in the country?"

She pulled her attention back to him and nodded. "My dad's a geography buff. My sister's name is France and my brother's is Scotland."

"You're joking."

"No. I leave that to others. Mr. Howard, I need to tell you . . ."

"Gage Langdon," he corrected. "I didn't mean to be disrespectful about your name."

"That's okay. I'm used to the comments. I thought the Howards lived here."

"They do. Jamison Howard, Sr. was my step-father."

She was about to explain he wasn't the only one mistaking a person's identity when the door on

3

the right opened and a middle aged woman burst into the foyer. Her plump cheeks were flushed and wisps of graying hair hung loosely from an untidy bun. She gave Holland a brief look before zeroing in on Gage.

"I'm sorry to bother you Mr. Langdon, but I'm at my wits end," she said raising her voice over the sounds of the infant cries coming from the tiny wrapped bundle she jiggled in her arms. "Little Jamie won't stop crying no matter what I do. I've no experience with babies, you see."

"It's all right, Colleen. It's probably his usual problem. The new nanny will take over now."

Nanny? Holland nearly jumped back when Gage suddenly thrust the crying infant into her arms allowing a very relieved looking Colleen to scurry away. Holland realized he must think she was the person they'd hired. She was about to hand the baby back when his legs drew up and a loud gurgling sound erupted from his stomach.

"Whatever his mommy ate before she nursed him must not have agreed with him."

"His mother isn't nursing him. He's been on a formula since birth, but we've not found one that he can tolerate yet. The pediatrician just gave us the names of a couple different ones to try. We had them delivered this morning. It'll be your job to try them out."

Holland opened her mouth once again to stop her unintended charade when the baby let out another piteous wail. Tiny fists waved in the air and his face looked pinched with obvious pain.

"He's really worked himself up. Rocking might help to calm him."

"There's a rocking chair in the nursery. I'll take you there."

"It might be better if his mother rocked him because he's used to her," Holland said, hoping to hand the baby over before she became anymore involved in the situation.

"She won't be rocking him."

The mother didn't nurse her baby and she didn't rock him. Was she ill? Or heaven forbid, had she died in childbirth? The thought of such a tragedy made Holland clutch the baby to her. She didn't know the unfortunate woman, but that didn't mean she couldn't grieve for the loss.

The baby's crying seemed to echo his own kind of grief. "Okay. Where's the nursery?"

Gage led her down a series of long hallways carpeted in dark colors and gray walls. He stopped at a door and pushed it open. Holland smiled when she saw pale blue walls decorated with framed pictures of baby animals. At least this room didn't remind her of a cave. She crossed the room to the rocking chair feeling her shoes sink into the thick blue carpet.

Holland settled herself onto the plush cushions and pressed the baby to her. She began to hum to him keeping her voice low in a steady drone. He stiffened and fought her attempts to soothe him until he finally closed his eyes. Gage watched from the doorway.

"He's never calmed down so quickly. He usually falls asleep from sheer exhaustion."

"Poor little guy."

"You've made a good start. I'll show you to your room when you've put him down." She shook her head making Gage frown at her. "I'll send someone to your car for your things right now if you that's what's bothering you."

"You don't understand. I'm not . . ."

"Who the hell is she and what's she doing in here?"

Holland suddenly felt the weight of being in the wrong place at the wrong time. A young man walked into the room bristling with obvious temper while she laid the baby in a cradle.

"You'll have to forgive the display of poor manners. Holland Wallace, meet my brother, Jamison Howard, Junior, better known as James. He's Jamie's father. This is the new nanny."

"Like hell she is." James motioned to an older woman hovering in the hall. "This is Mrs. Armstead, the one I hired. Jamie's my son in case you've forgotten."

Holland decided to intervene before tempers got out of control. It was time for her to make her retreat, anyway. "Why don't we go into the hallway, so we don't wake the baby?"

"Yes, why don't we?" Gage replied in a chilly voice.

She cringed inwardly at his accusing glare, but forced herself to face him as soon as they stood outside the room, reminding herself not to feel guilty for his mistake.

"I've been trying to tell you ever since you first saw me outside, but you never gave me a chance.

I'm visiting my uncle and aunt. They own the minimart and gas station in town. I heard about your house from them and was curious to see it. That's all. I'm sorry things went this far."

James stared at Gage.

"You let a stranger in the house without bothering to check who she is? How could you be so careless? I left word I'd gone to get the new nanny."

"Which I obviously didn't know about; why don't you show Mrs. Armstead to her quarters while I escort this impostor to her car?"

James shot one last scathing look at Holland, took the bewildered looking Mrs. Armstead by the elbow, and steered her back to the nursery.

Holland treated Gage to her own glare. "I may not be the nanny, but I'm not an impostor. It's not my fault you jumped to the wrong conclusion. But I'm not going to apologize for rocking that baby to sleep. Now excuse me while I show myself out."

She turned and started to stomp away, but his voice stopped her.

"You can't do that."

"Here's a newsflash for you, Mr. Langdon . . . oh yes I can."

"Not if you continue in that direction. It leads to a dead end." He pointed behind him.

"That's the way out."

Holland ground her teeth in frustration.

"You should post exit signs. A person needs a compass to find their way around this fortress."

"You're calling my home a fortress?"

"What else? You have bars on the windows, for crying out loud."

"To deter burglars from getting inside."

"Or to keep someone from trying to get out," she murmured under her breath.

"What did you say?"

"Nothing." She followed him to the front door and offered another apology.

"You may not have been guilty of trying to pose as the nanny, but you were trespassing."

"Well, I would have called for permission first, but your number is probably unlisted. I told you I was curious. Your house and family generate a great deal of gossip around here."

"Hardly an enviable distinction."

"What do you expect when you build a place like this?"

"I expect people to mind their own business."

"I'd say it's too late for that." She brought her anger under control. "Your nephew sounds like he's having digestive issues."

"You're right. How is it you know so much about babies if you're not a nanny? Do you have children?"

Her hesitation was so brief as to be almost unnoticeable. "No, but I've taken care of my nieces and nephews a lot. I'm sorry about Jamie's mother," she added on impulse.

Gage gave her a guarded look.

"What do you know about her?"

"Nothing. I just assumed she may be ill or may have even died."

"You assumed wrong."

He opened the front door.

"Goodbye, Ms. Wallace. I suggest you heed the no trespassing signs should you decide to wander this way again."

"You couldn't pay me to come back." she snapped, anger rising to the surface again.

She marched outside staring over her shoulder as she went. Gage stood in the doorway watching her with his arms crossed over his chest looking every bit like an alpha male guarding his territory. His demeanor irked her, but Holland reminded herself it had nothing to do with her if he wanted to protect whatever was going on inside those somber walls.

A sudden peculiar feeling that other eyes were observing her departure made Holland quicken her pace. She jumped into her car and sped down the driveway in her haste to leave.

May's eyes sparkled with anticipation, as soon as she found out Holland had been inside the mansion.

"What was it like? Are there specks of real gold in the ceilings? Are the walls covered in silk? Did you see Mrs. Howard? Come on honey, tell us."

"Give the girl a chance to have her tea," Leo admonished his wife.

Holland took a sip. "No gold and silk." She didn't miss her aunt's disappointed expression and hastened to add. "But the foyer has a fantastic Murano chandelier, lovely hand carved molding, and a beautiful parquet floor. I didn't see Mrs. Howard."

"Probably locked in her room. What about the rest of the house? You said you went to the nursery. You must have noticed other rooms on your way there," May pressed, hungry for more.

"We went through a maze of empty hallways. I needed help to find my way back out. I insulted Mr. Langdon when I called the house a fortress, but it sure felt like one."

"Gage Langdon, old man Howard's stepson," Leo said. "I hear tell he's a financial genius. Apparently the younger brothers have to answer to him for money and they don't like it."

"I got a sense of that tension when James Howard thought his brother interfered with hiring the nanny. What's wrong with the baby's mother? I thought something awful must be the matter by the way Mr. Langdon talked. But he practically bit my head off when I offered sympathy."

May's eyes widened. "Hmm, could be another mystery. I wonder if she's being kept a prisoner like the elder Mrs. Howard. Maybe they won't even allow her to see her own baby."

"Now May, don't go firing up that imagination of yours. The woman could be ill."

"Or just not interested. A fancy piece like her didn't strike me as the motherly type."

"You've seen her?" Holland asked.

"Once, getting out of a car in town. Pretty little thing and young with a cloud of blonde hair and a diamond wedding ring that must have cost the earth. Word is Gage was her lover before she ended up with the younger brother. Makes you wonder who fathered that baby of hers."

New Beginnings
Olivia Claire High

"You shouldn't be saying that. It's one thing to speculate about the house, but talking about personal relationships is getting into dangerous territory," Leo warned.

"You saw the two brothers, Holly. Who did the baby look like?"

Holland reached for a cookie and shrugged. "Like a baby."

She thought it best not to mention that Jamie's hair was the same color as his Uncle Gage's.

James pointed an accusing finger at Gage. "I still can't believe you let that woman in here."

"I never intended to let her wander without strict instructions on where she'd be allowed to go. The next time you hire a nanny be sure I have word when she's supposed to arrive."

"I'm sorry about the mix up; but even so, that woman could have disturbed Kim."

"If you ask me, your wife might be better off if someone did disturb her," Jonathan put in.

"You shut up about my wife!"

"Enough," Gage held up his hand. "Your wife wasn't in any danger."

"What about Mom? Did you stop to think how she would react to a stranger in the house?"

"I never stop thinking about how our mother will react to anything, which brings me to the point of this meeting. I want you to introduce her to Mrs. Armstead as soon as possible."

"If the woman stays," Jonathan reminded them.

"It's not my fault the others wanted to leave. No one else in the house heard or saw anything out of the ordinary except the screaming women. I hope Mrs. Armstead is made of sterner stuff."

Gage nodded.

"It's also important that she and Mother be comfortable with each other because they'll both be involved with the baby."

"Mom really likes being around Jamie, doesn't she?"

"I don't know how you can say that when the kid is screaming all the time," Jonathan said.

"My son does not scream all the time; and when he does he can't help it. You know darn well he's having trouble with his formula. I'm starting to think you're just jealous because I beat you to it and gave Mom her first grandchild."

"I am not jealous. I have no intention of procreating for several more years if at all, and it looks like old Gage here doesn't have any desire to add to the family tree any time soon, either."

"Suit yourself. Kim and I can always have another child in the future."

Jonathan snorted.

"Why bother when she can't stand the one you've got now?"

Chapter Two

The three brothers gathered again to discuss the previous night's episode and Mrs. Armstead's rapid departure after staying for only two days.

Jonathan twisted out of his chair and looked at Gage.

"Did Mrs. Armstead tell you she actually saw someone chasing her?"

"As a matter of fact, she did; waving a large butcher knife, I might add."

Jonathan whistled.

"She must have had one hell of a nightmare."

"Don't you think it's odd that all the nannies have mentioned being chased by someone insisting they leave or they'll die?"

"Maybe nipping a little too much sherry before going to bed caused their mass hysteria."

"All of them?" Gage shook his head. "I don't think so. It's got to be something else. I've asked Mrs. Armstead's permission to be tested for the possibility of drugs being in her system."

"Drugs!" James exclaimed. "You think she was drugged?"

"I don't know, but we need to find out why all these women thought someone in this house wanted to kill them. Whatever the reason, I don't want what happened to leave this room. The locals gossip about us enough as it is."

James nodded.

"Fine by me, but what are we going to do about another nanny for my son?"

"Why don't you see if Wonder Woman or Super Girl are available?" Jonathan joked, but sank back down onto his chair when Gage shot him a steely look.

"James, I have someone in mind if you'll allow me to take charge."

"That depends. Who are you thinking about?"

"I'd rather let you know after I find out whether or not she'd be interested."

Holland plunged her trowel into the soft ground, releasing the earthly aroma of slightly damp soil. She scooped out a weed, shook off small clods of dirt, and tossed it onto the growing pile in the large basket setting by her side. Her aunt's bad hip had made it too painful to keep up the vegetable garden and her uncle was too busy running their business.

They hadn't asked her to do this, but Holland wanted to neaten things up. It also gave her a chance to enjoy being outdoors after spending so much time inside seeing to her aunt's needs. The sun felt warm on her shoulders, but she knew come early evening there would be a cool nip in the mountain air. She watched a butterfly with tiny wings the color of pale butter flit by. Bees buzzed as they busily inspected plants. She waved her hand in the air when one started to investigate her hair. A wren chirped from its perch in a nearby tree and a jay scolded in return.

She spent the next two hours completing her task before she struggled to her feet. A thin line of sweat trickled down one side of her face. She wiped it away with her gloved hand, leaving a smudge of dirt on her cheek. She surveyed her handiwork, pleased to see the garden was weed free and ready to give up its bounty of vegetables without having to fight through a jungle of unwanted plants trying to wed themselves to the squash and cucumbers.

Holland walked to the house stretching sore muscles as she entered the kitchen. She put a few ice cubes in a glass and filled it with fruit juice. Her uncle picked the berries that grew wild along their back fence. Her aunt baked with them and squeezed some for drinking. Holland took a deep swallow before carrying the glass outside. She felt so good about the newly resurrected garden that she started singing a song from her youthful days at summer camp.

"I don't recognize the tune, but you sound off-key."

She whirled around at the unexpected sound of the male voice. Gage leaped back, but not in time to prevent the splash of juice hurling out of Holland's glass and landing across the front of his shirt. They both stared momentarily mesmerized by the rapidly spreading purple blotch.

"You scared the devil out of me and now look what you made me do to your shirt. What are you doing sneaking around here?" she demanded.

"I wasn't sneaking. I rang the bell and knocked at the front door several times. I came back here when I heard you," Gage said, pulling the wet material away from his chest.

"Your shirt's a mess. Come into the kitchen, so I can soak it."

"I don't want to trouble you. I'll take care of it later."

"The juice will stain if you wait. I have seen a man's bare chest before, so you needn't worry that I'll faint," she called over her shoulder.

He followed her into the kitchen while slipping the shirt buttons loose with a deft hand. Holland filled the sink with water and turned as Gage shrugged out of the garment. She may not feel like fainting, but the temptation to run her hands over his muscular, hair roughened chest took her by surprise. The last time she'd allowed herself to be physically attracted to a man she ended up marrying him and he turned out to be the bane of her life. She grabbed the shirt and pushed it down into the water with unnecessary force.

"I'd loan you one of my uncle's shirts, but it'd be too small."

"I'll be fine, especially now that I know I won't have a fainting woman on my hands."

Holland realized he was trying to be friendly. But her ego still felt bruised from his coldness when he'd dismissed her from his house. Who was the trespasser now?

"You're all sticky. Better wipe the juice off your skin," she tossed a damp towel at him.

He caught it in midair, rubbed the cloth over his chest, and walked to her. Holland moved back until her spine pressed against the edge of the counter. She put her hands out to stop him.

"What do you think you're doing?"

"You have a streak of dirt on your cheek."

His clean scent filled her nostrils making her embarrassed knowing she smelled of sweat and dirt. But it was the crazy things his nearness did to her pulse that made her jerk her head back.

Gage gripped her chin.

"Hold still." He wiped the towel over her cheek. "There. All clean."

She snatched the towel and flung it over a chair. "I don't like to be manhandled."

"I'm sorry. I didn't realize I was being too rough."

He hadn't hurt her, but his touch made emotions stir inside her that she didn't want to feel. She knew she was acting like a shrew, but he was lucky she offered to save his shirt and she was beginning to regret that bit of courtesy considering how jittery he was making her feel.

"You wasted a trip if you came to talk to my uncle and aunt. They aren't home."

"Actually, you're the one I wanted to see."

"I can't imagine why. You couldn't wait to get rid of me the last time you saw me."

Gage grimaced.

"I wasn't very nice to you."

"No, you weren't. If you're here to apologize, I accept. Now go away."

"Well, I would, but you have my shirt."

Damn, she'd actually forgotten that's why he was in the kitchen. The man was rattling her.

"I meant after I get the stain out."

"Right," he said with a smile twitching at the corners of his mouth.

She thought he was good looking before, but his smile nearly sent her into a swoon. She sank down onto a chair feeling annoyed with herself for reacting this way.

"I really am sorry for being so inhospitable to you. Please understand that part of my anger was because others have deliberately used various ruses to get inside my house. I had no idea James was out getting the woman he'd hired to be the new nanny."

"You have a nasty temper."

"Not really. I've actually been pretty patient when it comes to anything involving my brothers considering the predicaments they've gotten themselves into over the years.

"May I sit down?"

Holland waved a hand toward the chair across from her.

Gage sat.

"Are you through chastising me, or do you want to go another round?"

"I don't know what else you'd expect, but I suppose I can call a truce."

"Good, because I'd like to hire you to be my nephew's nanny."

Holland gaped at him.

"Well now, there's a twist. You don't even like me."

"I never actually said that."

"No, but your actions did. What happened to Mrs. Armstead?"

"She decided our little mountain town would be too confining. I know you're here to assist your aunt, so I won't ask you to work full time. But it'd mean a great deal to my family if you could come to the house even if it's only for a couple hours a day. You would be paid very well."

"Aren't you forgetting about me saying you couldn't pay me to come back?"

"I didn't forget, but I was hoping you would."

Holland drummed her fingers on the table. "You're already aware that I don't live here. I only planned on being with my aunt and uncle for a month. I have responsibilities back home."

"You told me you don't have children." Gage pointed to her left hand. "You aren't wearing a wedding ring. Can I assume a husband isn't one of those responsibilities?"

She gave an unladylike snort.

"Been there. Done that. Don't plan on doing it again."

"You look too young to be so cynical about marriage."

"I'm twenty-eight. Experience can be a real eye opener no matter how old you are."

"True. While I've never been married myself, I've witnessed enough bad unions among family and friends to know what you mean. But somehow they all keep trying again."

"I suppose some people still believe in happily ever after. How old are you?"

"Thirty-six."

"You act older."

A brief smile touched his lips. "First born children often do because more is usually expected of them – which brings me back to the reason for my visit. My brother is twenty-three and his wife is twenty-one. They're both finding parenthood a little more than they can handle right now and need help in taking care of their infant son."

"Your brother didn't seem to appreciate your interference when I was there."

"He doesn't. Nor does my other brother, but they need guidance since their father died. He asked me to look after the family, and I promised him I would. I'm trying to keep that vow."

"Sounds like you're their nanny. You mentioned another brother. How old is he?"

"Twenty-three. He and James are twins. His name is Jonathan. You may or may not meet him. He travels quite a bit and is gone right now. We never know when he'll show up."

"What about the women in your family? Why isn't Jamie's mother involved in his care? Or am I being too nosy again?" she asked, recalling his earlier rebuff on that subject.

"You've a right to know, since I'm asking you to take care of Jamie. Kim, his mother is suffering from postpartum depression."

"That can resolve itself in time. What about your mother?"

"She has her own health issues. She suffers from agoraphobia."

"What's that?" Holland asked, wrinkling her brow.

"She has panic attacks if she tries to leave the house. That's why we've added on so much. Because she won't go out into the world, the world has to be brought to her."

"Wow. That explains why no one ever sees her. How long has she been like that?"

"Since my step-father's death twelve years ago."

"What happened to him? You don't have to tell me if you'd rather not. But just so you know, I'm not a gossip."

"I appreciate that. They were vacationing in Mexico. He loved Mexico, especially out of the way places. They were in a small village when a couple of drug dealers arrived. One pulled a knife and demanded money from Jamison while the other tried to take off my mother's wedding rings. The villagers were too terrified to help, but my step-father tried to protect her."

"Did he get stabbed while he was trying to defend her?"

"Yes and getting immediate treatment wasn't easy. They were a long way from the nearest medical facility. He'd lost a lot of blood; and also his wound became infected. He wasn't a young man, and his heart wasn't strong. It turned out to be more than his body could take."

Holland's voice softened with sympathy. "I'm sorry for your loss."

"The experience threw my mother into a depression that she continues to fight. She hasn't left the house since Jamison's funeral. She's the one who insisted we have bars on the windows."

"What about your biological father? Did he die, too?"

"I don't know if he's alive or not." His voice held a definite tinge of antipathy now. "He left my mother when I was little and she never heard from him again."

"Haven't you ever been curious about him?"

"Not as curious as you seem to be," he replied, making her fidget. "As far as I'm concerned, he wasn't much of a father if he deserted me when I was so young. Jamison filled whatever void I may have felt because he was a wonderful father figure to me."

"Your mother's had it rough. Being afraid of something can be very crippling. I was bitten by a rattlesnake when I was a kid. My parents got me to the hospital in plenty of time, but I never got over the sheer terror I felt. Just seeing a picture of a snake makes my flesh crawl."

"I'm sorry you've had to carry that burden around all this time."

She felt his sympathy and stood up.

"Your shirt needs to go in the washing machine."

His thanks were interrupted by the sound of the living room door opening.

"We're back," a woman's voice called. "Do you have company? There's a car outside."

"I'm in the kitchen, Aunt May."

Gage looked down at his bare chest. "Well, this ought to be interesting."

"More than you think. You're about to be in for an interrogation. Most everyone in town, including

22

my aunt thinks you've been keeping your mother a prisoner in her own house."

He surged to his feet almost knocking the chair over.

"What!"

"It's true. Better get ready to defend yourself while I explain why the richest man in the county is sitting here in their kitchen half-dressed."

Holland walked with Gage to his car.

"Thank you for saving my shirt."

"I like to make things right if I can. Thanks for being so patient with my aunt's questions."

"Most uncomfortable hour of my life," he said, wiping imaginary sweat off his brow.

Holland laughed. "Somehow I doubt that. But think of it this way. Now that you've set the record straight people won't think you and your brothers are jailers. Of course, that probably means the gossips will end up inventing something else to keep your family in the limelight."

"Is that supposed to make me feel better?"

"Just trying to prepare you for the next time you're in town."

Gage opened his car door.

"Will you consider my job offer, Holland?"

She felt a little jab of pleasure hearing him say her first name.

"I don't know. You kind of sprung it on me out of the blue."

"I'd be willing to call your employer at home and ask them to give you more time off."

"That would be my dad. I've been helping in his secondhand store while I'm in-between jobs. My mom can continue filling in for me, but to tell you the truth, Mr. Langdon . . ."

"Gage, please."

"Okay, Gage. No offense, but your house is kind of creepy, except for the nursery."

"Only because you haven't seen it all. Let me give you a tour. I think you'll be surprised."

Here was the chance she'd been waiting for to satisfy her curiosity, but she hesitated.

"I don't know. Your brother made it pretty clear he resented me being there."

"He won't now. He knows how much we need you for little Jamie."

She sighed.

"You hit my soft spot. I'll come, but I'm not making any promises. What time?"

"Would ten o'clock tomorrow morning be convenient for you?"

"Fine, but I'd like to meet your mother and your sister-in-law before I make my decision."

He looked away for a moment before facing her again.

"That could be complicated."

"You've asked me to take care of your nephew. Surely you wouldn't expect anyone in that position not to want to have contact with these women, especially Jamie's mother."

"I'll need to prepare them first. My mother and sister-in-law are not used to strangers."

"All this isn't exactly enticing me go there. It sounds like those women won't want me."

"Try to concentrate on how much the baby needs you." He pulled a business card out of his wallet, flipped it over, and wrote on the back. "Here's my personal number. Please call me when you've made your decision. I'll understand if you'd rather not come, but I hope you will."

"Ah, the coveted unlisted number. A lot of people around here might pay big bucks for this. Aren't you afraid I'll sell it to the high bidder?" she teased.

"I just may have to throw you in my dungeon if you do," he quipped in return.

He drove away leaving her wondering what she should do about his job offer. Jamie clearly needed a mother figure since the females in his household didn't seem to be able to fill that role. She admitted her aunt and uncle weren't the only ones who wanted to know what went on inside that unusual house. But the job and house weren't the only things on her mind. Gage made her want to learn more about him despite her mistrust of men. He presented a hard businesslike façade, but he had a sense of humor and knew how to show sympathy.

The contrast was an interesting mixture that just might be too intriguing to ignore.

Gage answered the door himself and took Holland through one of the side doors off the foyer. She couldn't stop the quick giggle that escaped her when he led her to a golf cart.

"What's so funny?"

"Oh, come on. Not everyone has to have a golf cart to get around in their house. My uncle will be pleased to know he was right about that bit of gossip."

"Chalk one up for the town," he said with the dry humor she was coming to appreciate.

Holland twisted in her seat to look at Gage when they finished touring the house.

"I stand corrected. I thought my aunt exaggerated when she said all that stuff about you having a mini city inside here. Was it your idea to have so much?"

"My mother chooses what she wants, and I sign the checks."

"I noticed the newer additions have fake windows painted in place of real glass."

"Also my mother's idea," he frowned making it clear he didn't approve.

They left the cart and walked down an empty hallway until he stopped at yet another door. Holland decided a locksmith would have a field day in this place.

"My sister-in-law's room."

He knocked.

"Kim, it's Gage. I've brought Ms. Wallace."

He opened the door and stood back for Holland to go in ahead of him. She entered a large sitting room, dazzling in its rich décor. Her eyes were drawn to a young blonde haired woman dressed in a pale pink tight fitting sweater and hip hugging blue jeans. She sat staring at the phone in her hands and didn't look up when Gage made the introductions.

Holland cleared her throat.

"I'm happy to meet you, Mrs. Howard," she said, although she felt a little foolish being so formal knowing she was older.

"Kim, remember I mentioned bringing someone to meet you today who may be Jamie's new nanny," Gage said finally drawing her attention.

"Another one? What happened to the old woman?"

"She decided not to take the job. Ms. Wallace is thinking about it."

Holland worked up a smile.

"I've seen Jamie. You have a darling baby."

"He cries."

"Well, yes. Babies have a tendency to do that."

"It gets on my nerves. Where's James? I've called and texted, but he's not answering."

"He had some business in town, but he'll be back soon."

"I don't want to talk to her. Make her go away," she said pointing a finger at Holland.

Holland heard the shrill tone rising in Kim's voice and backed away.

"I'm going. It's been, um, nice meeting you," she blurted out and made a hasty retreat.

Gage immediately followed and closed the door. "I had hoped that would go better."

"Boy, she's really on edge. Has she seen a counselor?"

"Yes, and he's seen her." Gage looked at his watch. "Ready to meet my mother?"

Holland hung back. "Maybe we should skip that. I'm not feeling very wanted here."

"Don't take Kim's behavior personally. She's like that with everyone. I promise you my mother is looking forward to having you."

"Only because you need a nanny."

"That's part of it of course, but she trusts my judgment and I told her I like you."

Holland cocked her head to one side and looked at him.

"You're trying to butter me up."

"Is it working?"

She caught the quick gleam of amusement in his eyes and bit her lip to keep from smiling.

"I'm no pushover."

"Good for you. Shall we go?"

"Okay, but tell me, will you still think I'm a nice person if I don't take the job?"

"Why don't you hang around for a while and find out?"

Chapter Three

Gage shoved open double wooden doors and they entered a large room he'd skipped on the tour. Holland stopped and looked around. A large wall mural painted to depict windows caught her attention first. The artist had painted flowers, trees, birds, and butterflies against a false sunlit background. She let her eyes travel around the room. A polished mahogany bar with half a dozen barstools covered in dark brown leather took up most of the second wall. The bronze statue of an eagle sat at one end of the bar, its wings spread ready to take flight.

Another mural painted to represent people seated in booths filled a third wall. Holland glanced up and saw a painted blue ceiling with puffy looking white clouds and a bright yellow orb representing the sun. No doubt it was an attempt to give the illusion of something that wasn't allowed to exist for real here . . . genuine sky and sunlight.

A dark haired man with streaks of gray at his temples stood nearby as straight as a stick and looking just as thin in black slacks, a long sleeved white shirt, and black bowtie.

"Good morning, Mr. Langdon. Your mother is waiting for you and your guest, sir."

"Thank you, Jacob. This is Ms. Wallace. She may be taking the nanny position."

He smiled at her and Holland smiled back before her eyes were drawn to a tall, slender woman just pushing away from a table at the back of the room. Holland's first impression was how elegant she looked with her silver hair swept back into a neat chignon at the nape of her neck, a stylish linen apricot colored dress, and a double strand of pearls at her throat.

"Jacob, we'll have our tea now."

"Yes, Mr. Langdon."

Gage cupped Holland's elbow and urged her forward. He kissed the woman on her cheek.

"Mother, this is Holland Wallace. Holland, my mother, Marguerite Howard."

"I'm happy to meet you, Mrs. Howard," Holland decided not to extend her hand when she saw how rigid the woman held herself.

"Welcome to our home."

Her voice sounded strained to Holland's ears and her smile seemed forced. The woman was clearly struggling to play the part of a welcoming hostess. It didn't surprise Holland considering the years Gage's mother had kept herself in exile from the outside world. Gage pulled chairs out for both the women before sitting down himself.

"We've just come from Kim. I'm afraid she wasn't very receptive," he told his mother.

She looked at Holland. "I know why you're here, Ms. Wallace, so I hope my daughter-in-law didn't discourage you. Gage told me how wonderful you were with Jamie."

"I was only with him for a short time. He probably fell asleep because he'd been crying so long. I'm sure anyone else would have been able to do the same thing."

Jacob arrived with the tea tray. Marguerite's hand trembled slightly when she poured from the silver pot. She asked Holland if she preferred milk or lemon before offering dainty pastries.

"Try the blackberry tarts. I had them made especially for you," Gage said with a wink.

She rolled her eyes at him and plucked one from the plate. They drank their tea and made small talk until Holland decided to satisfy her curiosity about Jamie's nannies.

"I'm wondering about the other nannies. You said Mrs. Armstead didn't like mountain living, but who took care of the baby before she came?"

"We had a couple other women. They said they didn't sleep well," Gage answered. "I suppose the house can be a little scary at night given its size. We assumed they were having nightmares. Does the thought of that frighten you?"

"I don't frighten easily, but what makes you think I wouldn't have the same problem?"

"Because we're not asking you to spend the night here. We need you in the morning to start Jamie's day and a little time in the evening to settle him for bed."

"I didn't plan on staying around once my aunt is able to cope without me."

Marguerite set her cup down onto its saucer with a tiny click.

"But Gage said you'd be the perfect nanny for my grandson."

"I also told you nothing was settled yet, Mother."

"I understand that, but when you said Ms. Wallace was able to soothe Jamie so quickly I just assumed she'd want to take the position."

Holland remembered how miserable Jamie had been. It wasn't that she didn't want to help the baby, but her first priority had to be to her aunt.

"Even if I did agree to help that would probably make things worse when I had to go home."

"We'd appreciate anything you could do. Would it be easier if we made arrangements for a nurse to be with your aunt while you're here with the baby?" Gage asked.

"I'd have to talk to my aunt and uncle about that."

Gage's cell phone rang just then. He took it out of his pocket, glanced at the screen, and excused himself to walk across the room keeping his back to them. Marguerite startled Holland when she reached over, grabbed her wrist, and started squeezing with surprising strength.

"You've got to do this for us," she pleaded under her breath.

Her tense voice reminded Holland of Kim. Two females on the verge of hysteria in one day was a bit much and not a pleasant thought if one had to deal with them on a regular basis.

"I said I need more time to think about it."

"My grandson may die if you don't come. Do you want that on your conscience?"

Holland jerked her hand back.

"Shouldn't you tell his doctor if you really think your grandson's health is in that much danger?"

"The doctor isn't here enough to see what's going on." Marguerite twisted her pearls. "I feel something isn't right in the nursery, but no one stays there long enough to find out."

An uneasy thought crept into Holland's mind. "Mrs. Howard, are you saying the other nannies may have left because something happened with the baby to upset them?"

"I don't know. Gage assures me everything is fine. But I can't help wondering why all the women didn't want to stay. In the meantime, Jamie isn't thriving the way he should."

Gage returned to the table. Holland thanked them for the tea and stood up.

"I need to go."

He didn't question her until they were outside. "You're as stiff as a poker. Did something happen while I was on the phone?"

"Ask your mother."

"I'd rather have you tell me, if you don't mind."

She heard the hint of command in his tone and lifted her chin at a defiant angle.

"I do mind, but I will say this. Shouldn't you think about doing some serious housecleaning before you invite anyone else in to help with the dusting?"

"You obviously aren't referring to domestic chores. I don't know what transpired between you and my mother, but the bottom line is Jamie does need you."

"That's the one thing your mom said that made sense," Holland replied and walked away.

"I think you should take the job," May told Holland later that afternoon.

"I came here to help you, remember?"

"The doctor wants me to start doing more on my own, and Leo's not that far away if I have a problem. But if you're still worried then let the Howards hire me a nurse."

"May's right, we can work things out."

Holland frowned. "I still feel like I'm abandoning you."

"Don't be silly. Besides, they're convinced you're the one the baby needs."

"I don't know why they keep saying that. All I did was spend a few minutes rocking him to sleep, and you'd think I'd performed a miracle."

"Maybe it seemed like a miracle to the family. You've always had a way with kids, honey. I know you, and if you don't at least give the job a try, you're always going to wonder if you could have made a difference. Not only that, I have a feeling the women in that household are lonely and need you to be there just as much as the baby does."

Holland knew she'd probably set off a firestorm of new gossip if she mentioned the strange conversation she'd had with Gage's mother. She was still trying to sift through it herself.

"I guess I could handle taking care of the baby, but I don't want to be nanny to the ladies."

New Beginnings
Olivia Claire High

"Just be yourself. Those women are closed up in that house as well as in mind, body, and spirit by the sound of things. You'd be like a breath of fresh air."

"Don't let us hold you back," Leo added in an encouraging voice.

Holland pointed a finger at them.

"Why do I get the feeling you two are so anxious to have me go work in that house just so you can know firsthand what goes on inside?"

"Well, there is that," Leo muttered, and they all laughed.

But Holland wasn't in a laughing mood, while she cooked dinner that evening wondering whether or not she should go take care of Jamie. It would help if she could get the image of the baby's piteous cries out of her mind and how he'd snuggled against her when he fell asleep. She also couldn't forget his grandmother's words about the baby dying if she refused to take the job. Talk about emotional blackmail. Did Gage's mother suspect someone of deliberately trying to harm the baby? It certainly sounded that way.

She thought about Kim. The woman couldn't help her condition, but she didn't seem to have one iota of maternal instinct. She acted like she resented the baby. Well, she was young and probably spoiled. What about James? Was he going to be a problem? Gage didn't think so. But Holland couldn't forget how James said he wanted to hire the nanny himself.

35

She didn't like the idea that Gage may be forcing James to accept her. Gage said he signed the checks. Did that mean he was the one who'd be paying her? That probably didn't set well with his brothers if he was in charge of the money, as Jamison, Sr. was their biological father.

Holland wondered who she would have to answer to. Maybe Gage, since he appeared to be making the decisions for everything else in that house. There seemed to be a lot of inner tension within the family. Maybe that's why the other nannies left. Did she want to get involved?

Holland did a mental inventory of the principal people she'd be working with. An eccentric grandmother, unhappy new mother, resentful father, wayward twin brother, a handsome lord of the manor, and of course little Jamie.

He had to have someone take care of him. Everybody insisted she was the person he needed.

Holland closed her eyes for a moment, thinking of another time in her life when she would have sold her soul to have a baby need her.

"Have you heard from the Wallace woman yet?" James asked Gage.

"She just called. She'll come for a couple hours a day for a week and see how it goes."

"If she lasts even that long."

"I have a feeling she will. Holland Wallace strikes me as a woman with a lot of gumption."

"I still don't like the idea of having a local person snooping around here and blabbing to the whole town about our business. The people we have working here now probably do enough of that as it is. But I guess we should be thankful they don't bolt, since we need so much help keeping this place up. Come to think of it, why do you suppose they stay and not the nannies?"

Gage's eyes flared before he brought himself under control. "The nannies were drugged."

"You found out for sure?"

"Yes. Mrs. Armstead was tested and gave permission for me to know the results. I haven't had a chance to tell you. She'd been given a drug that caused her to hallucinate. It made her believe someone actually wanted to kill her. I'm assuming that's what happened to the others."

James gave him a shocked look. "How could something like that be possible?"

"The doctor explained it to me. A suggestion is made that they're going to die when the women have just blacked out from the drug, but are still coherent enough to hear. They could have been given it in something as simple as a cup of tea. The first thing they think of when they awake is the last words they heard before they went completely out."

"Are you saying someone in this house went around drugging the nannies?"

"It looks that way."

James swiped a hand through his hair. "For what reason?"

"Presumably to get rid of them, but I don't know why that would be."

"Mom's getting suspicious something's wrong because she asked me a lot of questions."

"Stick with the nightmare theory."

"I will, but what if this drug thing happens again? We'll be dealing with local relatives now, and they may demand an investigation. Can't Colleen just take care of Jamie?"

"Colleen isn't capable of being in full charge. There won't be any need for the police."

"How can you be so sure?"

"The women were always drugged during the night. Holland won't be staying over."

"Yeah, but what will we do if she ends up getting drugged in the daytime?"

Gage's eyes narrowed in determination.

"We're going to see that she doesn't."

Holland tucked the baby into his cradle and continued rocking it until he was deep in sleep. She wound the music box attached to the mobile above the cradle and walked across the room where she started to clear away his bath things. Jamie hadn't been too sure he liked the water. He'd only been on this earth a month and so far not much seemed to make him happy.

Hopefully that would change now that he was doing better with his new formula. Holland fed Jamie his bottle as soon as she arrived and was pleased that no unsettling gurgling sounds came from his tummy. Colleen was in charge of the baby's other feedings and said he'd done well for her, too.

Holland looked around the nursery, satisfied that everything was in order, and her charge was sleeping peacefully before she tiptoed out of the room. She looked at her watch and hurried down the hallway to Gage's office. She'd promised to get home to help her aunt wash and dry her hair before her lady friends arrived for their weekly game of Bunco.

Gage drew a map for her, so she'd be able to navigate around the confusing corridors. So far she'd managed to find her way to the nursery, the kitchen, and his office. She wanted to tell him she'd be leaving. Holland knew she could use the house intercom, but she liked talking to Gage face to face. And she wasn't going to delve too deeply into the reason for that.

It hadn't taken Holland long to realize she would be answering to Gage when it came to Jamie. She could only assume he would keep the rest of the family apprised of the baby's progress. James did show some interest in his son, but there'd been no sign of Kim.

Holland knocked on the door and Gage bid her to enter. She walked into the room and saw that he was on the phone. He motioned her to a chair in front of his desk. She sat admiring his profile, as she waited for him to finish. He ended the call and smiled at her showing even white teeth. She smiled back while trying to ignore the rapid tap, tap, tapping of her heart. She wondered if he had any idea how he affected her, or if he felt any kind of vibe between them.

Probably not. He had more important things on his mind.

"How did things go?" he asked, coming to sit on the corner of his desk.

She resisted the urge to push her chair back away from him.

"Everything went well. Baby's bathed, fed, and down for his morning nap."

He nodded in approval.

"A good beginning."

"I came to tell you I have to go back to my aunt's now. Will someone be with Jamie when he wakes up?"

"Colleen. My goal is to eventually get my mother and also James to perhaps feed the baby a bottle at least once in a while. I want Jamie to know his family cares about him. Would you mind if I had them come to the nursery sometime when you're here, so you can show them how you do things? I may even take a crack at it myself."

"Come whenever you like. Do you think Kim will want to join the rest of you?"

"Only time will tell. I think part of her bonding problem is that she was sick for most of the pregnancy. She also had a very difficult labor and delivery."

"I'm sorry to hear that. You're obviously taking a very active role in Jamie's care. Isn't that kind of unusual considering James is here in the house?"

"I'm merely trying to set an example for my brother, so he'll learn to accept more parental responsibility. He wants to be a good father, but he just doesn't know how."

"And you do?"

"Not exactly, but I am older and happen to possess more common sense."

"I'm surprised he doesn't resent you considering how he acted when he brought Mrs. Armstead here. I mean, doesn't he ever feel like you're infringing on his territory?"

"Maybe it's not so much his territory, as it is mine through default."

"That's an odd thing to say."

"Not so odd once you understand that my brothers choose to let me be in charge of anything that entails any kind of responsibility, despite whatever objections they make. If that gives me extra privileges, I've damn well earned them."

The phone rang.

Holland stood.

"I'm sure you want to answer that, and I need to go."

"Thank you for this morning," he said, and went back to sit behind his desk.

Holland puzzled over Gage's comment about extra privileges. She couldn't help wondering if James knew the baby may not be his, although he acted adamant about his fatherhood role. Was that the real reason for Kim's depression? Did she know who Jamie's true father was, but had to keep quiet for fear of some form of reprisal? What kind of a hold did Gage have over her?

Marguerite may be the matriarch, but Gage was clearly the one in charge of the household, including who took care of little Jamie Howard.

Or should she say, little Jamie Langdon?

Chapter Four

Holland scooped the crying baby out of his cradle and held him to her shoulder.

"Okay little man help is here. You need a quick pit stop for a diaper change and then it'll be feeding time."

She walked over to the changing table, replaced his soiled diaper with a fresh one, and opened the small refrigerator in the nursery that held bottles of formula. Holland turned on the warmer and shook the bottle like she always did to be sure the liquid was well mixed only to have formula leak out of the bottle and run down her arm.

"Oh for Pete's sake. Whoever made up this last batch didn't screw the lid on tight enough. Hang on, Jamie," Holland cooed when the baby began to whimper again.

She set the bottle aside, grabbed another one out of the fridge, checked the lid, gave it a shake, and put the bottle into the warmer. She wiped the liquid off her arm and hand talking to the baby to soothe him as best she could.

She lifted the bottle out of the warmer as soon as the timer pinged, hurried over to sit in the rocking chair, and eased the bottle's nipple into Jamie's gaping mouth.

New Beginnings
Olivia Claire High

"Feeling better now, sweetie?" she smiled, as he began to vigorously suck.

Holland wasn't sure who made up Jamie's bottles, but she assumed it was probably Colleen. She wasn't going to complain about the loose lid, but would let it be a lesson to her to be sure to check each bottle more carefully before she did the shaking.

She finished feeding Jamie, patted his back until he burped, cuddled, and talked to him until he fell asleep. She settled him in his cradle before checking the other bottles. One other lid was loose. Colleen must have been in a hurry. Holland felt guilty knowing things would be easier for the woman if she didn't have to take care of the baby and still do her other duties.

Holland decided it might be time to commit to more hours here, including preparing Jamie's bottles. Her aunt was getting along well and ended up dismissing the visiting nurse after a couple of days. Holland's parents were handling things back home and gave her the green light to stay here as long as she was needed when she told them about Jamie.

She stood looking down at the sleeping infant. His mother's continued avoidance of her son was troubling. Gage said the family hoped Kim's attitude would improve, but Holland had a feeling that wasn't going to happen any time soon. She hadn't seen Kim since her first visit here and couldn't forget how she'd complain about Jamie's crying. It certainly wasn't a very encouraging sign for developing a loving mother/child relationship.

Marguerite said she wanted the nanny to bond with her grandson. Didn't she want the same thing for her daughter-in-law? Gage's plan to have the women come to the nursery while she was there hadn't happened yet. He did come by once and enjoyed feeding the baby. She smiled thinking about it. James came, but only watched. Hopefully he'd come again.

Holland stepped away from the cradle reminding herself she needed to tell Gage she'd be willing to spend more time here. It felt like it was something she should discuss with James, but Gage was the one who hired her. She called Colleen on the intercom to come sit with Jamie.

"Is Mr. Langdon in his office?"

"Yes, miss."

Holland thanked Colleen and hurried through the winding corridors. She raised her hand to knock on the office door, but stopped in midair when she heard Kim shouting from inside. There was no mistaking that young woman's shrill voice. Holland knew she should walk away, but stayed riveted to the spot when she heard Kim say Jamie's name.

"You know you're his father. How much longer do I have to keep up this farce? I'm sick of being cooped up here. My fake depression is going to start being real if I have to hang around this stupid town and this mausoleum of a house much longer. You promised we'd be together if I had the kid. You know I never wanted him. There's something wrong with him. It's not normal the way he cries so much and don't start going on about the new nanny being a miracle worker. Wait and see what happens. I have a feeling she's about to run out of miracles."

The words tore through Holland like claws raking over exposed flesh. So Kim's depression was an act and she really did hate her own child. She'd referred to Jamie as 'the kid' like he was a bad tasting dose of medicine. The woman's heart was as evil as her soul.

Holland supposed she shouldn't be so shocked to learn of Kim's true feelings. But what about Gage? How could he allow Jamie to be conceived knowing the baby wouldn't be wanted? To speculate that the gossip about him being Jaimie's father was one thing, but to actually have it be proven was devastating. Holland believed him to be honest in his efforts to help his nephew. Nephew? My God, Jamie really was his son.

Holland made her way slowly to the nursery like a woman creeping through dense fog. She grabbed her purse and told Colleen she was going for a drive.

"All right, miss. Enjoy the fresh air. I'll stay with Jamie until you return."

Holland didn't have the heart to tell the woman she wouldn't be coming back.

May looked at the wall clock, as Holland cleared dishes off the table that evening.

"It's getting late. You need to go back to the baby. Leo and I can finish cleaning up."

"May's right, we'll do this," Leo said and began carrying dishes to the sink.

45

Holland's hands clenched on a dish. "I won't be going back tonight or any other time."

Leo and May exchanged startled looks. "Isn't that rather sudden?" she wanted to know.

"Yes it is, but something's come up and I don't want to talk about it."

"We're responsible for you while you're here. Did someone hurt you?"

"No, Uncle Leo. I just don't care for the way they do some things in that household."

"Maybe you should call and let them know you're not coming, so someone will feed the baby before he gets too upset," May suggested.

"I'm sure they'll figure it out on their own."

"It's only fair to the little one that you don't wait, Holly. He's going to be hungry."

Holland set the plate aside she'd been holding. Hearing her aunt refer to Jamie as 'the little one' struck a sensitive cord. Jamie was an innocent pawn caught up in a web of deceit fashioned by the guilty. The slow drip from the kitchen faucet seemed unnaturally loud to her ears.

She felt Leo and May's eyes on her knowing they would continue to interfere on Jamie's behalf. Holland gripped the edge of the counter reluctantly realizing they were right and despising herself for not championing the baby herself. But it wasn't easy getting beyond the disgust she felt for Gage and Kim.

"All right. I'll call and let them know someone should take over. But I'm not going back."

She turned away before their disappointment peeled away her resolve. Holland left the kitchen

46

feeling her nerves tighten as each step brought her closer to the phone and the prospect of what she would say. She paused for several seconds before making her call. The relief at having Colleen answer the phone instead of Gage helped to relieve some of her tension.

"Oh Ms. Wallace, I was just getting ready to call you. Jamie's having terrible tummy problems again and he's barely stopped crying every time I feed him."

Holland forced back her initial sympathy and made herself harden her heart.

"You'd better call the doctor."

"I did. I've tried his suggestions, but nothing's helped. I don't understand why Jamie's tummy is so upset after he's been doing so well. His grandmother asked me to call you."

"Did she? I would have thought it'd be Mr. Langdon's idea to contact me."

"He had to leave for an unexpected business trip and will be gone for a few days."

"Oh? Well, I'm sorry, but I won't be coming there again. I'm giving my notice. I would have done it with Mr. Langdon, but since he's not there please tell his mother for me."

"You're not coming back? But who is going to help me take care of the baby?"

"Why don't you see if Jamie's mother will help? It's time she does something for him."

Holland felt disgusted with herself as soon as the words were out. She didn't sound anybetter than Kim. She was being deliberately cruel and she tried never to be mean to anyone.

"I did. She . . . she called me terrible names, threw a shoe at me, and told me to get out."

Anger at Kim fought with her own mounting guilt. Holland knew she wouldn't find any kind of peace if she turned her back on Jamie. He was fighting, possibly for his life if he continued to be unable to eat without being sick. How could she turn her back on him?

Colleen broke into her thoughts.

"I have no idea why you've decided to quit, and it's not my place to ask. I do hope it isn't because your aunt has taken a bad turn. But I'm begging you to please come back if it's at all possible. I can't fix what's wrong with the baby, but perhaps you can."

Colleen and Gage's mother must think she had some kind of special attributes when it came to Jamie. Holland wished she did for the baby's sake.

"Jamie was fine when I fed him. Did you change his formula?"

"No. I used the bottles in the nursery refrigerator, but the baby is in misery."

Misery. Holland felt sick hearing that and even more sick with herself knowing she'd been willing to turn her back and let Jamie suffer. Who was the monster now?

"All right. I'll be there as soon as I can. Try rocking him until I get there."

"Oh, thank you, Ms. Wallace. Thank you."

"Colleen, I think it would be best if you didn't mention to Jamie's grandmother that I'd considered not coming back. I'll discuss it with Mr. Langdon when he returns."

"Whatever you say, miss."

Holland hung up and hurried to the kitchen to tell her aunt and uncle about the phone call.

"Oh that poor little lamb," May murmured in sympathy. "That child needs mother's milk."

"I agree, but that's not going to happen. I told you his mother isn't nursing him."

Leo stood up. "That doesn't mean he can't get mother's milk from someone else."

Holland lifted a brow at him. "Any suggestions?"

"Yes, as a matter of fact. One of my customers, a young widow is having a real hard time paying all her bills. Her husband was killed in a logging accident and the insurance company has been dragging their feet with the settlement. People in town have stopped extending her credit. She's run up a huge bill with me, but I can't bear to turn her away."

May nodded. "Janet Carl. She's a sweet girl."

"I feel very sorry for her, but I don't see what that has to do with Jamie's situation."

"The Howard baby needs breast milk and my customer needs money. She's nursing her three-month-old baby. I heard her tell the girl who works for me how she has so much extra milk she could pay off some of her bills if she could find someone willing to buy it."

A big grin spread over Holland's face when she realized what this meant. She hugged him.

"You're a genius, Uncle Leo. Will you call her and ask if she'd be able to pump her breast so I could take some milk to Jamie tonight? I'll pay her out of my own pocket."

His face turned red making May smile. "I'd better do it. Leo's too embarrassed. But I thought you said you were quitting the nanny job."

Holland shook her head.

"I changed my mind."

Holland set the empty bottle aside and began to pat Jamie's back until he let out a couple of good burps. She smiled and continued rocking him, stealing kisses on his head. She hummed to him until he closed his eyes in sleep. She put him in his cradle just as the door to the nursery opened. Holland didn't have to turn around to know it was Gage's mother. The woman was evidently partial to roses. She kept them in vases around the house and wore the scent on her person. Putting her finger to her lips, Holland motioned Marguerite to follow her from the room.

Marguerite spoke first.

"I want to thank you for helping Jamie. I owe you an apology for doubting that you really do care for him."

"That's okay."

"No, it isn't." Marguerite began to wring her hands. "I overreacted, but only because I love the baby and want what's best for him. My three sons mean the world to me and I would do anything to ensure their wellbeing. That's why I'm having such a difficult time with . . ."

She stopped, as though she was reluctant to finish and reveal feelings that she thought should be kept locked inside. Holland waited allowing Marguerite to either get her secrets out in the open, or tuck them back into the safety of denial.

"I can't understand how my daughter-in-law can continue to reject her own child."

"You're aware of her doctor's diagnosis," Holland said, trying to be tactful.

"Yes, and we've all been hoping she'll recover and be a mother to her son. I know postpartum depression is real, but I'm beginning to believe that isn't Kim's problem. You'll think me shameful, but every motherly instinct I have tells me she is putting on an act."

Marguerite's children meant everything to her by her own admission, and to have her grandson be rejected by his own mother was obviously beyond her comprehension. Holland could see that and had no problem agreeing with Marguerite's assessment after the things she'd heard Kim saying in Gage's office. She wondered what else Marguerite might suspect her daughter-in-law of, and if she had any clue to just how much Gage really was connected to Jamie.

But it wasn't her place to discuss something so personal, especially with a woman who already had enough complications in her life.

"I guess only time will tell what happens. In the meantime, I'll be here to take care of the baby. I was able to get a local woman who is breastfeeding her own baby to give me some of her milk for Jamie."

"This is what he's needed all along. Is there any way you could work something out with the woman to continue to supply her breast milk without denying her own child? I'd gladly pay her."

Holland nearly sighed, glad the subject of money had come up without her having to approach the idea herself.

"The woman is more than willing to help for Jamie's sake. But she's also a widow in dire need of some extra money. Whatever you choose to pay her will be appreciated."

Holland explained the situation and how her uncle had been trying to help the woman by continuing to give her credit in his store.

"It sounds as though the poor girl is having a very difficult time."

"Yes she is. I saw her and her baby tonight. They're both very healthy and the baby is thriving, so I don't think you have to worry about the quality of the breast milk."

"We must make arrangements right away to see that she is compensated."

"I'll talk to her and work out some kind of payment. Um, Colleen said Gage is away on business. I'd rather not have to make the woman wait for her money until he returns."

"My son isn't the only one capable of writing a check." She paused, as though choosing her next words carefully. "Ms. Wallace, I know you don't usually stay, but would you consider spending tonight since Jamie was so upset earlier?"

"Sure. I'll call my aunt and uncle and tell them not to expect me home."

"Thank you so much. I'll rest much better knowing you're here. What is the name of the young woman supplying her breast milk?"

"Janet Carl."

"I'll go make the check out to her right now." Marguerite named an amount. "Do you think that will be enough?"

"That's more than generous for the first month. I'm sure Janet will be very thankful."

"I want to give her that for each week."

Holland shook her head. "I'm pretty positive she wasn't expecting so much."

"She's helping my grandson. No amount of money would be too much, Ms. Wallace."

"As long as I'm going to be here taking care of Jamie, and we'll be seeing more of each other, won't you please call me by my first name? It's Holland."

"Yes, I remember. I would like us to be on a first name basis. It sounds so much friendlier than using titles. So I hope you'll be comfortable calling me Marguerite."

"Thank you. It's a beautiful name."

"I was named after a great-grandmother on my mother's side. Gage told me how you and your siblings came to have your names. I find that fascinating. Your father sounds like a very interesting man."

"He is. I guess people think he's probably a little eccentric at times, but he's a very good man and I love him to bits."

"I envy you that connection. I barely knew my own father. He had his reasons. Perhaps I'll tell you about it sometime." She fingered the pearls she almost always wore. "I won't keep you standing out here in the hallway any longer. Will you join me for breakfast in the morning? You can get the check for your friend then. Just come when it's convenient."

"Thank you. Where should I meet you?"

"The room where we had tea the first day we met. Let Colleen know via the house intercom when you're ready."

"I will. Would you like to kiss your grandson goodnight?"

Holland knew she'd done the right thing in asking when she saw the woman's face light up.

"I'd like that very much," she said and followed Holland back into the nursery where she kissed Jamie and stood for several moments looking at him before leaving the room.

Marguerite turned to Holland once again when they were back in the hallway.

"I'm going to enjoy being a grandmother, especially with your help. Goodnight, Holland. I hope you sleep well."

"Thank you, you too."

Holland awoke the next morning feeling logy. She hadn't slept well. She couldn't stop thinking about Gage and the big lie he was living. She'd begun to think they could be friends, but not now knowing what she did about his connection to Kim and Jamie.

That wasn't the only reason she had such a restless night. She didn't have a clue why the other nannies might have had their nightmares, but this

New Beginnings
Olivia Claire High

house wasn't what one would call cozy. Holland heard odd creaking and groaning noises throughout the night. Her dad once told her that *old houses talk* at night; and the bigger the house, the more it has to say.

She left her door open besides using the baby monitor, so she could see into Jamie's room. She had a strange sensation during the night that someone was in the nursery. Whoever it was hovered around the refrigerator. Had she imagined the clinking sound of bottles? Holland stumbled out of bed and staggered into the nursery, but if anyone had been there they'd vanished. She decided it must have been a dream probably caused by the situation with Jamie's feeding problems.

Holland kicked back the blanket and sheet when she heard Jamie's first cries letting her know he was awake. She walked swiftly into his room, lifted him into her arms, and carried him to his changing table, talking to him the whole time. Jamie seemed to recognize her voice and managed to stop crying while she changed his diaper.

Holland held him and went to the refrigerator to get a bottle. She plucked one off the shelf and made sure the lid was on correctly. She was just about to put the bottle in the warmer when she took a second look. Frowning, she held the bottle up to the light and felt her body stiffen. The bottle held the creamy colored liquid that she knew had to be formula, instead of the paler looking breast milk she expected.

Holland bit her lip. Maybe she hadn't been dreaming last night when she thought she saw someone in the nursery's semidarkness hanging around the refrigerator. She'd brought extra bottles with Janet's breast milk, but each one she checked turned out to be filled with formula.

The day she'd spilled formula on her hand when she'd shaken the bottle came to mind. Jamie hadn't done well after that feeding and now it was becoming clear why he'd suffered from his earlier digestive problems. The formula he was able to tolerate must have been replaced with the one that caused his stomach upsets.

Whoever did that was probably responsible for this latest exchange. That miserable excuse for a human being was deliberately trying to make Jamie sick. The realization hit Holland like a slap in the face. The knowledge made her feel ill herself until her anger began to build making her shake with the force of her fury.

Jamie whimpered. Holland looked at the baby and knew what she had to do.

Chapter Five

Marguerite stared in surprise when Holland pushed her way through the doors carrying the crying Jamie. The cup in her hand clattered onto the saucer and she rose quickly from her chair.

"Is something the matter with the baby?"

"He's hungry," Holland said, barely controlling her anger. "Is James in the house?"

"No, he went with Gage. Why? What's wrong? Why aren't you giving Jamie his bottle?"

"The breast milk I brought is gone. Since James isn't here, I want your permission to take Jamie to Janet. I'd rather not ask Kim."

"I thought you said there were enough bottles. Did he go through all of the milk already?"

"I said the breast milk was gone. I didn't say Jamie drank it."

Marguerite frowned.

"I don't understand."

"I'm not sure I do, either. We can try to figure it out later. Right now your grandson needs to eat. Will you let me take him to Janet's house?"

"Of course. There's a car seat in his closet. I know I should probably go with you, but I. . ."

"It's all right, Marguerite. You don't have to worry. He'll be safe with me."

"Bless you. Let me at least help you get ready. I also have the check for your friend."

Marguerite insisted they take a golf cart. Holland didn't argue when Jamie's crying became more insistent. She called Janet and told her she would explain the reason later, but right now the baby was in dire need of more breast milk. Thankfully that good woman didn't ask questions, but instead said she'd be more than willing to help.

Holland grabbed a tote bag and began filling it with the items she thought Jamie would need while Marguerite brought the car seat out of the closet. They piled everything into the golf cart and drove to the foyer.

"I'll have to leave you here. I apologize for putting this in your hands, but I'm just a useless old woman."

"You mustn't say that."

"Well, it's true." She reached for Jamie. "I'll hold him while you go set up his car seat."

Holland ran out to her car and worked quickly thankful she'd done this before with her nieces and nephews. Jamie was crying with a great deal more gusto by the time Holland raced back into the house. Marguerite handed him over.

"Please call me as soon as you can. I'd like to know if he's all right."

"He'll be fine once he's been fed."

Holland slung the tote bag over one shoulder and took the baby.

"I think it would be best if you didn't mention to Kim about the bottles, or that I've taken Jamie out."

New Beginnings
Olivia Claire High

"I wasn't intending to, and you needn't worry about her wondering where Jamie is because she never asks about the baby."

Holland left with those sad words ringing in her ears along with Jamie's steady crying. She looked in the rearview mirror at the house. The heavy stone facade loomed large and forbidding, shrouded in the gray morning mist. Windows stared back like black holes with their iron bars reminding her of long scars. No wonder the other nannies hadn't wanted to stay.

She knew taking Jamie to Janet would only be a temporary fix for his feeding problems. It wasn't just the situation about his food that had Holland so worried. She'd told Marguerite about the breast milk being gone. But who else could she confide in about the bottle tampering without putting Jamie at more risk?

Marguerite appeared sincere in her efforts to help her grandson, but she was too emotionally fragile, and might not be able to handle more upsetting news concerning the baby's welfare. James may be okay as long as he continued to believe Jamie was his son. But what if he allowed Gage to influence him? He seemed inclined to go along with anything his big brother suggested after a mere token show of resistance.

Gage would have been the first one Holland went to if she hadn't heard that disturbing conversation with Kim in his office. She hadn't actually heard his voice, but it had to be Gage. It was his office and he was the one the town gossips said might be Jamie's real father. He also made decisions about the baby's care that were unusually involved.

Colleen did try to be helpful in her own bumbling way, but she might not appreciate having Holland ask her to spy on the members of the household. Her loyalty went too deep. Holland was in a quandary what to do. But how could she take Jamie back to a house where someone was deliberately trying to make him sick?

She knew she'd have to think of a way to keep him safe. But short of kidnapping the baby, nothing else came to mind.

Janet ran out to meet Holland. "Oh my, he's really in a state. I actually thought I might just nurse him, but I ended up using the breast pump while I waited. I started warming the bottle as soon as I heard you drive up."

"Thank you. He's been crying for a while. I'm afraid it's going to be hard to quiet him."

Holland unhooked the car seat and followed Janet into her small cabin. Janet pointed to an overstuffed chair.

"That's where I nurse my baby, Mimi. Make yourself comfortable while I get the bottle."

"I hope we aren't going to wake your little girl."

"She can sleep through most any noise."

Holland sat in the chair and did her best to soothe Jamie, but it wasn't until he had the bottle's nipple in his mouth before he stopped crying. Even then his little body shook and he hiccupped, as he tried to suckle. Holland reached into her pocket and handed Janet the check from Marguerite.

"That's your first payment and you should be getting a check like that every week."

Janet's eyes widened. "This is way more than I expected. I don't think I should take it."

"I told Mrs. Howard that, but she insisted it's a small price to pay for helping her grandson."

"She's being very generous. God knows I need the money." She set the check on a nearby table. "Did Jamie drink all the milk I sent with you?"

"No." Holland paused to gnaw her bottom lip before making her decision. "I'm going to tell you something and you must promise me that it won't go any further than this room. I don't mean to sound rude, but I know how the people in this town gossip."

"Oh lord, yes. You have my word that whatever you say will be safe with me."

"Someone exchanged your breast milk with formula. I don't know if it's the brand Jamie can't tolerate, but I wasn't taking the chance after Colleen told me he got sick after I left."

Janet sat down.

"You mean someone deliberately did the switch?"

"That's what I'm thinking."

"They should be shot."

Holland nodded.

"I'd aim the gun myself if I knew who was responsible."

"What are you going to do to protect Jamie?"

"I actually thought about kidnapping him, but I know that won't work."

"You got that right. The Howards would be all over you like fleas on a hairy dog."

"I know. Besides, the only way I'm going to have a chance to find out who's doing this is to stay at the house and be with Jamie as much as possible."

"Do you think that's why the Howards haven't been able to keep a nanny?"

Holland shrugged. "I was told the women complained of having nightmares."

"Well, the house does look to be a perfect setting for such things."

"It's not so bad inside."

"Does it really have a theater and all the other things everyone talks about?"

"Yes. It's like a miniature city with a garden, a gym, indoor pool, and café, plus a lot more."

Janet shook her head in amazement.

"Sounds unbelievable."

"I guess it's okay to tell you the reason for all those rooms. Mrs. Howard has an illness that makes her afraid to go outside. It has to do with her husband being killed while they were on vacation in a remote part of Mexico. She never got over the trauma."

"So she stays inside because she feels safer. That's very sad."

"It is." Holland finished feeding Jamie and rocked him to sleep.

Janet smiled at him.

"He really is a cute little guy. Might make a fun play companion for Mimi, although I doubt if the Howards would ever allow that to happen."

"You never know."

"Would you like a cup of coffee, Holland?"

"Thanks, I sure would. I left the house before I had a chance to grab one."

"I made a couple of pies yesterday and took one to your aunt and uncle. Could you go for a slice right now? It's apple."

"Sounds wonderful."

Holland put Jamie in his carrier and followed Janet to the tiny kitchen where Janet insisted she sit down while she warmed the coffee and cut the pie.

"Your home is so warm and inviting."

"My husband built it. We were planning to add on after I had Mimi, but then he . . ." her voice trembled.

"I'm so sorry," Holland said and waited until Janet composed herself enough to bring the pie and coffee to the table.

Holland took a bite and made a yummy sound. "This pie is sheer heaven. Thank you for making one for my aunt and uncle. She hasn't been able to do much baking with her bad hip, and I'm not much of a baker myself."

"It's the least I can do. They've been so wonderful to me. I'm glad I'll be able to pay on my bill, thanks to Mrs. Howard's generosity. I don't know if you're aware of this, but your uncle is the only one who still lets me buy on credit. I would have had to go on the dole otherwise. I guess I should have, but my silly pride kept getting in the way. I really do think my insurance money will arrive any day now. But even when it does I'll still be happy to look in on your aunt and help in any way that I can if you do decide to spend more time at the Howards."

"I'd appreciate that and I know they would, too. They think of you as a daughter."

"That's so sweet. Leo told me one time that they wanted kids, but it wasn't meant to be."

They drank their coffee and finished their pie in silence until Janet cleared her throat.

"So, how do you plan to protect Jamie and keep the sicko away from his food?"

"I'm thinking of putting a coded lock on the nursery refrigerator."

"That's going to take some explaining. What will you tell the family?"

"I'm not sure yet. The lock might be enough to make the person stop messing with Jamie's bottles now that they know I'm on to them."

"I just don't understand why someone would do something so cruel."

"I don't either, but I'm going to do my best to find out."

Holland called Marguerite before taking Jamie to her aunt and uncle's house for the rest of the day. She told them she wanted to spend more time with the baby and they agreed it was a good idea. Holland had a feeling she'd have to go through Gage before anything was settled. The idea of having to talk to him filled her with indignation. She couldn't stop thinking about what she'd heard

New Beginnings
Olivia Claire High

Kim say in his office. The one good thing she could say about Gage was that since he was away he couldn't be the one responsible for messing with the baby's bottles.

Holland also decided to tell him one of the stipulations for her taking the nanny job would be to allow her to take Jamie to Janet's as well as her aunt and uncle's at least a couple times a week. She had a feeling she would need the outings and it'd probably be good for the baby, too.

She waited until she'd given Jamie his last bottle of the day and packed a suitcase for herself before she called Marguerite again to tell her she was on her way back.

Marguerite hovered in the foyer, when Jacob answered the door.

"Is the baby all right?"

"He's fine. Sleeping for the moment. I'll take him to his room now."

"Whatever you think is best. Jacob will get your things and put your car away."

"Why don't you come with me and help tuck your grandson in for the night?"

Holland handed Jamie over once they were in the nursery.

"You can put him in his cradle. He's all fed and changed."

Marguerite cuddled him in her arms and kissed his forehead before laying him down. Holland watched her gently stroke his cheek.

"Jamison Howard III. My husband would have been so proud. He's a beautiful little boy."

"Yes he is."

"I'd like to stay with him a little longer if you don't mind."

"This is your house and your grandson. You can stay as long as you like. I think it'd be a good idea for you to visit him on a daily basis. It'll be a great way to get to know him."

"That would be wonderful. I wanted to spend more time with the baby from the very beginning, but I didn't want Kim to think I was intruding. I'm sure it can't be easy for her having to live in her mother-in-law's home."

"You don't strike me as a very intrusive person."

Marguerite smiled.

"I try not to be. Would you like to join me for a cup of tea before bedtime? I find a cup or two is very soothing in the evenings. I'll have a tray brought to your room, so we can keep an eye on the baby."

Holland decided this would be as good a time as any to start laying out her plans for how she intended to take care of Jamie. But she wanted to be careful in how she introduced the idea to Marguerite without upsetting her. Hopefully things would be easier over a cup of tea.

"I'd like that very much. I know I can use a baby monitor to check on Jamie, but I prefer to stay with him as much as possible."

"My grandson needs mothering. Whether or not Kim will ever step into that role is anyone's guess. I will do what I can, but I'm a nervous old woman. You are what he needs."

New Beginnings
Olivia Claire High

"Please don't underestimate yourself. You love Jamie and that counts for a lot."

"Thank you. Gage said you would be good with the baby, and he was right."

"I couldn't help noticing that you rely on him quite a bit."

"He's my rock. We all lean on him probably more than we should. It's a good thing he is able to handle so much. Oh, here's Jacob. Just put the suitcase in Ms. Wallace's room."

"Yes, Mrs. Howard."

She looked at Holland. "I'll order our tray now. I prefer herbal tea in the evening, but I'll have regular sent for you if you'd like."

"Herbal will be fine."

"Any particular favorite?"

"I like mint or peach flavor if you had either of those, but if not, please don't worry."

"Two of my favorites."

Marguerite walked over to press the intercom button in the wall. Holland thanked Jacob as he left and went into her room to start unpacking while she chatted with Marguerite. She managed to put away her few belongings by the time the tea arrived.

Colleen carried the tray into Holland's room and set it on a table. She arranged the dainty cups with the pink rose pattern on their saucers and set out a basket filled with different flavored tea bags followed by a dish of thin flower shaped sugar cookies and tiny ginger snaps. A ceramic teapot with the matching rose pattern held the boiling water. She put down small silver spoons and pale pink linen napkins.

"Shall I pour for you, Mrs. Howard?"

"We can manage. Thank you, Colleen."

Colleen smiled, bobbed her head, and walked over to close the connecting door to the nursery, but Holland's voice stopped her.

"That's all right, Colleen. I'd rather keep it open."

"I thought you might be afraid of waking the baby while you two did your visiting."

"My goodness Colleen, we're two soft spoken women, not carnival barkers," Marguerite said with just enough humor in her voice to let her hireling know she wasn't angry.

"Oh, I would never think that, Mrs. Howard," she said and went away.

"Actually, I can yell pretty loud when I need to," Holland informed Marguerite.

"So can I, but that'll be our little secret."

Holland smiled, liking the fact that her employer was beginning to show that she had a sense of humor. She didn't want to shatter the light mood, but she knew she couldn't wait too long before she requested to have a coded lock put on the refrigerator in Jamie's room. Her chance came when Marguerite asked if Holland brought enough bottles of breast milk to get Jamie through the night and the next morning.

Holland set her teacup on its saucer with care.

"I brought enough and I know you'll have one of the servants bring more from Janet, but I'd like to take Jamie to her house sometimes. I think it'll do him good to be out now and then. I'd also like to stop in to see my uncle and aunt. Do you think that will be a problem?"

"I wouldn't think so. Kim won't care. I'd like you to discuss it with James, though. I'm sure he'll approve, but it'd be nice to let him know you're asking him to make decisions for his son."

"How about Gage? Do I have to get his permission, too?" Holland just had to ask.

"I don't think that will be necessary. You must understand that Gage doesn't want to have so much responsibility, but it just seems to be thrust upon him. Jamie was obviously not doing well, Kim wasn't any help, and although James protested at first he ended up going along with Gage's idea to hire you. We all go to Gage when we need advice, and probably more than we should."

"Gage does have that authoritarian presence about him, but I have to know how much authority I'll have myself when I need to make decisions on Jamie's behalf without having to go through the family every time I feel it's necessary to try something new."

"I would think you'd have the freedom to do whatever you feel is necessary, as long as it's for the sake of good. The main thing is to be sure Jamie is well cared for and starts to thrive after having such a difficult start in life."

This was the opening Holland had been waiting for. She took a deep breath and silently let it escape, hoping she was approaching such a touchy subject in the best way possible.

"Then I'm going to ask you to let me put a coded lock on the refrigerator in the nursery. Not only that, I don't want anyone handling Jamie's bottles except myself."

Marguerite raised carefully sculpted eyebrows.

"Why on earth do you want a coded lock?"

"Do you remember the first time I met you and you implored me to become Jamie's nanny because if I didn't he might die?"

"I'm afraid I was being overly dramatic, but I was so desperate to have you take the job."

"You love your grandson and you want what's best for him; and so do I. The only way I can keep his food supply safe is to be in charge of his bottles myself. That's why I want the lock."

"You said safe. Does this have to do with the breast milk being switched?"

"Yes. You suspected something wasn't right when the other nannies left in such a hurry. If you'll recall that's one of the reasons you wanted me here to keep an eye on Jamie."

"True, but I never thought that would entail keeping his food under lock and key."

"I wish I didn't have to say this, but the lock is necessary because someone has been filling your grandson's bottles with the formula that makes him sick."

Marguerite's hand shook and she set her cup down.

"Oh my dear heaven. Are you sure?"

"Yes. I saw the difference myself. Jamie would have suffered his usual ill effects from the formula if I had given him the wrong bottle."

"I can hardly fathom the implications of what you're saying."

"I'm merely telling you what I know. Short of nursing Jamie myself, the lock on the baby's refrigerator is the only way I can think to keep his food source safe as long as he lives in this house."

"Do you have any idea who is responsible for this . . . this villainy?"

Holland knew she had to be careful with her answer since she'd upset Marguerite enough already.

"Not really. That's why I need to have the lock."

She watched Marguerite's expression as she struggled with a reply. No doubt the woman was wishing Gage was here to consult. But Holland wanted to gain Marguerite's support before he returned and possibly tried to talk his mother out of it. Holland had a feeling she was going to need all the backup she could get.

"You wanted me to save your grandson and that's what I'm trying to do. But I can't do it alone."

"I know, but what you're asking seems so drastic."

"It's the only way." Holland leaned close enough to squeeze the other woman's hand much as Marguerite had done with her the first time they met.

"Will you help me get the lock for Jamie's sake?"

Chapter Six

Gage stared at the lock on the nursery refrigerator, his anger at a slow smolder. His mother informed him that Holland had taken Jamie to the woman who was providing the breast milk for the baby. He didn't have a problem with that, but he did have a problem when anyone, whether it be employee or family member who caused his mother to worry.

She became agitated when he asked about the lock, insisting he'd have to find out from Holland why it was necessary. Anyone who upset his mother had to answer to him. That was an unwritten rule in the house. The price they paid depended on the offense. Holland may not have known that at the time she was doing her manipulating. But by God, she was about to find out.

He stared at the refrigerator again. Why was Holland going to such an extreme? Did she expect someone other than Jamie to drink the breast milk, for God's sake? He thought James was joking when he ran into his office to tell him about the lock.

Gage admitted to feeling a big relief when his mother told him Holland agreed to be Jamie's nanny. But now he wasn't so sure. Maybe he didn't do the family any favors by bringing her here. Who did Holland think she was putting locks where they shouldn't be needed and telling his mother as Jamie's nanny she wanted full charge in taking care of the baby?

A few days away from the house and he comes back to find important decisions being made without his input. Holland clearly took advantage of his absence and used his mother's vulnerability to steamroll her way into getting her demands met. She also used his mother to write a rather large check to the woman providing the breast milk for Jamie. Gage was happy the baby was doing so well, but he didn't care for the way Holland was handling things.

He and Ms. Holland Wallace were going to have a talk before she spent another day under his roof; and if he didn't like what he heard . . . she would be gone.

Gage was waiting in the nursery when Holland finally returned that evening with Jamie. She paused in the doorway when she saw him, before she entered the room.

"You're back."

"As you can see. I came to talk to you as soon as I had a free moment."

"My hero," she mumbled under her breath.

He frowned.

"What's that supposed to mean?"

She ignored his question and set Jamie's carrier down before slipping the tote bag off her shoulder. Gage watched as she pulled out three bottles, set one aside, and unlocked the refrigerator to put two more inside.

"Care to explain that?"

"Explain what?"

"You know perfectly well what. My mother became quite agitated when I asked her why you insisted on having that lock. I don't like it when she's upset. She told me I would have to ask you. So I'm asking, what's with the damn lock?"

Holland lifted Jamie to the changing table and began getting him ready for bed. She kept her back to Gage while she talked.

"Your mother isn't upset because I put the lock on the refrigerator. Rather, she's upset because of the reason I had to put it there."

"And what reason would that be?"

"Someone has been tampering with Jamie's bottles."

He gave her a baffled look.

"Tampering, how?"

"They were exchanging the formula he could tolerate with the one that made him sick. I saw someone in here the first night I stayed over, but I was half asleep and thought I'd dreamt it. The next morning one of the bottle lids wasn't screwed on tight enough and I spilled the formula."

"That doesn't prove anything."

"It does when Jamie suffered his old stomach upset after being fed from those bottles. But I still wasn't one hundred per cent sure of my suspicions until I started giving him the breast milk and the bottles had been messed with again. I knew immediately that someone replaced the breast milk with formula because there's a different look between the milk and formula."

"Are you implying someone did the switch because they wanted to make the baby sick?"

"I'm not implying it, I'm saying it."

"Is that why his cradle has been moved next to your bed?"

"That's right. Whoever is doing this will have to crawl over me to get to him."

"I see. Who came up with the idea to give him breast milk?"

"My aunt and it just so happens my uncle knows a young widow in town with a three-month old baby. The woman mentioned she had more milk than her daughter needed and how it'd be helpful if she could sell some. I told your mother and she was more than willing to pay."

"So I noticed by the check she wrote. Is that the going rate for breast milk these days?"

Holland turned to face him, fighting to maintain her composure at his sarcasm. She carried Jamie to the rocking chair and began to feed him.

"Take a good look at this baby. He hasn't been this healthy since he was born. This breast milk is what he needed. Are you going to begrudge him that?"

"Of course not. What do you think I am?" he demanded.

"I think you're a control freak," she said, throwing all caution aside.

Gage drew in a sharp breath and gave her a warning glare, but Holland was too worked up to stop now.

"You've been making all the decisions around here for so long you don't even give anyone else a chance. Your mother wants to have a say so in her grandson's care. Neither I nor the woman providing the breast milk named a price. The amount was your mom's idea. She wants to feel needed. She's not made of glass and she won't break if she does a few things on her own."

"Are you saying I don't allow my mother freewill?"

"I'm sure you mean well, but you've wrapped her in cotton wool all these years until she thinks she has to ask your permission before she does most anything."

"That's ridiculous. All I've ever tried to do is keep her from being upset."

"Being upset now and then is part of living. I'm sure she can become stronger if you'd let her try to exert a little autonomy once in a while."

"I've known my mother all my life and you think you're an expert after knowing her for such a short time. You'll pardon me if I don't agree with your assessment."

"I'm not claiming to be an expert, but sometimes it takes an outsider to see what you don't. You're too close to her and stuck in the way you've been handling things," Holland retaliated.

"Aren't you afraid I'll fire you for the way you're speaking to me?"

"You probably will, given your need to be in charge. Just make sure Jamie is safe. I don't care how you do it whether by a security camera or sleeping in here yourself. Whatever means you use is up to you, but please do something to protect him."

"My mother refuses to have security cameras in the house because she says it makes her feel like she's being watched, but let's talk about Jamie. You honestly believe he's in danger?"

"Yes I do."

Holland put Jamie to her shoulder and patted him on the back.

"So much so that I contemplated taking him away from this house completely to keep him safe."

"I'd see you in hell first."

"Naturally. The best I can do is keep him with me as much as possible."

"My God, you're really serious about this crazy idea that someone wants to hurt Jamie."

"It's not crazy. I'm beginning to wonder if those other nannies discovered the same thing."

Holland carried the sleeping baby into her room to put him in his cradle and missed Gage's expression as he followed her.

"That's not why they left," he said keeping his voice low.

She faced him. "Oh, right. Nightmares. What did you do, read them scary bedtime stories?"

"I've had just about enough of you mocking me."

His voice held a dangerous tone and his eyes glittered with anger barely held in check.

"Fine. I'll pack my things and be out of here. I can only pray that you care enough for Jamie to protect him because believe me you have a maniac bent on doing him harm."

New Beginnings
Olivia Claire High

Holland walked to the closet and took out her suitcase. Gage's long legs took him to her in three strides. He grabbed the bag out of her hand.

"Jesus!" he hissed under his breath. "Wait just a damn minute, will you? Come away from the baby, so I can talk to you without waking him."

She trailed after him, but stopped just inside the doorway, waiting.

"You've been making some pretty serious accusations. You call me a tyrant, tell me I'm stifling my mother's spontaneity, and insist there's a psycho in the house."

"I didn't call you a tyrant."

"As good as. I have no idea who you suspect, but it can't be Jonathan because he's not here. James and I were gone when the tampering took place, so we aren't guilty. I get the sense that you feel my mother isn't the culprit. That leaves the servants. They've been with us for years and I'd bet my fortune that none of them are in on this."

"You forgot about Kim."

"Kim?" Gage snorted out a sardonic laugh. "She doesn't care enough about Jamie to come into this room, let alone go to the trouble of bothering with what he eats. Not only that, she probably doesn't have a clue how to prepare formula."

"Well, it's not too difficult. The directions are right on the can, so I'm sure even she'd be able to figure it out. I agree that she doesn't care for Jamie, but she's not above using him to get her revenge for being forced to give birth to him."

Gage shook his head in disbelief.

New Beginnings
Olivia Claire High

"You're saying James forced Kim to give birth to their baby? Now you really have flipped your lid."

"I wasn't referring to James. Goodnight, Mr. Langdon," she said before closing her door.

Gage immediately lunged forward just as the lock clicked into place. He knew he couldn't pound on the door and demand that she open it, without waking Jamie. He stared at the door for a few more seconds before storming out of the nursery grinding his teeth in frustration.

Holland leaned back against the door while her heart beat like a wild thing ready to burst from its cage. Her whole body shook as she walked across the room where she slumped down onto the bed. She hadn't intended for their conversation to go so far where she actually brought up the part about Kim using Jamie for revenge.

She sat there gnawing on her thumbnail. What would Gage do now that he realized she suspected James might not be the baby's father? She'd definitely gone too far. She'd called him a control freak, practically said he wasn't a good son, and accused his sister-in-law of doing something horrendous.

Holland stared at the sleeping baby and felt tears burn at the back of her eyes. Would Gage make sure Jamie was going to be all right if she left? Had her blabbing everything ended up putting the child in more danger? Maybe she should have put the lock on her big mouth instead of the refrigerator. But she couldn't take back the things she'd said and wasn't one hundred per cent sure she'd made a mistake in letting Gage know she was aware of the situation.

Holland looked at her suitcase and decided she may as well pack her things now because come morning she was pretty sure she'd be out of a job here. But first she walked over to the cradle and placed a soft kiss on the baby's head.

"I'm sorry I couldn't be the miracle worker you needed, sweet Jamie," she whispered

Gage walked briskly down the hall toward the nursery the next morning, his jaw set in determination. He'd barely slept going over Holland's outrageous claims. She definitely had some explaining to do about Kim being forced to have Jamie. He also was damn well going to get her to tell him what the hell she meant about her crack that James wasn't the guilty one. Just what had she been alluding to?

He was about to enter the nursery when he heard his mother laughing. He froze. Gage couldn't remember the last time he'd heard her laugh like that. He peered around the corner and saw her standing with Holland by her side, as the two women bathed the baby.

He leaned back so they wouldn't spot him. He couldn't help noticing how the two women called each other by their first names. They were acting more like mother and daughter, than employer and employee. Gage stood there listening to his mother tell Holland about an amusing incident from her childhood. It'd been a very long time since she'd had a female friend to share a story like that. The women from her past had stopped coming to visit a long time ago, and he suddenly realized how lonely she must have been for female companionship.

The female servants in the house liked their mistress and were very respectful, but it wasn't the same thing as having a personal friend to confide in, as women were prone to do. He'd actually come here to tell Holland her services were no longer needed. But now seeing how happy his mother sounded he was beginning to have second thoughts.

How could he sack Holland now that he knew how good she was making his mother feel? It would be cruel to take that away from his parent. Perhaps Holland was right, and he had been sheltering his mother too much.

She was in a real snit last night and he sensed it wasn't just about what was happening with the baby. A lot of that anger had been personally directed at him. They were on friendly terms when he left for his business trip. So friendly that he thought about her a lot while he was gone.

Now the good vibes they shared were gone and Gage didn't have a clue why. What really bothered him was the look of disgust she'd given him before she shut the door in his face.

Holland trusted him and now she didn't. It could turn out to be awkward as hell having her live here if he couldn't regain that trust.

But as much as he wanted to solve that mystery, the bigger priority was Jamie's safety. Gage knew he had to stop whoever was responsible for switching the baby's formula if Holland was right about that. He still couldn't believe it. But why would she make something like that up?

A terrible thought just came to him making his breath back up in his lungs. Did Jamie's bottle tampering have anything to do with the person who'd drugged the nannies? Did this mean the monster was back?

Or perhaps they'd never left.

Marguerite wrapped Jamie in the fluffy towel. "Oh Holland, I'm so glad you invited me to give the baby his bath. I'd forgotten how pleasant it could be to do this. I was a very hands-on mother with my boys, and bathing them was one of my favorite things."

"I know what you mean. I always get a kick out of it with my nieces and nephews. Wait till Jamie gets a little older and starts splashing all over the place. We'll have to use the big bathtub."

"I know. I used to wear a plastic apron to protect my clothes and the boys still managed to get me wet, but I didn't really mind. It was all part of the fun for me."

Marguerite laid the baby on the changing table and stepped back indicating she wanted Holland to diaper and dress him.

"Did Gage have a chance to talk to you last night?" she asked in a casual voice.

Holland's hands stilled for a moment. She hoped Marguerite wouldn't bring up her son's name when she showed up in the nursery this morning. Holland felt uneasy wondering just how much she should confess, but decided to just get everything out in the open. At least this way Marguerite would hear both sides of the story.

"Yes. I planned on telling you, but you were enjoying the baby so much I didn't want to spoil it for you. Our conversation didn't go very well. I said a lot more than I should have. I'm pretty sure he's going to give me the boot today.'"

"Nonsense. I am the head of this household and I want you to stay."

"Thank you for that vote of confidence, but you may not think so when I tell you I called Gage a control freak."

Holland waited fearing she was about to lose Marguerite's friendship when much to her relief the older woman chuckled.

"You did? Well, I never think of him like that, but I suppose he must seem that way to others at times. Never mind. It doesn't hurt a commanding person like my son to be brought down a peg or two if he needs it."

Holland's fingers fumbled with the snaps on Jamie's clothes. She really was nervous wanting to get this conversation over with. "That's not all. I accused him of stifling you."

"Oh dear. How did he take that?"

"Not very well."

"I don't imagine he would, but it's not so much smothering me as being overly protective, and I'm guilty of letting Gage carry on that way. Did you mention the problem with the formula? He wanted me to tell him why the lock was on the refrigerator, but I told him he had to ask you."

"Yes, we did talk about that, and I didn't mean to say so much, but I was angry and told him I believe Kim is responsible. I'm sorry."

"Well, what's done is done. I've been thinking about my daughter-in-law's behavior, and I'm beginning to think her depression is just an excuse, so she doesn't have to have anything to do with her son."

Holland peered at Marguerite out of the corner of her eye. "Why do you think that?"

"Even if she is depressed I think she should feel some amount of guilt over not being a mother to her son. I believe she let herself become pregnant because she wanted James to marry her. My son is very much in love with her, more's the pity because I truly believe Kim doesn't care about anyone but herself."

"Don't be too sure."

"Why do you say that?"

Holland picked up Jamie and walked over to where she'd put his morning bottle. She sat in the rocking chair and nodded toward a nearby chair silently inviting Marguerite to sit down.

"I've probably already said more than I should on the subject of Kim, but I may as well go all the way. I didn't mean to be listening, but I couldn't help overhearing Kim say she never wanted Jamie and she demanded the father keep his promise and go away with her. Apparently she went ahead with the pregnancy to please this person. And I don't mean James."

Marguerite's eyes widened. "Where was this? Who was she talking to?"

"I'm sorry to have to tell you, but she was in Gage's office."

"Did she say anything else? You may as well tell me," she said when Holland hesitated.

"She said he was the baby's real father."

Marguerite looked stunned.

"There is no way Gage would do such a thing. He knows how much James loves that girl. You must have misunderstood. What did Gage say to Kim?"

"I never heard his voice, but they were in Gage's office, so who else would it be? I'm sorry, Marguerite. I don't want to cause trouble in your family, but you have to admit things aren't going well with this business about someone fooling around with Jamie's formula and Kim acting the way she does. Maybe you're too close to your son to see his flaws."

"That may be, but nothing will convince me that Gage fathered Jamie."

"Jamie's hair is the same color as his. James and Kim are both blonde."

"My hair was the same color as Gage's before I turned gray."

"It was?" Holland dragged her bottom lip between her teeth. "I hadn't considered that."

"One more thing you haven't considered is although we call it Gage's office or the study, he's not the only one who uses it. I go in there sometimes and so do his brothers."

"I see. But I didn't imagine Kim's voice and she was ranting to someone."

"She could have been talking on the telephone."

"I hadn't thought of that. Now I feel stupid. I hope I haven't alienated myself from you, too because right now I'm sure I'm not exactly one of your son's favorite people."

"You must tell Gage about the things you heard Kim say. He has a right to know and also the right to defend himself."

"I was pretty belligerent to him last night. Please, won't you tell him?"

"I think it would be better coming from you."

"Why do I get the feeling I'm getting ready to face a firing squad?"

"I'm sure it won't be that bad. He may bluster a bit at first, but Gage is a fair-minded man. Let me take care of Jamie while you go and talk to my son."

"Now?" Holland gulped.

"You may as well get it over with. He's in the office."

"How apropos." Holland reluctantly handed the baby over. "Wish me luck."

"You'll do fine. Just tell him everything the way you told it to me."

Holland wished she had Marguerite's confidence, as she stood in front of the office door.

She wiped her damp hands down the side of her jeans and knocked on the door.

"Come in."

Holland opened the door and stepped inside. Gage sat behind his desk, writing.

"I, um, think we need to talk about last night."

"I agree," he said without looking at her. She waited until he finished writing and tossed his pen aside. He fixed her with a cold glare when he finally gave her his full attention.

"Let me start off by saying you're fired."

Chapter Seven

Holland stiffened. She wasn't surprised he was firing her, but she hadn't expected to feel so shocked hearing him actually say the words. Her legs felt wobbly as she turned to leave.

"Sit down."

She whirled to face him again.

"But you said . . ."

"I said what I should be saying after the way you spoke to me last night, but my mother just called on the intercom and informed me she wants you to stay."

Holland did her best to harden her own expression in an effort to salvage her pride.

"You obviously don't agree with her, so I'll go tell her now, and spare you the trouble."

"Damn it woman, sit down!" Gage bellowed in a combination of anger and frustration.

Startled, Holland sat, suddenly feeling like a cowering dog being scolded for chewing one of its master's favorite slippers. Hopefully if she apologized she could ease some of the tension she'd caused and make things a little easier for them both.

"I owe you an apology for the way I talked to you. I didn't mean to be so disrespectful."

"Like hell you didn't. I may be a control freak, but I'm not an idiot. You had something to say and you said it. I don't need your apology, but I do want an explanation as to why you verbally attacked me; and also what you meant about James forcing Kim to have the baby."

"You're not going to like it."

"I didn't expect to."

"I told you, I believe someone is trying to harm Jamie."

"We'll come back to that. What about the rest?"

Her breath came out in a nervous little sigh.

"I was outside the office before you left on your business trip. Kim was complaining to you. At least I thought it was you, but I never heard anyone answer her. I guess she could have been on the phone."

"What was she going on about?"

"She said you, or whoever she was talking to was the baby's real father and that she never wanted the baby. She had Jamie because she was promised if she did, that person would run off with her leaving Jamie here. I also heard her admit that her depression was fake."

"Anything else?" he ground out.

She saw the flare of temper in his eyes and dreaded having to tell him more.

"She said she knew the family thought I was some kind of miracle worker with Jamie, but that my miracles were about to run out. I was told later the baby became ill right after that."

"Were you gone by then?"

"Yes. I intended to quit, but I couldn't stay away when Colleen called and said Jamie was sick again. That's when my uncle told me about Janet Carl."

"The lady providing her breast milk?"

Holland nodded.

"She's struggling financially. But she didn't name a price even though she needs the money. The important thing is how much Jamie needs her milk. I'm scared that something worse than an upset tummy is going to happen to him if I don't keep watch."

"Hence, the lock on the nursery refrigerator."

"That's right. Can you blame me now that you know what I heard?"

"I blame you for jumping to the wrong conclusion, but not about wanting to protect Jamie."

Gage rested his elbows on the surface of his desk and made a steeple with his long fingers.

"You told me what you think you heard about me. Now you'll hear the truth. First, let me say emphatically that I have never donated any of my sperm to Kim intimately or in any other fashion. Second, I'll arrange to have some testing done to prove that James is Jamie's biological father if that becomes necessary. And third, don't ever shut a door in my face again."

Holland had the grace to look ashamed.

"I won't. I only did it last night because you looked like you wanted to throttle me."

"The thought had crossed my mind, but despite our differences I'd like you to stay."

"Only because your mother told you she wants me."

"That's part of it, but not all. You're not the only one who listens at doors. I went to the nursery this morning to have it out with you when I saw you two giving the baby a bath. I haven't seen my mother look or sound that happy in too long to remember."

"She loves her grandson."

"Yes she does. But you're partly responsible for her good mood. I realize my mother's been lonely for female company other than the servants, and you seem to be filling that void."

"I'd like to think I'm doing some good. I've become very fond of your mother and Jamie."

"But you think I'm a first class jerk," Gage said in a dry tone.

Holland flinched.

"No I don't. I mean I did, but not now."

"Well, that's a big load lifted. I'd hate to be on the same crap list as your ex-husband."

"You'd have to be pretty bad for that to happen."

"Perhaps you'll tell me someday what went wrong with your marriage," he said, softening.

"What went wrong was I married the wrong guy." Holland rose from her chair. "I think I should go back and check on how your mother is doing."

Gage came from around his desk to face her. "I'll want you with me when I confront Kim."

"Oh boy, now there's something to look forward to."

He smiled.

"I'm glad you still have your sense of humor."

"My dad always says *leave 'em laughing*. Are we done here now?"

"One more thing before you go."

"What?"

"This."

He pulled her against his chest, seized her mouth in a kiss so sensual it made her feel like her toes were about to curl. He let her go and she stumbled back touching a fingertip to her lips.

"Wh . . . why did you do that?"

The intercom buzzed to life before Gage had a chance to answer. The sound of Marguerite's frantic voice cut through the earlier erotic moment.

"Come to the nursery. Hurry!" Her voice broke on a sob.

"Mother, what's wrong?"

"Jamie's gone!"

Gage grabbed Holland by the hand "We're on our way."

They dashed out of his office and took off running. Marguerite met them at the door, but she was crying so hard by now she couldn't talk. Colleen stood by nearly in tears herself.

"What happened?" Gage demanded of Colleen.

"Your sister-in-law contacted your mother and said she needed to talk to her. Your mother called and told me to find out what was wrong. Mrs. Howard, your sister-in-law that is, insisted she had to talk to your mother in person. I came back to the nursery. Jamie was asleep. Your mother told me to stay with him."

Gage put his arm around his mother's shoulders.

New Beginnings
Olivia Claire High

"Go on."

"I saw that the baby's bathwater was still there, so I took the little tub to the bathroom to empty it. I was only there a few minutes when your mother returned and found Jamie missing."

"What about Kim? What did she want, Mother?" Gage urged.

Marguerite managed to stop crying enough to answer him. "I don't know. She wasn't in her room when I arrived. I thought she must have decided to come here and I missed her."

"Holland, come with me. Colleen, you stay here with my mother."

"Yes, sir."

Marguerite wiped her tear stained face with a lace trimmed handkerchief.

"No. I'm not going to stay here wringing my hands like a helpless ninny. I want to help. The more people we have looking for my grandson the sooner we'll find him."

Gage nodded before turning to Colleen. "Do you have any idea where James might be?"

"I believe he's working out in the gym."

"I think it'd be best if I went there rather than call him on the intercom. You ladies each take a wing and we'll meet back at the gym. With any luck James will know where we can find his wife and son. If not, then he can help us look for them."

Kim set the carrier down and pointed to the sleeping Jamie. "Here's your precious son."

"This is no place for a baby. He should be back in the nursery."

"I'm beginning to think you care more about him than you do me."

"I just don't want you taking unnecessary chances with him."

"I still don't know why you were so set on me having the baby when I told you how I felt."

"It didn't seem right to have an abortion and you wouldn't have gotten pregnant if you'd been more careful with your birth control. Did you get pregnant thinking you could trap me?"

"No. I would have come up with a less painful way for us to be together. You're not the one who had to go through months of puking and having your body swell up like a damn balloon. I wished you were dead while I suffered through the agony of labor."

"You wouldn't want me dead and you know it."

She let out a harsh breath.

"I've kept my part of our bargain and I'm getting tired of waiting around for you to keep yours. You wanted the kid. You can have him. I'm leaving."

"Brave talk, Kim. You had the baby because I told you to and you'll stay put until I tell you it's time to go."

"How much longer, damn it?"

"I told you I have plans for us, but I need more time."

"I'm going out of my mind waiting."

"Hang on a little while longer. Now take the baby back before someone comes looking for him.

We don't want anyone to discover our hiding place."

"I know, but I can't help wanting to be with you," she whined.

"I've told you before I'm the one who decides when it's safe to be together. I can't keep sneaking in and out of here on your whims. You put us both at too much risk, especially when you said there's a new nanny hanging around. When are you going to do something about her?"

"I've just been waiting for the right opportunity. I don't know why you're so worried about her seeing us together. She never comes to my room. But I have an idea how we can see each other without her knowing. She's been taking the baby into town a couple times a week. You can come to my room while she's gone."

"During the day? Are you nuts? You'll blow our secret."

"Will you at least come to me tonight, then?"

"I still don't want to take the chance the nanny will see me sneaking into your room. I know you said she doesn't go there, but that doesn't mean she won't. She sounds like the snoopy type."

Kim let out a frustrated breath. "You won't come to me, so I'm forced to come to you. I'm completely recovered from the pregnancy and birth. I need you to make love to me."

"All right. I'll try to see you tonight."

Her eyes sparkled with anticipation. "I'll drug James like before."

"You be careful doing that. I don't want any problems. Now go."

"I will, but kiss me first."

"You sound pathetic, do you know that?"

"Only because you've made me this way."

Kim leaned against him and kissed hungrily at his lips, thrusting her tongue into his mouth before he finally pushed her away.

"You'd better go before the baby wakes up."

"I'm going. I can't wait to be in your arms again."

She picked up the carrier, blew him a kiss, and hurried away.

He watched her go and rubbed a hand across his mouth. Kim was becoming too demanding. Having her show up with Jamie was proof of her recklessness. Her growing resentment towards the baby worried him. He would have taken Jamie by now, but he had to be sure the child was healthy enough for what he had in mind.

Kim would ruin his plans if he couldn't get her to hold herself together a while longer. She had amused him once, but not for a long time now. Her pregnancy caught him off guard. He shouldn't have trusted her when she claimed to be using birth control.

She tried to use her pregnancy to force him to marry her and threatened to have an abortion when he told her now wasn't a good time for them to wed. While he may not want her he had an inspiration for what to do with the baby for reasons he could never share with Kim. He promised to marry her later, but convinced her to seduce James and get him to marry her. He didn't want to take the chance the family might not let her stay without a Howard ring on her finger. He also suggested she pretend to be depressed after the baby came when she claimed she hated the idea of being a mother. He knew she wouldn't have to try very hard to snag James because she'd tried to make him jealous by saying James would do anything to have her for his wife.

Now Kim had a child she didn't want and a husband she didn't love. But she was determined to keep him as her lover. His insides churned at the thought of being with her tonight. She wasn't the only one growing weary of their charade, but he would do what he had to do until Jamie was strong enough to be taken away from here.

And it would have to be soon, or he'd be the one going out of his mind.

Kim hurried along heedless of the precious burden she carried. All she could think about was having her lover join her tonight. She decided she'd wear her new silk nightgown or better yet, nothing but a few dots of perfume. She smiled at the thought and carelessly jostled the carrier against her leg as she entered one of the side entrances of the house. Jamie awoke and began to whimper.

"Oh, shut up," she snapped, shaking the carrier and causing him to cry harder.

"Where have you been?" Kim stopped at the sound of Marguerite's angry voice. "Everyone has been looking for you," she said and reached down to unbuckle the straps to lift the crying Jamie into her arms.

"I took him for a walk. You let London, or whatever the nanny's name is to take him anywhere she pleases. I'll just bet you don't subject her to an inquisition."

"I'm happy that you're finally taking an interest in your son, Kim. But it would have helped if you'd let someone know you had him with you."

"Oh, so now I need permission? Are you saying I can't be trusted with my own baby?"

"No. It's just that we were all concerned. Would you please call James on the intercom at the gym and let him know everything is all right? He's very worried. I'll take Jamie back to the nursery if you'd like while you do that, shall I?"

"Do what you want. I can't stand his crying. I try to do one thing and this is how he reacts."

"Kim, he's only a few weeks old and he's had a hard time with his digestive problems. You must learn to be patient with him."

"I'll leave that to the nanny you're so enthralled with. That's what you're paying her for."

Kim stabbed a finger against the intercom pad and connected to the gym to let James know she was back. She stopped him when he began to go on about how worried he'd been. She told him she'd be in their room and his mother had taken charge of getting the baby to the nursery.

Marguerite held her temper, as she watched her daughter-in-law flounce away. Holland met Marguerite a few minutes later outside the baby's room and peered anxiously at him.

"Oh thank God you found him. Is he all right?"

"I think so. He's just a little frightened I imagine. Kim took him for a walk."

Holland's brows arched. "Really? Well, I hope that's a good sign."

"I wish I could say differently, but Kim is Kim. Nothing has changed."

Gage sat with Holland and his mother in Holland's room that evening. He drank coffee while they had their nightly tea. They kept their voices low not wanting to wake Jamie.

"Did James come to see the baby?" he asked Holland.

"Yes, he left just before you got here. I got the impression he's angry we upset Kim."

Marguerite sniffed.

"Upset her? It seems to me he should be more worried that his wife took their son out of the house without letting any of us know."

Gage nodded.

"The fact that one of the servants saw her going into the tunnel bothers me. Why would she take the baby in there, I wonder?"

"What tunnel?" Holland asked, looking at them.

"The original part of the house has some tunnels beneath the foundation leading to the outside. My step-father wanted them as an escape route in the event there was ever a threat of kidnappers coming here. The twins used to enjoy playing in them. The only one used now leads to a wine cellar."

"I had no idea Kim even knew about them," Marguerite said.

"Nor did I. James must have told her."

"How odd that she decided to take Jamie with her after not wanting to touch him since his birth. Although the doctor did say she could come out of her depression at any time. I suppose I should apologize for being so hard on her."

"You were worried," Gage replied.

"I know. But what if she wanted her first outing with Jamie to be private? The more I think about it the worse I feel. I practically accused her of kidnapping her own son."

He reached over and squeezed his mother's hand.

"Now don't go putting yourself on a guilt trip. Your first reaction was the same any of us would have felt. We'll talk to James tomorrow and see how Kim is doing. Maybe you can get him to encourage her to come to the nursery again now that she made an attempt to take Jamie out with her."

"That's a good idea. Perhaps if we continue to encourage them both to have a relationship with Jamie together it will help them to see how much we want to have our family be united."

Holland cleared her throat.

"I don't want to discourage Kim, but have you forgotten about the formula tampering? We never did find out who was responsible."

"You still think Kim's involved?" Gage said.

"I'm not ruling her out and neither should you. I don't know why she took the baby off on her own, but I sincerely doubt if it was a step toward bonding with him."

"You seem determined to believe she's a threat. I don't know why when she's never shown any interest in him. Today was a first. I agree it was a little strange the way she went about it, but hopefully it'll be a start of something good."

"I doubt it. I believe she's very calculating."

"I have my doubts about her depression, but calculating? Isn't that being a bit harsh?"

"You're forgetting that I heard her say her depression was fake. I don't know what her agenda is, but as far as I can tell it has nothing to do with being a mother to Jamie. We need to find out the real reason she took the baby with her today."

Marguerite gave a strained chuckle. "You sound more like a detective than a nanny, Holland."

"Maybe that's because I need to be both."

Chapter Eight

Gage sat in the small dining room off the kitchen, ignoring the coffee in front of him. James had just left. For a man who rarely drank alcohol and very little when he did, James looked and sounded like someone recovering from a hangover. His hands shook as he poured himself coffee from a carafe. He complained of a pounding headache when Gage asked if he felt all right. Their conversation hadn't gone well after that.

James spent several minutes ranting about how the entire household was against Kim. He seemed especially intent on singling out Holland. He accused her of taking control of his son and denying his wife access to the baby, shouting down any words Gage attempted to offer in Holland's defense. He stormed out of the room, but not before threatening to take Kim and Jamie somewhere else to live if Holland wasn't out of the house by tonight.

James had a tendency to let his temper take over whenever he felt he needed to defend his wife. His brother was so much in love with her that he never saw any of her flaws, including the fact that she would sleep with any man who'd have her. Gage felt disgusted remembering how she'd come on to him. He'd made short work of letting her know he wasn't interested, which certainly didn't endear himself to her.

Gage knew she'd gone after Jonathan next who treated her advances as a joke and merely laughed at her display of female wiles. Gage couldn't help feeling sorry for James. The man was desperate to make his marriage succeed, but how he would ever manage that feat with a wife like Kim was beyond understanding.

His thoughts turned to how James demanded that Holland be fired. Gage rubbed his forehead in frustration. How many more nannies were they going to have to hire before Jamie was old enough not to need one? The truth was, he didn't want Holland to leave. She'd not only managed to stay longer than the other women, but she was genuinely fond of Jamie, and he was definitely doing much better under her care.

It troubled him that Holland remained convinced someone wanted to harm Jamie. Gage understood with their kind of wealth, kidnapping would be the biggest danger to his nephew. But having someone switch his formula knowing it would make him ill was an unexpected and disturbing development. What did the person hope to gain by doing such a terrible thing?

Holland thought Kim was the guilty one. Did she really hate her own child that much? It made Gage sick to think so. What if Holland was right? He couldn't let James take the baby away and have Kim be in charge of Jamie. It didn't take a child specialist to see that she wasn't fond of being around her own son.

Gage got up and shoved his hands in his pockets. Jamie wasn't his child, which meant he didn't have the legal right to say who should care for the baby. He'd been able to have Holland here because James had allowed it, but now that was about to change unless he could convince his brother otherwise.

Either Holland was sent packing, or Jamie would be taken away from here into an unknown situation. Gage wanted his brother to be more independent, but damned if the man didn't choose the most inopportune times and causes to exert his fledging independence. James continued to be gullible where his wife was concerned, and maybe the rest of them were just as naïve in believing she was suffering from depression.

Holland insisted she heard Kim say she was faking her condition, so she wouldn't have to be around the baby, which made it all the more worrisome how Jamie would get on if James took him away. Another concern was what would having her grandson be gone do to his mother? He noticed she was spending more and more time in the nursery and taking a more active role in his care under Holland's tutelage.

Nor did he want to speculate on how he'd feel if Holland left. He thought about their kiss and the feel of her soft lips. He'd kissed her on an impulse, but had to admit it was something he wouldn't mind repeating. Gage knew Jamie wasn't the only one who wouldn't be happy if she wasn't here. He'd have to find a way to convince James to let Holland stay.

James looked daggers at Gage.

"No! I told you I don't want Holland here. I promised Kim she'd be gone. How else is my wife ever going to be able to be a proper mother to Jamie with that . . . that warden controlling every minute of our son's life? Must I remind you again that he's my son, not yours? This isn't your decision to make."

"Just hear me out. Please," Gage added while keeping a tight rein on his own temper.

"All right, but nothing you say is going to make me change my mind."

"I understand how you feel. I'm happy that Kim is willing to take a more active role in caring for Jamie, but I think you realize your wife's emotions are still very fragile. She also doesn't have any experience in taking care of a baby."

"How could she when she's been so ill? You know what the doctor said about her depression going away. Well, she's trying to be better, but no one will give her the chance."

"That's what we're going to do now. She can go to the nursery every day to watch and learn until she's comfortable enough to be on her own."

James shook his head.

"It won't work. I keep telling you Kim can't stand Holland."

"I didn't mean for Holland to be there at the same time. Mother and Colleen will assist Kim. I'd also like to encourage you to be available. I think it would help your wife if you're willing to make this important adjustment together. I have a feeling there's nothing like changing a baby's soiled diaper to help you bond with the child."

"I guess learning to take care of Jamie together might work. I'll do anything to help Kim even if it means changing diapers. But what did you have in mind about Holland?"

"She knows more about the baby than anyone. I think it'd be best if she's in the house in case we have any questions."

"No, damn it. I'm telling you, Kim doesn't want her here. Period."

"We won't tell her Holland is still hanging around."

James snorted.

"Oh, like that's going to work. I'll never hear the end of it if Kim finds out. She hates the woman."

"So you keep saying. Why is that?"

"The servants talk. Kim heard them saying Holland thinks Kim's the one responsible for messing with Jamie's formula. How do you think that makes her feel being accused by a stranger of trying to hurt her own baby?"

"Not very well, I imagine."

"You got that right." James shoved his hands in his pockets and rocked back on his heels while Gage waited. "Okay, we'll keep Holland's presence here a secret and by God you'd better make damn sure she stays out of sight. I'll talk to Kim and see if she's willing to try the rest of your plan, but only on one condition."

Gage raised his brows.

"Which would be?"

"No more locks on the refrigerator in my son's room."

"James, I don't think . . ."

"No lock or you can forget about everything else. That's my final word. Either do what I say, or Holland goes."

Holland gave Gage an incredulous look. "Are you out of your mind?"

"What did you say?"

"Oh, don't get all haughty on me. Let me see if I've got this straight. You want me to make myself scarce while James and Kim take over the care of their son?"

"My mother and Colleen will be helping them. He is their child, Holland. They've got to start taking some responsibility for him some time. The longer things go on the way they are now I believe the harder it'll be for them to bond with the baby."

"I get it. I'll be sent on my way after they've got the hang of being parents."

"Not at all. I still want you to be in charge of making sure your friend's breast milk gets here and have you be in the house if questions arise about Jamie. You just can't be around Kim."

"What am I supposed to do, sit in a closet twiddling my thumbs?"

"Don't be ridiculous. There are plenty of things you can do around here to make the waiting more pleasant. Swim in the pool. Walk in the atrium. Use the library. Watch movies in the theater. Or anything else that you'd like."

"What I'd like is to not be around when Jamie starts getting sick again."

"You seem very sure that will be a foregone conclusion."

"Let's just say it's a judgment call. Have you ever thought of putting a hidden camera in the nursery like people do when they suspect a babysitter of abusing their child?"

"Yes. I suggested it to James, but he nixed the idea after talking to Kim because she said it'd make her feel like we were spying on her."

"Which ironically would be true. God forbid we should hurt her feelings. You could have snuck the camera in if you hadn't mentioned it to James."

"I doubt it. He's been keeping a closer eye on the nursery lately."

"So you're willing to let the baby suffer in order to keep peace with his parents."

Gage's jaw tightened.

"Stop trying to make me out to be the villain here. Of course I don't want Jamie to suffer."

"I'm sorry. I didn't mean that. I'm just so frustrated."

"And you think I'm not? The bottom line is we have to do what Kim wants."

"That little snot knows how much we care for Jamie, so she's using emotional blackmail to keep us all under her control."

"I suppose she is in her own way. I'm doing the best I can to keep Jamie here, but the fact remains he isn't my child and I can only do so much to help him. Kim convinced James you should be fired. I talked him out of it by saying you wouldn't be around her. I discussed this with my mother and she agreed we should give the plan a try."

"Why do I get the feeling I'm a rotten tooth that you all want to pull?"

"That's not a very nice image and it certainly isn't true. Please try to see my side of the situation. My options are limited. James originally threatened to take Kim and the baby to live somewhere else. I couldn't allow that. Not only would it upset my mother, but we'd also be constantly wondering if Jamie was all right. James promised to stay if you keep out of sight."

"Okay, I'll frolic in the pool, or whatever, during the day while Kim plays mommy, but what are you going to do about the nights? Will Colleen stay with Jamie then?"

Gage shook his head. "No. That will still be you. Someone will give the all clear and you can go back to your room. You just have to be gone before James and Kim go to their son in the morning. I couldn't get him to negotiate on that point."

"Wonderful. All that sneaking around is going to make me feel like I'm a criminal."

"I'm sorry. Also, I hate to ask, but you need to remove all your belongings from your room. That's the only way we'll be able to convince Kim that you're no longer in the house."

"Well, jeez. Am I allowed to have my nightshirt, or do I have to sleep naked?"

A quick surge of heat flickered in his eyes. "Now that's what I call a very nice image."

Holland flopped over from her stomach to her back. She looked at the bedside clock and sighed. She'd been in bed for over an hour and still hadn't fallen asleep, thanks to having too much on her mind. She tugged at her nightshirt smoothing out the wrinkles and felt her entire body go warm remembering Gage's reaction when she mentioned sleeping in the nude.

She'd sworn off men and didn't want to have these random urges that Gage aroused, but the man was just too darn sexy for her to ignore. Holland couldn't deny that she'd thought about what he'd look like in the buff ever since she saw him without his shirt at her aunt's that day. But fantasizing about Gage being naked wasn't the only thing keeping her from sleep tonight.

She shoved that enticing image away and turned her head to peek at Jamie. Concern for the baby was another thing preying on her mind. She still felt nervous about leaving him anywhere near Kim, but she supposed the family couldn't be blamed for wanting things to work out. Holland just wished she didn't feel so certain about Kim being a threat to the child.

She was determined not to let anything happen on her watch, but what about when she was relegated to hiding while James and Kim spent time with Jamie? Gage said his mother or Colleen would be with them. She hoped they'd be vigilant. Everything would probably be all right as long as James didn't insist his wife be on her own with their son. The man was so nuts about the woman she could tell him to go dance naked in the snow in the dead of winter, and he'd probably do it.

Naked. Now why did she have to think of that word? She groaned and turned over to bury her hot cheeks in the pillow. She'd told Gage she wasn't keen on marriage after her bad luck. Now she had to wonder if he thought that meant she was off men completely. Not that it would matter in his case because she was pretty sure a man like Gage could have any woman he wanted. Holland seriously doubted if that choice would include a lowly nanny like herself.

Gage found himself doing his own tossing and turning. He chose to get up rather than continue to roll around in bed. He pulled on a pair of sweatpants and a tee shirt before going to the office where he now sat at his computer. He thought he'd do some work there until he felt sleepy enough to go back to bed. So far he wasn't having much luck. His brain kept bringing up images of Holland no matter how much he tried to concentrate on the data in front of him.

When he wasn't thinking about Holland his mind plagued him with the situation involving James and Kim and their infant son. His lips pressed into an angry line recalling what his mother had told him earlier about the attempt at family bonding in the nursery.

James had to practically drag Kim there, but it turned out to be a waste of time. She refused to so much as touch her son, let alone change a diaper or feed him a bottle. Marguerite said it was almost a relief when her daughter-in-law insisted on leaving after only ten minutes. James had apologized and hurried to follow his wife.

Gage moved his hands away from the keyboard and sat back in his chair. He hadn't cared for the plan he'd proposed in the first place, but he couldn't think of any other way to keep James from taking the baby away. He also continued to remind himself he didn't want Holland to go.

He didn't flatter himself that Holland stayed because she wanted to be around him. He knew Jamie was the real reason she'd agreed to hide out during the day and return to the nursery at night to watch over the baby.

Once again he thought about Holland's theory that Kim was guilty of trying to harm Jamie. Holland also insisted she'd heard some pretty damning proof that James wasn't the baby's father. Both were serious allegations that could have dire consequences if she was correct.

Jamie's birth should have brought nothing but happiness to the household. They'd all been pleased when James announced he and Kim were expecting. Gage smiled, recalling his mother's excitement at becoming a grandmother and how she had offered to help decorate the nursery.

Sadly, Kim didn't want to have anything to do with the project. That was the first red flag that she wasn't pleased about becoming a parent. James blamed it on her not feeling well. He'd stayed close to her doing everything he could to make her comfortable during the pregnancy

New Beginnings
Olivia Claire High

Gage never saw his sister-in-law when she wasn't complaining and how much she couldn't wait for her ordeal to end. His mother had been appalled that Kim thought being pregnant was an ordeal. He didn't miss how James winced every time she whined about her condition.

Jamie arrived three weeks early, but luckily he was healthy and at a good weight. Thinking of that made Gage wonder again about Holland's claim that the baby hadn't been fathered by James. What if she was right? It would certainly devastate James. He felt his anger rise when he thought of Holland's accusation that he was Jamie's biological father. He'd put her straight on that notion, but it did get him to wondering who may have fathered his nephew if it wasn't James. It was difficult to tell at this point who the baby was going to look like because he was still so young.

The fact that Kim prowled around men like a tigress needing to feed didn't make it easy to believe that she'd been totally faithful to James. Had she gotten pregnant by someone else and lied in order to have James marry her because her real lover dumped her? If that was the case, then why didn't she have an abortion? His body cringed at such a distasteful thought.

He didn't care for the path his thoughts were taking, but it was difficult not to suspect his sister-in-law. Kim wasn't an easy person to like. Gage didn't think he'd ever seen her happy; and he had to force himself to keep his mouth shut when he saw how she treated James. There were times he wanted to shake his brother for allowing himself to become her whipping boy.

He was tempted to challenge Kim about her behavior after what Holland told him. But of course no one wanted to upset her because of her so-called fragile state. Was her depression real like her doctor claimed, or was she just a good actress? How much longer would the entire household have to tiptoe around her as though she might have a breakdown at any moment?

Gage turned off his computer and stood up. He'd only made his sleeplessness worse by filling his head with so many unresolved issues. He knew he shouldn't wait much longer to find a way to expose Kim if she really was a fraud, or to finally settle in his own mind that she actually was just a sick, unhappy woman who hated her life here.

Holland was in the laundry room helping Colleen the next morning. She wanted to be useful in some way during the hours she was banned from taking care of the baby. She started to fold Kim's clothing, but Colleen quickly took over saying things had to be folded a certain way or she would be in trouble. It made Holland angry to see how nervous the poor woman was over something as simple as folding laundry. Kim's demanding behavior obviously wasn't endearing her to anyone, including the servants.

Gage found them there.

"Good morning, ladies."

"Oh, good morning, Mr. Langdon."

114

Holland didn't miss the fact that Colleen was much more at ease with Gage than his cantankerous sister-in-law. But then he didn't seem inclined to call her bad names and throw shoes at her, either. She smiled at him to acknowledge his greeting and went on folding clothes.

"Colleen, will you excuse us, please? I'd like to talk to Holland in private."

"Certainly, sir."

He waited until she left before turning to Holland.

"What are you doing in here?"

"Jamie's laundry. I offered to help Colleen since she's taking on my duties in the nursery."

"She told my mother you helped prepare our dinner last night. You didn't have to do that. We're paying you to be the nanny, not a scullery maid. Please don't feel you have to do anything else while you're here. I'd rather see you go back to your uncle and aunt's to help them."

"I went there, and then I came back here. How'd things go with Kim and Jamie yesterday?"

He raked his hands through his hair.

"It didn't. She was barely there before she left. James told my mother she was practically hysterical by the time they got back to their own room."

"Sorry to hear that. But I had my doubts that your idea would work. So what's plan B?"

"James told me this morning he wants you back. It didn't take him long to see Kim wasn't up to doing what she claimed she wanted, which on the plus side means he won't be taking Jamie away. I told him I'd talk to you. My mother's with the baby now. She enjoys helping, but she and Colleen aren't capable of his fulltime care. Do you mind picking up where you left off?"

"That's why I hung around. What are you going to do about Kim, though? She hates me."

"Oh the hell with Kim. I've had it with her attitude. Like you, I heard some things I wish I hadn't. I went to talk to them and was standing outside their bedroom door when I heard her yelling at James. My God, I don't know how the man puts up with her tantrums."

Holland shrugged.

"He's in love and he'll do anything to keep from upsetting her, especially if he still believes she's suffering from depression."

"Does that so-called depression include saying she wished she never had the baby?"

"It can; and if I'm wrong about her and she really is ill, I'm going to feel pretty terrible. But I can't forget the fact that I actually heard her say she was faking."

"I'm beginning to feel like we're sitting on a bomb that's going to explode any day now. If Kim hates the baby, and probably James, the way she talks, I can't believe she's stayed around this long. I honestly believe James and Jamie will be better off without her if this keeps up, but it's going to tear my brother apart if she does leave."

"It's demoralizing to love someone and find out they don't love you back."

"Is that how things were with you and your ex-husband?" he asked keeping his tone gentle.

"Something like that."

"I'm sorry."

"Don't be. So, should I go relieve your mother now?"

Gage didn't miss how Holland changed the subject, but he knew he had no right to probe and bring up unhappy memories for her. It made him sad to think she'd suffered because of an ill-fated love, just as his brother was doing.

"I think she'd appreciate that. I have one more thing I need to tell you. I know you're not going to like it, but as I said before, I can only do so much."

Holland paused at the door holding the basket of Jamie's clean laundry in her hands.

"I don't like it already. What's the problem now?"

"James still insists the lock stays off the refrigerator in the nursery. He says it will make Kim angry if she sees it. He's convinced it's a clear message that we don't trust her."

"It doesn't sound like Kim will be going back to the baby's room any time soon if her last trip was an example of her behavior. But okay, no lock. I'll move the refrigerator into my room."

Gage shook his head.

"That won't work, either. She'll still see it as a vote of no confidence."

Holland's hands clenched on the basket. "Kim doesn't want to be a mother to her son, but that doesn't stop her from wanting to keep anyone else from trying to do what's right for him. All right, I'll play it their way. Tell James and his precious Kim there won't be a lock, but I'm still going to do what

I can to keep anyone from tampering with Jamie's food."

"I'd be interested to know how you plan to do that."

"I'll let you know when I figure it out."

"Holland, one more thing before you go. Not about Kim," he quickly added when she scowled at him. "I don't mean to pry when I ask you questions about your ex-husband. I just want to get to know you better."

She paused, as though she might be making a decision about how to answer him.

"I want to get to know you better too, especially since I had a dream about us last night."

Gage raised an inquiring brow.

"How did that go?"

"I'll have to let you know when I figure that out, too."

New Beginnings
Olivia Claire High

Chapter Nine

Holland walked out of the bathroom the next morning into the nursery carrying Jamie after cleaning up his bath things. She stopped at the sight of the man standing there, looking down at the baby's cradle. He wore faded jeans, a bright red tee shirt, tennis shoes, and a baseball hat with the bill turned to the back. Something about him reminded her of James.

"May I help you?"

The man spun around to stare at her.

"You startled me."

"That makes two of us, but now that I see your face I can relax. You're obviously Jonathan."

"That would be me, and you must be Holland." He grinned, and held out his hand. She set Jamie in his bouncy chair and shook hands.

"You have a cool name."

"Thanks. I didn't realize you and James were identical twins."

"Yeah, but I'm still the better looking one."

His friendly manner had Holland smiling. She watched, as he crouched down and slipped a finger into Jamie's tiny fist, grinning when the baby grabbed on.

"Hey buddy, do you have a smile for your Uncle Johnny?" He stood up after a few seconds.

"He's looking good. I just got home last night. Gage filled me in. Great idea you had to get Jamie breast milk, but you wouldn't have to go elsewhere if he had a decent mother."

"Everyone is hoping she'll eventually be well enough to accept her responsibilities."

He rolled his eyes.

"Don't count on it. She could care less about Jamie and my brother. She treats James like a trained circus dog. It's enough to make you gag."

"Maybe part of that is because she senses the family doesn't like her."

"I'm surprised you'd defend her, especially considering what I heard concerning how she feels about you. The family, myself included have bent over backwards to be nice to Kim because we know how important she is to James and also that she's Jamie's mother. We've never shown her, to her face, how we really feel about her. But no matter how much we try to do for her she's never satisfied. She'd rather go on about how terrible her life is. She pretends she's sick, so she doesn't have to have anything to do with her son or I suspect sleep with my brother."

"I take it you don't believe her depression is real."

"I know it's not real. She told me she was going to fake it."

Holland couldn't hide her surprise.

"Kim actually told you that?"

"She was pretty wasted at the time, otherwise I doubt if she would have let her plan slip. It happened right after Jamie was born. I'd just finished a late night swim and was going to bed when I remembered I left my phone in the dining room. I found Kim there along with a vodka bottle in one hand and a glass in the other."

"Did James know about the incident?"

"No. He wouldn't even know she was out of bed. Kim insisted they sleep in separate bedrooms when she found out she was pregnant. I'd never tell him. She's hurting him enough as it is. I'd like to shut her up every time she badmouths him. We're twins and we used to be close."

"Are you saying Kim has changed your relationship?"

"Yeah. He's definitely not the same because of her, but he doesn't see what she's doing to him. Someone needs to kick her out of this house."

"It sounds as though you'd like that someone to be you."

"Oh hell yes. I'd even pack her bag. Unfortunately, it's not my decision."

Holland sat rocking Jamie and thought about her conversation with Jonathan. He was one more person in this house who didn't care for Kim. Who could blame any of them when she went out of her way to do her best to alienate everyone?

Colleen was terrified of Kim, and she wasn't the only servant who would rather not have anything to do with the woman. Holland found out there were a lot more people working here than she realized, and they all had an unpleasant experience to tell about the young Mrs. Howard.

New Beginnings
Olivia Claire High

She knew Marguerite and Gage tried to support Kim for James and Jamie's benefit. But Holland could see their patience was wearing thin. Jonathan clearly had no love for his sister-in-law because of the way she treated his brother. James seemed to be the only one who continued to show her affection, although his efforts didn't seem to be appreciated by his wife.

James obviously adored Kim and would do anything to defend her against any and all derogatory comments. Holland suspected a big part of him trying to make the marriage work was for Jamie's sake. One had to wonder if his efforts were worth the struggle considering how much Kim disliked her own child. And apparently her husband as well if Jonathan was to be believed.

Had Kim altered Jamie's bottles because she really hated the baby that much, or did she want everyone to think Jamie was sickly? Holland thought about that and realized she knew the answer. Recalling what she'd heard outside Gage's office, Kim was desperate to leave here with her secret lover and it sounded like she was trying to convince the man that their son was too frail to take with them. Why was the man stalling? Could it be that he wanted Jamie?

Holland thought Kim also stayed because she lacked enough money to live in the affluent lifestyle the Howards could afford. But according to the servants she came from a very wealthy family herself. Holland did an inventory in her head. Kim hated living here. She didn't want her son. She didn't love her husband. His family annoyed her.

She didn't need their wealth. But she suffered through all this because she wanted to leave with her lover.

Was she so in love with him that she couldn't bring herself to go away without him? That made sense when Holland considered Kim claimed he was Jamie's real father and she had the baby because that's what he wanted her to do. The big question was, who could that someone be who not only fathered her child, but had such a hold on Kim that she'd rather have a baby she didn't want and stay in a house she detested until the man was ready to take her away?

Jamie would be better off if Kim did leave him here and according to Jonathan, so would James. God only knows what lay ahead for this household if Kim stayed spreading her bitterness and ripping into everyone with her angry tantrums.

Holland stood up and carried the sleeping Jamie to his cradle. She laid him gently inside and smiled down at him. She really was becoming seriously attached to the child. It made her feel sad knowing he had a mother who cared nothing for the sweet baby boy. For a moment that sadness turned to actual pain inside making her chest ache until she forced the feeling away.

Holland's attention was drawn away from so many swirling thoughts when she heard a soft tap at the door. She smiled when Marguerite entered the room.

"Is he asleep?" she whispered pointing to the cradle.

"Yes. I put him down a few minutes ago."

"Would it sound selfish of me if I said I can't wait until he's a little older and able to stay awake longer, so I can have him smile at me and eventually hear that first little tentative laugh?"

"Not at all. I remember how much my family enjoyed it when my nieces and nephews allreached those milestones."

"I came up to relieve you. I thought you'd like to go and spend some time with your aunt and uncle. We've been keeping you away from them far too much."

"They understand, but it'd be nice to go have lunch with them if you're sure that's okay."

"Of course, dear. Colleen and I can handle things here. I know there are enough bottles in the refrigerator for his next couple of feedings."

"That's right. I'll also give Janet a call and see if I can stop by for more."

"She's been such a Godsend for Jamie. He's doing so much better since he's had her breast milk. I would love to meet her. Do you think you could arrange a time when she would be willing to come here? Tell her to bring her baby with her. I want to see her little one, too."

"I'm sure she'd like that. Your money has really helped her."

"I'm glad. She sent me a lovely thank you note. Now off you go. Jamie is in safe hands."

Holland knew this was Marguerite's way of saying Kim wouldn't be allowed to be alone with the baby. It made her feel good to see the fierce determination in the older woman's face. At least

New Beginnings
Olivia Claire High

Jamie could count on his grandmother for love and support.

"I'll be back for his evening feeding."

"Enjoy your visit and please give my best to your aunt and uncle."

Holland took her purse and left. She stopped when she saw Gage by the front door.

"I'm going to my aunt and uncle's for lunch."

"I know. I'm taking you."

"Who says?"

"I've been invited, so I'm driving."

She tilted her head to one side and looked at him.

"Did you and your mother set this up?"

"She did suggest that you should have some time off and we both agreed it'd be nice if some of that time was spent with your family. I called and told them to expect you and received an invitation to lunch. Is that going to be a problem?"

"Nope. But just so you know, don't worry if my aunt looks at you kind of weird."

"You mean because I was shirtless the last time I was in her kitchen?"

Holland shook her head.

"She broke her glasses and hasn't received her new ones yet."

"Oh I see. She's having trouble focusing, is that it?"

"Yes. Uncle Leo said she beat two raisins to death with a wooden spoon and drowned a chocolate chip yesterday thinking they were bugs."

Gage's shoulders shook with laughter, as they walked outside.

"I have a feeling this is going to be a very enjoyable afternoon."

"Don't expect filet mignon or lobster tails."

"You're making me sound like a snob, Holland."

"I didn't mean to, but I doubt if your favorite lunch is a baloney and cheese sandwich."

"It isn't. I like peanut butter and mayonnaise with lettuce on white bread."

She wrinkled her nose at him. "Peanut butter and mayonnaise? Yuk."

"Don't knock it until you've tried it."

"I'll pass."

Gage held the door while Holland climbed into the passenger seat. He turned toward her after he slid behind the wheel. "Don't you like to try new things?"

"It depends on what the things are. By the way, my favorite sandwich is BLT on rye."

"A good old standard. Isn't it nice how we're getting to know each other?"

"Is that what you call this?"

Gage started the engine.

"It's a start, but I plan on finding out a lot more about you."

"Why?"

"You're not the only one who had a dream about us. The difference is I've figured mine out. The next step is for me to try and make it come true."

Holland was proud of her aunt and uncle for not trying to impress Gage by *putting on airs,* as

May would say. They welcomed him into their modest home without apologizing for the worn carpet in the living room, the scarred furniture, or the fact that they ate at the kitchen table and not in their small dining room.

Leo served fluffy omelets filled with fresh vegetables from their garden and eggs from their chickens. May set out slices of her crusty brown bread and a bowl of homemade applesauce. They followed the main meal with coffee and fresh baked chocolate chip cookies. Gage cleared every morsel off his plate making her uncle and aunt beam with satisfaction.

They stayed a little over two hours. Gage suggested they take a drive before going back to his house. Holland agreed knowing Jamie was being well cared for. She realized she was looking forward to the opportunity to be with Gage on her own. Her eyes strayed to him and she took her fill.

He was a big man, wide of shoulder and long limbed, but there was nothing clumsy about him, despite his size. She looked at his hands on the wheel. They were large, strong looking hands, but she knew they could be gentle when she saw how carefully he held Jamie.

"I enjoyed myself."

"Oh good. I know my aunt and uncle enjoyed having you."

"I'd like them to meet my mother."

"They've speculated about your home for years, so I'm sure they'd leap at the chance. But don't get me wrong, my aunt and uncle would treat your mother with the respect she deserves."

"I wouldn't have suggested the meeting if I didn't believe that."

"I was wondering if you felt claustrophobic today, as their house is so much smaller than what you're used to."

"No I didn't. Bigger isn't always better. Would you believe there are times when my mother actually feels closed in despite the size of our house?"

"I'm sure that's because of her illness, but that seems odd since your place is so enormous."

"My house may be a sprawling mansion, but it still reminds her that no matter how big it gets, it still has walls. I dread it every time she tells me she wants more added on because I know she's feeling smothered. It makes me feel as though I'm putting another nail in a coffin. We keep her as comfortable as we can, like so many people do when dealing with a long term illness; but the quality of life just isn't what you'd wish it could be for her."

"I'm sorry, Gage. It must be very hard for you."

"Worse for her. Another reason, besides her illness that keeps my mother inside, is because she says it makes her feel closer to Jamison. But I hate all the damn additions. That's why I stay in my old bedroom in the original part of the house."

"I see your point. My aunt and uncle's house may be small, but they can always go outdoors if they ever feel closed in."

"Exactly. Do you live in a house or an apartment when you're back home?"

New Beginnings
Olivia Claire High

"I'm in my grandmother's little house. I moved in with her after my divorce. She'd had a stroke and needed someone to stay with her. I needed a place to live, so it worked out for us both. My dad says she's doing better now, but I'll still go back to her house when I leave here."

"You seem to do a lot of that kind of thing."

She didn't hear any censure in his tone, but frowned, not understanding his meaning.

"What kind of thing?"

"Taking care of people. Your grandmother, your nieces and nephews, your aunt, and Jamie."

"You do the same thing with your family," she reminded him.

"I suppose I do. You also said you help your father in his store."

"I've worked there off and on since I was a kid. But this time I used it for my own therapy."

"May I ask if you needed the therapy because of your divorce?"

"I needed all the help I could get."

Gage glanced at her before pulling his eyes back to the road. She spoke barely above a whisper, but he heard the strain in her voice.

"Would you like to talk about it?"

Holland turned her head away from him and stared out the window. Walls of greenery from the forest flashed by. Light flirted with shadow, as the sun filtered through the trees. The road stretched out before them winding its path among the wooded landscape. Seconds slid by.

Gage looked at her again. Her cheeks were pale. Tiny lines bracketed her mouth. Her expression looked pinched as though her skin had been pulled too tight.

His hands pressed against the steering wheel. "Now I'm one who's sorry. I didn't mean to upset you, Holland."

"I know you didn't."

"I realize I've asked you about your husband before. I don't do it out of morbid curiosity, and I certainly don't want to torture you. But I can't help noticing how you seem to be holding so much hurt inside. Sometimes it helps people to talk about what's troubling them; and sometimes it makes the pain deepen. You're the only one who can decide which would be best for you."

Her fingers toyed with the zipper on her jacket. More seconds passed. Gage drove in silence now respecting her need to make her own decision. Holland finally inhaled, dragging air into her lungs, and began to speak slowly at first, but with determination.

"Ray, my ex-husband managed a big insurance firm. I was his personal assistant. He hired me right out of college. I'd just turned twenty-two."

"How old was he?" Gage inquired, relaxing his hands now that Holland began to talk.

"Forty. Handsome. Suave. He started coming on to me right away, and I fell like the proverbial ton of bricks. We dated for a few months before he proposed. A couple of the guys working in the office tried to warn me about Ray being a womanizer, but I foolishly thought I was going to be the one to change all that. I convinced myself that at his age he was ready to settle down and give all his attention to me. I tried to make him into someone he could never be. Talk about being naïve."

"Let me guess, he cheated on you."

She swallowed, and nodded. "Big time."

Gage's eyes turned as cold as ice and each word came out as slivers of glass.

"You thought I was like him when you accused me of sleeping with Kim."

"Well now you know why I'm so sensitive to that kind of thing. I married Ray believing we were building our relationship on love and mutual trust as a firm ground for our future together."

"I take it that firm ground turned into shifting sand," he replied, losing his momentary anger.

"More like quicksand. The marriage began to sink almost immediately. I should have left him right then, but I wanted to prove to my family that I could make it work. They were very much against the marriage. I wished I had listened to them."

"It must have been pretty awkward for all of you on your wedding day."

"We eloped to Las Vegas. I heard my mother crying in the background when I called to tell my parents. I knew she'd always planned for me to have a church wedding like my brother and sister. But I let Ray talk me into the elopement because I knew how my parents felt about him."

"What about his family? Didn't they have a say in the matter?"

"His parents had passed away. He didn't have any other relatives that he knew of."

"Maybe a part of you felt sorry for him being alone and wanted to give him a family."

"You're very astute. That definitely was there all mixed up with my feelings for him. I come from such a loving family that I wanted him to have the same kind of connection. What I didn't realize before we got married was that he didn't want strings, as he called them."

Gage looked at her.

"Strings?"

"According to Ray my attachment to my family allowed them to dictate my life, to pull my strings. He didn't realize those strings are what binds my family together. He never understood the love my family shares because he'd never had the same kind of thing. He told me his parents were older and their philosophy was that a child should be seen and not heard."

"I suppose that kind of upbringing could either make a person hunger to be loved, or turn them into someone who had no idea how to love."

"The latter would be Ray. I forgave him when I discovered his first affair, but I packed my bags after two years and God knows how many other women he'd slept with."

"Hell of a way to prove he didn't want any strings."

"It wasn't just the cheating," she murmured.

If he'd thought she looked pale before, Gage felt concern coil in the pit of his stomach when he saw how positively white she'd gone, as though every bit of color had drained out of her face. What else had her ex done to make her look as though someone had just driven a knife into her heart? He waited, almost dreading to hear what she would say next.

"We were going to have a baby."

Holland kept her head down and didn't see Gage's quick, startled glance.

"The pregnancy didn't go well from the very beginning. I was spotting blood, cramping, and forced to spend a lot of time in bed. I was in my last trimester when the baby came. She . . . she was already dead, but I got to hold her for a bit."

She spoke so softly now, Gage had to lean his head toward her to catch the words.

"I named her Angel because that's what she was to me. Ray was in the Caribbean supposedly for a conference, but I knew he was with his latest girlfriend. I called and told him about the baby."

"I hope he came home to be with you, so you could grieve for your child together."

"No. He said there wasn't anything he could do, so he stayed away."

A sudden flash of anger so strong in its intensity made Gage want to strangle the man.

"Oh, Holland." He slowed the car and pulled off the road onto a shoulder. He reached over and taking her hands in his, squeezed them offering comfort.

"I'm so sorry."

"Ray reminded me that having the baby was my idea. I stopped taking the birth control pill without telling him. I know I shouldn't have, but I was so desperately unhappy. I thought if we had a child he would take more interest in our marriage. I was very naïve, like I said."

Gage rubbed his thumbs over her knuckles unconsciously offering her comfort.

"You mustn't be so hard on yourself. Most men would have been very happy to hear they were going to become a father."

"I have a feeling Ray thought being a father might inhibit his chances of scoring with other women. I didn't think about that until it was too late. Losing my baby was the end to everything. I buried Angel, filed for divorce, and went back home to my family. I know you can't live in the past. But sometimes it's hard not to remember, especially about Angel."

"Angel will always matter. It can't be easy for you being with Jamie and not think about her. I feel selfish for asking you to be his nanny now that I know about your child."

"Please don't worry about that. I love taking care of him."

Gage pulled his hands away and clenched them into fists.

"Why the hell did Ray bother to get married if he was going to treat you like that?"

"I asked him the same question once. He thought it sounded good to clients when he told them he had a wife. Oh, and he needed someone to do his dirty laundry."

"Jesus. Didn't he feel even the slightest bit of obligation to you?"

"The only obligation he ever felt was to himself."

"You aren't still in touch with him, are you?"

"Lord, no. Why would you think that? Ray has no wish to see me, and I certainly have no desire to be anywhere near him, either. Being married clearly didn't suit him."

"Well, marriage isn't for everyone, that's for sure."

"Including you?" Holland asked, curious to know and also anxious to stop talking about her personal life. "Don't tell me there haven't been any women because I won't believe that."

"I'd like to be married, but I've been too busy taking care of my family and business concerns to date much. There have been women." His mouth twisted. "My wealth assures me of that, but I'd like to find someone who'd be interested in me and not just my money."

"Well, having your kind of wealth would be a big lure."

"What people don't realize is after a while it's just money."

"Uncle Leo says you're a financial genius."

"I don't know about that, but I do enjoy working with numbers. My step-father put me in charge of everything. I keep trying to get my brothers to take an interest. James tries sometimes, but Jon could care less. He's happy as long as he has enough money to do his running around."

"Does it concern your mother that they aren't more mature about their future?"

"Yes. I know she wonders if things would've been different had their father lived."

"Was he close with the boys?"

"Yes. Very. My step-father was married before and didn't have any children. His wife died. He was quite a bit older than my mother and he was absolutely over the moon when she gave birth to the twins. He was a good father to them and to me as well."

"I'm surprised he didn't adopt you."

"He wanted to, but my mother refused because she said the only thing my father left me with was his name."

"She told me she wasn't close with her own dad."

"Not for lack of trying on her part. She was an only child and her father never let her forget how disappointed he was that she wasn't the son he'd wanted."

"It's nice to see that didn't turn her into a cold parent. She loves you all very much."

"I know; and she'd like to see us all happily married, but she knew Kim wasn't the best choice for James. We keep trying to accept their relationship, but it's not easy."

"I feel sorry for Jamie considering the way his parents are acting. It might have been better if you really were his father."

"I'd rather you didn't bring that up again."

Holland regretted saying it, but she couldn't deny that she really did believe Gage would be the more suitable parent to Jamie. Kim was too self-absorbed to care about the baby and James acted like a teenager going through the throes of first love rather than the twenty-three-year-old father of a child.

"I meant it as a compliment."

"Are you still in doubt as to my nephew's parentage?"

"No. It's just that I've grown very fond of the baby, and it hurts me to see how messed up his parents are. I know you love Jamie, and you only want what's best for him. What I meant to say earlier was that he should have a father like you."

"I suppose I am still a little miffed given that you did think I'd fathered Jamie."

"Do you want to wash my mouth out with soap for bringing it up again?"

Her comment made him chuckle.

"There are things I'd like to do with your mouth, but using soap isn't one of them."

Holland's cheeks turned a pretty shade of pink. She fidgeted and cleared her throat.

"Tell me something else about yourself, other than you like weird sandwiches and you're good with numbers."

"Nice evasion. Hmm, let me see. Well, I enjoy playing the piano."

"You do? I've never heard you. I'm envious."

"Don't be. I'm not a true musician. I haven't had any lessons. I play by ear."

"Well, I had lessons, but I didn't have the knack. I bet you play classical music."

"I sense that snob label you keep trying to hang on me coming out again."

"Sorry. I don't know why, but I just thought classical music and money go together."

"Interesting theory, but I don't think one's income bracket necessarily has to dictate what kind of music you like. My step-father was especially fond of jazz. I happen to prefer music from the fifties and sixties myself."

Her eyes lit up with approval.

"That's my favorite era, too! There's nothing like Bobby Hatfield of the Righteous Brothers singing 'Unchained Melody' to send chills through me."

"I know, or some of the Platters' hits like, 'Only You'."

"For sure. I think this is going to be the start of a beautiful relationship."

"I certainly hope so," Gage said, as he opened his door and climbed out.

Holland looked at him when he came around and opened her door.

"What are you doing?"

"I thought it might be nice if we took a little walk. Do you mind?"

"No. I could do with some exercise after our lunch."

He surprised Holland by reaching for her hand as he led her down a slight embankment into the deeper cover of the woods. They wound their way around trees and bushes finally stopping when they came to a small clearing. The sun beamed through the trees leaving delicate patterns over the forest floor reminding Holland of the crocheted shawls her grandmother wore.

Gage still held her hand. The little glade sheltered them in a womb of privacy lending an air of intimacy. Holland tried to relax, but the way he studied her was beginning to make her too aware of their isolation and much too aware of him. She tugged her hand free and looked around.

"It's quiet here. Kind of like the stillness you might find inside a little chapel."

"A good place to talk, which is why I chose it. I'm not sure if I should say what's on my mind after what you just told me about Ray, but I'd like to get it out in the open."

"What is it?"

"I wanted you to be Jamie's nanny because you're good with him. You already know that, but I also wanted to have you in my house because I needed to be able to see more of you."

"I have needs, too, but I'm just not sure what to do about them given my history."

"I won't rush you. I just want to know if we're anywhere near being on the same page."

"Well, since you brought it up, I may as well tell you I wanted to get to know you, too. Especially after you had me buzzing the day you took your shirt off in my aunt's kitchen."

"I hope it was a good buzz."

"Yes which was a surprise to me, because I'd been doing my best for a long time to avoid feeling anything like that."

"I did wonder if you would be interested in having a relationship with another man after your unhappy marriage. That makes sense now that you've told me about your ex."

"I let Ray ruin things in the romance department. I've lived like a nun since my divorce."

Gage studied her for a moment.

"Could you ever imagine making love with me?"

"Actually, I um, was working up to that in my dream about us."

"That sounds encouraging. How far did you get?"

"Your shirt was off and you were working on my blouse after we shared a few kisses."

"I dreamed about us being together, too. But I got a lot further than you did."

"Oh? How far?"

"Far enough to know that I wanted to have you for real and not just in my dreams."

His expression had Holland's insides doing flip flops. It'd been a long time since a man made her feel this way. The buzz she'd experienced in her aunt's kitchen began to intensify.

"Is that why you kissed me in your office?"

"I don't know why. All I know is I couldn't stop myself and I'm about to do it again."

The words were barely out before he tugged her into his arms and his mouth descended on hers. Her body instantly began to throb creating a hot ball of need in her belly. She parted her lips surprised at the fierce hunger he'd awakened in her. Gage kept their bodies close while he teased and tasted. He stopped and stared at her in a gaze smoldering with heat.

She stared back.

"You make my body feel like it's on fire."

"What the hell do you think you do to me?" he said in a hoarse voice. "I think I'd eventually like to try your strings."

New Beginnings
Olivia Claire High

"Is this what you call not rushing me?"

"I did say eventually," he reminded her.

"You already have strings."

"My family can't hang onto me forever. I'd like to start building a life for myself." He tucked a lock of hair behind her ear. "With you."

Holland bit her lip and stepped away from him needing the space, so she could concentrate without the heat radiating from his body to confuse her brain.

"I'm flattered, and I'm not saying no to your offer, but I'm not sure if I'm ready right now."

"I can wait."

The promise was there in the depth of his eyes. He held her gaze until she finally looked away. He said he could wait, but could she? The way her treacherous pulse reacted to his hard masculinity suddenly gave her cause to wonder.

Chapter Ten

Marguerite smiled when Holland walked into Jamie's room later that day.

"Did you enjoy your outing?"

"Yes, thank you. Did Jamie give you any trouble?"

"Not a bit. Colleen and I took turns changing and feeding him. Everything's gone well."

"Good. I brought some more of Janet's milk for him."

"Bless her. I hope you weren't angry that Gage went with you to lunch."

Holland felt her heart pound remembering that wasn't the only thing Gage did. She turned away when she felt a blush coming on. She took the bottles out of the small ice chest and opened the refrigerator, keeping her back to Marguerite. She hadn't realized how uncomfortable it would be talking about Gage with his mother, now that she knew how much he wanted her.

"No, I wasn't mad. He, um, seemed to enjoy himself. We took a drive afterwards."

"How nice. I hope you were able to become better acquainted."

"I think it's safe to say that we're well on our way there."

Holland spent the rest of the day with Jamie. She ate dinner in her room. She half expected Gage to come and see her and tried not to be disappointed when he didn't show up. Maybe he was too busy with work. She touched her fingers to her lips remembering all too well the intense physical awareness his kiss had evoked.

Colleen arrived carrying a tray, explaining Marguerite had a headache and went to bed early.

"Oh, I'm sorry. I hope taking care of Jamie wasn't too much for her."

"She loved every minute of it and she wanted me to be sure and tell you that her headache has nothing to do with the baby. She just gets these migraines now and then. The best thing for her to do is go to bed. She's usually fine by the morning."

"I hope so. Does Gage know his mother isn't feeling well?"

"Oh yes. He always checks on her every evening. He saw her for a few minutes before he went back to his office to make some business calls. He's been in there working all evening."

Holland felt a flutter of relief knowing he was genuinely busy and not just avoiding her.

"I was busy helping Mrs. Howard and sent word that one of the girls in the kitchen should prepare your tray, but I see whoever set things up filled the pot with one kind of tea instead of sending hot water and assorted tea bags. Oh dear, they forgot to include the lemon bars I made."

"That's okay, Colleen." Holland lifted the teapot lid and sniffed. "Mint. This will be fine."

"I'll leave the bars on a covered dish in the kitchen if you change your mind. Just put the tray outside the door when you're finished and someone will pick it up."

"I'll do that and thank you for bringing the tea."

Colleen nodded and walked to the door. "Goodnight, miss. Sleep well."

"Thanks. You, too."

Holland picked up the teapot and filled a cup, inhaling as she took a sip. She started to drink more, but thinking about Colleen's lemon bars suddenly sounded too good to pass up. She didn't like leaving Jamie, so she'd have to make a fast trip.

She hurried through the halls, but skidded to a halt just outside the kitchen doorway when she heard voices. She peaked around the corner and had to slap her hand over her mouth to smother the gasped that sprang to her lips. She had little difficulty recognizing the two people standing beneath the glow of the soft overhead lighting. Once again she'd innocently subjected herself to something she would have much rather avoided. Gage had kissed her this afternoon and now here he was a mere few hours later with Kim. The sight of them together sent her whirling around and running back to her room.

Holland plunked herself down onto a chair in stunned disbelief thinking about the scene she'd almost interrupted. Kim on tiptoes with her arms around Gage's neck and her mouth raised toward his lips to be kissed. The image burned at the back of Holland's eyes. Gage swore he wasn't with Kim in his office before, but there wasn't any mistaking his identity tonight.

After going through this kind of thing with her cheating husband the heartache felt all too familiar. Sometimes things from your past could bring comfort, but in her case Holland couldn't bear the thought of once again seeing a man she cared about turn to another woman while pretending to be personally interested in her.

Her insides churned with anger and hurt. She reached for her tea with a trembling hand, drained the cup, and poured another. She gulped it down hoping the mint would settle her jittery stomach. Gage made her believe he wanted her. She'd fallen for his glib tongue, damn him.

Holland sat there continuing to fret when she suddenly became so sleepy she could barely hold her eyes open. It seemed an odd reaction considering the shock she was suffering. Maybe a splash of cold water would keep her awake long enough to change into her nightshirt

She stood up, and her surroundings began to spin making her feel as though she was riding on a merry-go-round gone out of control. She grabbed the back of the chair and swayed. Her body began to shake. She realized she was going to have to sleep in her clothes because there was no way she'd be able to change. Just getting into her bed seemed like it was going to be a major challenge.

She moved away from the chair and stumbled her way across the room. She managed to get within a few feet of her bed before her legs gave out and she fell to her hands and knees. She started to crawl, but even that proved beyond her control and her body sank to the floor.

Her last coherent thought was that this couldn't be any ordinary sleepiness.

Gage awoke to the sound of a woman's screams. He bolted upright in bed. Had he been dreaming? He sat, listening. Night sounds. The creaking of the house. The rustle of his sheet and blanket as he shifted his legs. The scratching of a tree limb against the side of the outside wall. He heard more screaming. No dream, then. His heart jerked, as the disturbing sound continued to penetrate his senses.

"Holy God, not again," he muttered, thinking of the other nights when he'd been awakened by the nannies ear-piercing screams.

He kicked his blankets away, hurled himself out of bed, and pulled on the pair of sweatpants he'd tossed aside earlier. He flung open his bedroom door and stood shirtless and in his bare feet, listening more intently trying to pinpoint where the screams were coming from.

Another shriek shot through him sending chills rippling over his skin colder than the night air. He stood there straining to catch the location of the sound. It came again vibrating in undulating waves of terror. His forehead creased in a deep frown when he realized the ragged cries were coming from beneath the house.

The tunnels. Had he heard correctly? He paused, listening so intently his muscles tightened.

Yes. A woman was inside one of the tunnels; and whoever it was obviously needed help.

"What the hell is someone doing below the house this time of night?" he muttered.

But he didn't have time to think about that, as he sprinted down the hallway into an empty room where he opened a drawer in a chest, and grabbed a large flashlight before tossing back a rug to reveal a trapdoor. He knew there was a more accessible entrance to the tunnel that led to the wine cellar, but this entrance was closer to where the screams were coming from.

He descended the ladder feeling his way over each rung until his bare feet touched ground. The only tunnel lit by electric lights was the one leading to the wine cellar. The others hadn't been used in years, so the lights were no longer hooked up.

He wasn't afraid of the dark or the tunnels himself, but whoever was down here certainly was, as another earsplitting yell echoed, reverberating against the walls. He felt his gut quiver as the pathetic woman began to sob between her screams. Gage realized the poor thing was terrorized and beyond hysterical by the sound of things.

He couldn't imagine who on earth the person could be. The servants were only aware of the wine cellar tunnel and the only new hireling was Holland. She'd sounded curious when they mentioned Kim using the tunnels, but surely Holland wouldn't be down here exploring at this time of night. The flashlight cut a small swath through the inky darkness giving him barely enough light to see while he followed the sobbing until he came to a startled halt.

The sight of Holland running in circles and throwing herself against the wall, jumping, and slapping her legs would have been comical, if it wasn't for the fact that she appeared to be having a full blown panic attack. A sense of urgency raced through him as Gage rushed forward and grabbed her by the upper arm while holding the light in his other hand.

"Holland, it's okay! It's Gage. You're all right. I've got you now."

"Watch out for the snakes." She clawed at his bare chest and face, dragging her nails over his flesh and making him grunt in pain.

"I've been bitten. Oh God, I'm going to die."

He grabbed her by the shoulder and shook her.

"You're not going to die."

He passed the flashlight around the area in a quick sweep just to make sure she hadn't seen a mouse or perhaps a rat and mistook it for the reptiles she seemed so certain were attacking her.

"Holland, there aren't any snakes here."

"Yes there are! They're everywhere. Help me. Please, help me!"

The more she kept pounding on his chest and fighting him, the more Gage knew he had to get her out of the tunnel. He had a feeling no matter what he said wasn't going to convince her that she wasn't surrounded by snakes. Whatever was going on with her was more than a dream.

Just like what had happened with the other nannies, he grimly reminded himself.

New Beginnings
Olivia Claire High

He slung her over his shoulder and ran with her back to the entrance. Holland continued to scream while her nails raked over him, then herself, as he climbed the ladder. They were both bleeding and panting by the time he reached the top and shoved her into the room.

She continued to cry and slap at what he could only assume were her imaginary serpents. Gage hefted himself up and punched the intercom buttons to both Jacob's and Colleen's quarters summoning them to his bedroom. He knew the sound of Holland's screaming in the background was enough to make them both understand that this was an emergency.

It nearly broke his heart when Gage saw how terrified Holland looked as she suffered through her ordeal. He picked her up and quickly carried her to his bedroom where he laid her gently on his bed. But she scrambled to her feet and continued to flail about batting at her invisible demons. Jacob ran into the room, followed closely by Colleen. They were both dressed in their nightclothes with uncombed hair and sleepy looking eyes. But it didn't take them long to become totally alert when they saw Gage's bloodied flesh and Holland's bizarre behavior.

"Jacob, use my phone, call the emergency number at the clinic and tell them to send a doctor here right away."

"Yes, Mr. Langdon."

Gage turned to Colleen next.

"Get the first aid kit out of my bathroom."

She bobbed her head and whirled away casting a startled look at Holland as she went.

Gage reached for Holland. It took a lot of strength to hold her still while trying to keep her from hurting herself or him any further. He did his best to talk to her, but the glazed look in her eyes and the fact that she couldn't control her terror made him realize his efforts were in vain.

The other nannies were drugged into thinking someone was trying to kill them. They'd all ran from the nursery into the hallways, but Holland had ended up in one of the unused tunnels. How did she get there? Had she gone down there lured into thinking somebody was in trouble? It would be so like her knowing how much she always wanted to help people.

The doctor explained that whoever drugged the other women knew ahead of time what to say to make them afraid. Someone must have discovered Holland's fear of snakes and used that fear against her. Gage finally ended up having to wrap her in a blanket in an effort to subdue her, while Colleen did her best to dab antiseptic cream on Holland's face.

He turned down her offer to help him, saying he'd wait for the doctor. Trying to keep Holland still was taking all his attention making him grit his teeth, as she continued to fight him.

Holland fought to wake, as consciousness slowly began to return to her muddled brain. She kept her eyes closed, struggling to ignore the throbbing going on inside her head. Her throat felt raw when she swallowed and she ached all over, as though someone had been pounding on her.

New Beginnings
Olivia Claire High

Her face hurt in places, too. She tried to think *why*, and reached up to touch her cheek only to have fingers gently, but firmly wrap around her wrist stopping her hand in midair. Her eyelids lifted, and she saw Gage sitting there staring at her.

"Gage? What . . . what's going on?" She looked around.

"This isn't my room. Where am I?"

"In my bedroom."

Holland looked down to where he still held her by the wrist. Her eyes darted back to his face and she noticed his scratches for the first time.

"My God, what happened to your face? You look like you've been in a fight with a cat."

"Never mind me. How do you feel?"

"Exhausted and sore. Why do my cheeks hurt so much?"

"I'm going to let go of you now; but you mustn't touch your face."

"All right. But please, may I have some water?"

Gage reached over to the bedside table, picked up a pitcher, filled a glass, and handed it to her. She drank deeply emptying it. He set it aside while she struggled to scoot up into a sitting position.

"Let me help you," he said, as he placed a couple of pillows behind her.

"Thank you. Can you tell me why I feel as though I've been punched?"

"I'll try, but first I need you to answer a couple questions to help me hopefully give you the answers we're both looking for. Colleen said she brought you tea last night. Did you drink it?"

"Yes, two cups before I started feeling extremely sleepy. I got up to walk to my bed, and my legs gave out. I knew something wasn't right because I couldn't stay awake."

"Do you recall what happened after that?"

"It's all kind of jumbled. I was having some really mixed up dreams. I kept hearing this voice telling me I didn't belong here and I needed to leave and never come back."

"Was the voice a man or a woman's?"

"I'm not sure. It sounded distorted like it was coming from a long way off. The last thing the voice said was that I'd be put into a pit full of poisonous snakes because I had to be punished for meddling too much in this household's personal business."

She began to tremble.

Gage patted her on the hand.

"I think I must have really gone under after that. The next thing I remember is waking up in darkness. I couldn't see anything, but I knew I wasn't in my room."

"What made you think that?"

"It smelled different. Earthy. Musty. I took small steps, feeling around until I touched what must have been a wall. I used it to get to my feet and steady myself. That's when I . . ."

Her breath started coming faster and her hands clenched. Gage kept hold of her hands when her fingers tried to grab the sheet.

"You're going to be all right. Nothing can hurt you now."

"Snakes. I felt lots of snakes. I couldn't see them, but I knew they were there. They were crawling all over me, biting and hissing. I heard the sound of rattling. Dear God. Rattlesnakes. I remember thinking that this time I wouldn't be able to get help to save me. I kept trying to get away, but it was so dark. I screamed and screamed. I guess that explains why my throat hurts."

Perspiration sheened her forehead. Gage helped her drink more water before using a cloth to dab at the sweat on her brow.

"You're safe. You weren't bitten. There weren't any snakes. Do you understand me? There weren't any snakes. I'm sorry I had to make you talk about what happened, but I needed to know, so I could help you. Someone wanted you to think that you were being attacked by snakes because they wanted to scare you into leaving here."

"Well, they certainly made me scared enough. You said there weren't any snakes. But why did they seem so real?"

"Your tea was drugged," he told her after a moment's hesitation.

"Drugged? Well, that explains a lot. Who did this to me?"

"I don't know. That's another reason why I had to ask you questions."

"Colleen said someone else prepared my tea tray. Did you ask her who it was?"

"Yes. She thought it was Carol, one of the girls who helps with the housework, especially in the kitchen and stays late to clean up. When she returned from taking the trash out the tray was setting on the counter ready to go. Carol assumed Colleen must have taken care of everything.

She knows Colleen takes the tray to you and since her shift was over, she left to go home. Colleen came into the kitchen, saw the tray, and thought Carol had prepared the tea."

"Do you think Carol may be lying?"

Gage shook his head. "No, not after talking to her, and neither does Colleen."

"I know why my throat hurts, but why does my body ache and my face feel so sore?"

"You were clawing at yourself and throwing your body against the wall trying to get rid of what you thought were snakes. That's how I found you after I heard you screaming."

Holland leaned forward and peered closely at him.

"Did I do that to your face?"

"Don't worry about it."

"Oh God, I did, didn't I? I'm so sorry, Gage."

"You couldn't help yourself."

"I wouldn't have believed I was going to die down there in that tunnel if I'd been in my right mind, but obviously the drugs took care of that."

She shuddered causing him to tug her into his arms, wincing as her body pressed against the raw scratches beneath his tee shirt. He held her until she leaned back on the pillows again.

"I hate to keep bringing this up, but do you think you could stand to have me ask you one more question? It's important," he added.

"Ask away if it'll help you find out who did this to me."

"Who else did you tell besides me that you were afraid of snakes?"

"I don't know." She closed her eyes for a couple of seconds and then opened them again. "Wait. I remember now. It was when I helped out in the kitchen with Colleen and some of the other staff. Someone saw a little spider and killed it, but not before Colleen let out a yelp. She confessed that she hated spiders in any way, shape, or form."

"Interesting. I'll have to remember that."

"I could see that she was embarrassed, so I told everyone I had a great fear of snakes after being bitten by a rattlesnake as a child. One of the girls said she couldn't stand thunderstorms. Someone else said they were afraid of the dark. But I really can't imagine any of those women drugging me and putting me into an imaginary pit of snakes."

"I'll still have a talk with Colleen."

"Does your mother know what happened to me? Because if she doesn't, I'd rather you didn't tell her. I think it'd be too upsetting for her."

"She knows you were drugged, but not about the tunnel and the snakes."

Gage stood up.

"I think it would be best if you tried to get some rest now. I can take you back to your room if you'd like, or you're welcome to stay here."

Holland looked around the big room with its masculine furniture. She saw a large bookcase filled with books, a desk with a laptop, a couple large comfortable looking chairs, a widescreen television, and the wooden valet with one of his suit jackets draped over the hanger. A few brightly colored paintings added relief to the taupe walls and cocoa colored carpet.

"Where will you sleep if I stay here?"

"There are several guest bedrooms in the house, but I think it'd be better if I stayed here with you in case you need help. If that's okay with you."

"I'd rather not be alone. I feel like a baby, especially after telling you I don't scare easily."

"I'm sure you wouldn't under normal circumstances."

"Gosh, I forgot Jamie. Who'll be with him if I stay here?"

Gage hesitated for a moment. "I was hoping I wouldn't have to tell you this until you had more time to recover."

"Tell me what?" She gave him an imploring look. "Is the baby all right?"

"He's gone, Holland. And so is Kim. They disappeared sometime during the night."

"So James decided to take them and leave after all you did to keep them here."

"No." Gage stood up. "My brother is in the hospital. He's in a coma. Someone drugged him, too."

"Oh, God. I can't believe this," Holland said and sagged against the pillows.

Poor, defenseless Jamie somewhere outside the house with his mother who hated him. Was he hungry? Cold? Still alive? Her stomach churned at such thoughts. What about James being in a comma? Would he be able to recover?

She looked at Gage. He sat in a chair now. She couldn't see his face. He was bent over with his elbows on his knees and his fingers buried in his hair, as he stared at the floor. Holland knew him to be a strong man, but right now he looked filled with all the anguish he was being forced to go through. And why shouldn't he be suffering? His brother may be dying and his psycho sister-in-law had run off taking a very vulnerable baby with her.

It'd be enough to upset anyone.

"I'm so sorry about James and the baby. If only I hadn't drank that tea I'd still be there to keep Jamie safe. Kim wouldn't have been able to take him if I'd been keeping watch the way I was supposed to. I feel terrible that I let you down."

Gage jerked out of his chair. His eyes burned with anger. She shrank back further into the pillows thinking that he was about to shed his cloak of sympathy and let her know what he really thought of her and the outrageous tale of attacking snakes.

"You did not let anyone down. You're a victim."

The notion suddenly occurred to Holland that James and Jamie might not have fallen prey to Kim's evil scheme if Gage hadn't been so busy rescuing her from the tunnel.

"This is all my fault."

"No, it's not your fault. Stop saying that. You couldn't know your tea might be drugged. The blame is mine," he said and began to pace the room.

"How did you come to that conclusion? You couldn't know my tea was drugged, either."

He stopped and looked at her. The bleakness had returned to his eyes.

"That's where you're wrong. I did know it might happen. I should have explained to you the real reason the other nannies left."

What did he know about what happened with the other nannies? What had he kept hidden from her? Studying him now he looked very tense and the scratches on his face stood out in angry red stripes. Holland reminded herself she'd done that to him while he was trying to help her. But he looked guilty. What did Gage have to feel guilty about?

"I started to tell you about the other nannies the night I asked why you put a lock on the nursery refrigerator, but I got sidetracked by our argument."

"Well, don't you think it would be a good idea if you tell me now?"

Chapter Eleven

Gage stopped prowling and stared at her, unease flickering in his eyes. "Do you recall me saying the other nannies left because they had nightmares?"

"Yes."

"Their nightmares were drug induced, just like yours. But in my own defense I didn't know that until the last woman had her episode," he said when he saw Holland grab a fistful of sheet and squeeze until her knuckles stood out like hard white stones.

"I really did think the others were somehow spooked being here in the house. The place creaks and groans at night, as you well know. I gave the women a very generous payoff, asked them not to share their experiences, and sent them back to where they came from."

"Why did you ask them to be quiet about what happened to them?"

"The locals already gossiped enough about my family and this house. The last thing I needed was to have word get around that the place was haunted or some such nonsense. I was trying to keep as much privacy for us as I could. We've had plenty of people from town working inside during all the additions, plus the servants, and that opens us up to enough talk."

"Is that why you hired the other nannies from outside the area?"

"That's part of it, but there weren't any suitable candidates here until you came."

"When did you decide to look into the possibility the nannies were drugged?"

"It didn't seem right to me that this kept happening, so I asked Mrs. Armstead's permission to be tested. That's the first evidence I had as to what was going on. The doctor said it could have been given to her in her tea. I checked and found out that the other women also drank tea before having their episodes."

"Didn't you try to find out who prepared their trays?"

"Of course I did."

Holland raised her eyebrows. "And?"

"It was Colleen. Put yourself in my place. Would you suspect her now that you know her?"

"No, but people aren't always what they seem."

"I realize that, but I've known Colleen too long to suspect her. That left me trying to find out who might be guilty."

"Did you come to any conclusions?"

"No. I put it aside when you came here and started in about Kim wanting to make Jamie ill. A part of me still thought her depression would keep her from going anywhere near the baby. When you told me about hearing her say James wasn't the baby's real father, I didn't want to believe that, either. I knew what it would mean to James if you were right."

"Or you were more worried about generating gossip about who was sleeping with whom."

A quick flash of anger swirled in his eyes. "That's not worthy of you, Holland."

"I'm afraid I'm not feeling very worthy at the moment. What about after you said you believed me about Kim? Why didn't you do more to protect Jamie from her?"

"I didn't think it was necessary with you keeping such a close eye on him. There weren't any more problems with his feedings after you got the breast milk. That took care of his health issues. Kim didn't want to be around the baby unless we forced her. Everything was going well."

"What about when Kim took Jamie out of the nursery? Weren't you worried?"

"Naturally, but I wanted to believe she was finally showing some interest in the child."

"A child whose biological father is in question."

"Why do you insist on bringing that up again?"

"I'd think James would want to know for sure."

"He is sure, but even if he wasn't, some things are best left alone. What about my mother? Would you throw something like that up to her? She's been in a dark place for a long time. More than you know, Holland. Jamie's birth finally began to shed a little brightness into her life."

"I'm sorry for your mother. She deserves to have some peace. But she also deserves to know what's going on. Because let me tell you something I learned the hard way, Gage. It's a lot easier to know the truth up front instead of going on living a lie."

"We're not talking about your marriage," he said in a gentle voice.

Her head pounded; and she ached all over, especially in her heart. Raw emotion mingled with the knowledge that every second ticking by made her feel as though a wedge was being driven wider and deeper between her and Gage, splitting their friendship asunder.

"No, we're not talking about my marriage. Maybe you're right to let things stay as they are here, especially if your family would rather go on living a lie rather than know the truth."

Holland sat up and eased back the blanket and sheet. She swung her legs to the side of the bed, slowly lowered her feet to the floor, and stood up.

"Holland, for God's sake, what are you doing?"

"I'm going to my room to pack my things. I want to go back to my aunt and uncle's."

"The doctor said you needed to rest."

"I'll rest at their house," she replied, taking slow, halting steps toward the door.

Gage reached her in two long strides.

"I don't think you're recovered enough to go."

"Do you really think I'd want to stay here after what happened to me? Besides, there isn't any reason for me to stay. You no longer need a nanny. I'm heartsick about Jamie. I pray he'll be all right. Tell your mother and Colleen goodbye for me. I'll keep James in my prayers, too."

"I'll drive you." She shook her head. "Then please call and let me know you're okay."

"You can take my word for it that I'll be fine once I get out of here."

"Don't do this. Will you stay if I tell you how much I need you?" he asked in a hoarse voice.

She gripped the doorknob.

"You don't need anyone, especially not me. But even if I did believe you, I can't be with a man who lied to me. You knew how important honesty is to me."

"I already explained why I didn't tell you about the other nannies being drugged."

"I'm not referring to them. I'm talking about your ongoing relationship with Kim."

Gage froze as though she'd just hit him with a bucket of ice cold water.

"For God's sake. Not that again. I thought we'd settled that particular misconception."

"So did I until I saw you two kissing in the kitchen before I was drugged."

"Holland, you have to listen to me. I did not kiss her. If you had stayed a moment longer you would have realized that. She was the one coming on to me. It was one-sided on her part."

"Kim taking advantage of poor little you?" she mocked. "Odd how you two just happened to be in the kitchen together that time of night."

"I can explain that."

"Don't bother. I heard enough excuses from my lying, cheating ex-husband to last me a lifetime. I thought you were different. But I can see that I was wrong." Holland fought to still the trembling that wanted to take over her body, as she pressed her forehead against the door.

"Damn you for making me believe in you, Gage."

A muscle jerked in his cheek.

"Don't go. Not like this. I don't want to lose you, Holland."

"You can't lose what you never had," she whispered and stumbled out, belatedly recalling her promise never to shut a door in his face again.

May watched Holland fold another sweater into the suitcase.

"Are you sure you're up for the long drive home. What about that drugging business?"

Holland couldn't keep what happened to her a secret and begged her aunt not to repeat anything about the ordeal.

"It's been three days. The doctor said I'm fine. Don't forget I wouldn't have been here this long if I hadn't taken the nanny job."

"That little baby needed you, honey."

"Well now Granny needs me, and I agreed to go back to her after you were okay."

"I know. I heard James Howard came out of his coma and is expected to recover."

Holland felt some of her worry lift from her chest.

"I'm glad."

"I wonder how he's going to feel when he finds out his wife and child are gone."

"Jamie being gone will be hard on him, but hopefully he'll think he's well rid of Kim."

"Shouldn't you call Mr. Langdon to see if he's had any news about the baby?"

Holland closed the suitcase and swung it off the bed.

"No. I don't want to talk to him and I'm pretty sure he doesn't want to talk to me. But please let me know if you hear anything about Jamie."

Leo came to the doorway.

"Got your gas tank filled and tires checked. You're all set."

"Thank you, Uncle Leo," Holland hugged them both.

They all walked to the kitchen where May picked up a small brown paper bag.

"I packed you a lunch. Here's a couple bottles of water. Call us when you get home."

"I will. Thank you for everything."

Holland went out the backdoor almost tripping on the steps, as she fought the tears that blurred her vision. Leo put her suitcase in the trunk, while she slid into the driver's seat. She waved goodbye and headed down their driveway fighting the emotions she'd kept in check.

She wiped a hand over her eyes smearing salty drops over her cheeks that still bore the marks from her fingernails. She knew those blemishes would fade in time, but she had a feeling the scars on her heart were too deeply etched to ever heal.

She gulped back a sob and made herself focus on driving. She traveled through thick forest surrounding the road on either side coming into open areas by a swift rushing river where the sheer size of huge boulders made her feel like she was driving a toy car. Hours later she stopped by a small lake to stretch her legs and eat her sandwiches. The sun was just inching its way downward. She watched, mesmerized as the giant red ball cast its fiery glow across the water turning the surface the color of blood.

Holland tore her gaze away from the brutal beauty of the scene, stuffed the uneaten food into the paper bag, and got into her car. She had to concentrate on what lay ahead now. Whatever life she'd begun to build over the last few weeks was gone along with a fragile dream of the future.

Holland went back to helping take care of her grandmother and working in her father's store. The month since her return flashed by in a blur. She thought about Jamie constantly wondering if he was all right, but she couldn't work up the courage to call for any news.

Thoughts of Gage also filled her head. She couldn't dismiss the fact that he should have told her about the other women being drugged. But that didn't make her stop thinking about how she felt when they'd kissed. She craved the taste of him despite knowing he wasn't good for her.

She hadn't wanted to be with a man after her divorce, but Gage started to change that making her believe she could love someone again until she caught him with Kim. She got why he lied to her about the other nannies, but she couldn't forgive him for lying about his ongoing affair with his sister-in-law. Holland didn't know who she felt the most upset with – herself for succumbing to her attraction. Or with Gage for enticing her.

She'd foolishly tried to put Gage up on a pedestal after the way Ray had destroyed all her girlish illusions about love. Sadly, she was wrong about Gage being Mr. Perfect, although she reminded herself he did rescue her from the tunnel. She also couldn't dismiss the fact that he'd sent Colleen to her room to help her pack and drive her back to her aunt and uncle's house that fateful night. It was during that drive that Colleen innocently mentioned how Gage's chest was a bloody mess from Holland clawing at him.

Holland felt terrible about that. But she was just as quick to defend her actions when she reminded herself she would have been more careful with her nighttime tea and maybe saved herself that horrendous trip to the tunnel if she'd known the other nannies had their tea drugged. The continual back and forth kept her mind in turmoil.

"You're going to break that vase if you keep squeezing it like that."

Holland snapped out of her musings at the sound of her father's quiet voice. She was dusting the vase and hadn't realized how tightly her fingers gripped the fragile glass.

"Oh! I would have felt terrible if I broke it."

"I'd feel a lot worse if you cut yourself. You still thinking about that missing baby?"

She knew Aunt May had called her parents explaining about Jamie's disappearance.

"I try not to, but I just can't help it. I really care about little Jamie."

"Have you called his family to get an update?"

"No. I doubt if they'd want to hear from me, especially Gage. He's the one who hired me to be the nanny. I didn't leave him on good terms."

"You worried about what he thinks, or the rest of his family?" He pried the vase carefully from her hands when she started to squeeze it again.

"Do you have feelings for this man?"

"No! Yes," she amended just as quickly with a ragged sigh. "But I already fell for the wrong man once and look what it cost me. I don't want to succumb to a lie again."

"You calling this Gage a liar?"

She lifted her chin at a stubborn angle.

"He should have told me about those other nannies."

"You said he didn't because he knew you wouldn't take the job. There's nothing that says you can't like a person even if you don't happen to like what they say, or don't say in this case.

His motives weren't dishonorable. He was thinking of the child. You won't find out what either of you feel by moping around here. Call him."

"He might hang up on me."

"Or he might not."

"I don't know. I said some pretty terrible things to him."

"Sounds like he deserved it; and if he's any kind of a man, he'll own up to that. You're making yourself miserable. Go to my office and think about what you need to do to feel better."

"I'll probably end up making myself feel worse."

New Beginnings
Olivia Claire High

He pointed to the vase in his hand.

"I sold a woman a vase similar to this one once. She asked me if it was an antique. It wasn't, but I told her it was because I could see she really wanted it to be. I made sure not to overprice it. She came in the store a couple of weeks later and told me how much she was enjoying that old vase. Now, if I had told her it wasn't an antique she might not have bought it and missed out on having the pleasure of ownership."

"That's sweet Dad, but I don't know how that story applies to me."

"If Gage told you about those other women being drugged you wouldn't have taken him up on his job offer and you'd have missed the joy you felt when you took care of that baby."

Holland entered her father's office and closed the door. The room smelled of his aftershave, tobacco from the pipe he sometimes smoked, and dust from nearby shelves laden with old ledgers, and bits and pieces of small personal mementoes. She sat in his chair behind the old battered desk as she'd done so many times since her childhood.

She stared at the phone. Hopefully she could find out something about the baby before Gage hung up on her. But deciding to call and following through were two different things. Would calling make her feel better, as her father suggested, or worse, as she feared?

Gage might tell her to go to hell. She'd made him beg and then walked out on him. No man, especially one as proud as Gage would appreciate having their pride stomped on. She'd spent several nights crying remembering his devastated expression when she left.

Holland sat up, and decided she would concentrate on finding out what happened with Jamie and hoped she'd be able to deal with Gage's reaction to her call. She picked up the phone and steeled herself to make the call before she lost her nerve. Gage might not be the one to answer she reminded herself, but that didn't stop her heart from pounding with each passing second. Her summons was answered just after the fourth ring and a moment before she almost gave up.

"Holland, is that you?"

She let out a sigh of relief. "Yes it is. How are you, James?"

"You know what Kim did. How the heck do you think I'm doing?"

"I'm sorry," she said thinking how she'd already botched the call. "That was stupid of me."

"I shouldn't take my frustrations out on you. I heard you were drugged, too. Are you okay?"

"Pretty much, but ironically I sometimes have to take sleeping pills at night because I'm still having trouble with nightmares. I hope you're not suffering any ill effects yourself."

"That depends on how you look at things."

It seemed as though she couldn't say the right words. She did want to offer James comfort, but it sounded like she was making him feel sadder.

"I didn't call to upset you. I just wanted you to know I've been thinking about you and wondering if you had Jamie back. I'm sorry I bothered you. I won't keep you any longer."

"Don't hang up! I didn't mean to upset you, either. It's just that everything is in total chaos around here, and I'm kind of on edge."

"Does this mean Jamie isn't with you after all this time?"

"No, but at least we know where he is now. The trouble is I can't do anything about it because I was in an accident a couple of weeks ago. Banged myself up pretty good, including breaking my damn leg. "

"Oh James, I'm so sorry. You're certainly having your share of trouble. You said you know where Jamie is. I hope that also means he's okay."

"We got a call from some woman in Mexico."

"Mexico? I wouldn't have expected that. What did the woman say? Is Kim with her?"

"She has Jamie, and he's fine, but she claims she neither saw nor knew anything about my wife."

He bit the word *wife* out, as though it left a bad taste in his mouth.

"I'm happy to hear Jamie is all right. Hopefully Kim will be okay, too."

"All I care about is getting my son back alive and well. I don't give a damn what happens to Kim. I've been a blind fool turning my back and making excuses for all the trouble she caused around here. If I hadn't been so stupid and in love with her none of this would have happened. It took me long enough, but I'm finally seeing her for the person she really is."

"I wish you didn't have to find out about Kim in such a painful way."

"Some people have to get knocked in the head before they come to their senses."

Poor James. And to think she was complaining she'd had it bad – which just went to show that some betrayals were much worse than others.

"How are you going to get Jamie back?" she asked steering his attention away from Kim.

"We're in the process of working things out. The woman insists she had nothing to do with taking him, and she's being very cooperative. The complicated part is going to be getting my brother back. I should let him rot in hell for his part in this, but I can't do that to my mother."

Holland frowned.

"What does your brother have to do with this?"

"He had things set up before the baby was even born to take him to Mexico. That's why you and the other nannies were drugged. You all had to be kept away from the nursery."

Holland couldn't be sure, but it sounded as though James must have thrown something. She thought she heard what sounded like glass breaking.

"God knows how many times they must have drugged me, so she could be in bed with him while I couldn't get so much as a peck on the cheek from my own wife!"

How had Gage told her with a straight face the night he saved her from the tunnel that Kim and Jamie were missing, when he was the one responsible? Holland realized he must have joined Kim in Mexico after she went back to her aunt's house. But could she be jumping to conclusions? Her fingers wrapped tighter around the phone.

"James, which brother took off with Kim and the baby?"

Chapter Twelve

"Which one do you think? Jonathan, of course. Gage would never do anything so underhanded. He's too busy trying to protect our family. He's the only one who can ever make any sense out of this crazy household. Jonathan tells everybody we're so close, because he and I are twins. The truth is he's always been in competition with me. He gives the impression that he's Mr. Happy Go Lucky, but he's a real rat underneath all those lazy grins."

"I . . . I thought maybe Kim and Gage ran off together."

"No way. She was always throwing herself at him, but he refused to rise to the bait. I thought she did it to make me jealous, but it was Jonathan she wanted to rile. You can't believe how many times she put Gage in a compromising position, including right up until she left."

Holland felt her heart thumping heavily against her ribs. "What do you mean?"

"She called Gage on the intercom saying she cut herself and needed him to come to the kitchen. She said I was asleep and she didn't want to wake me."

"But she didn't hesitate to wake Gage," Holland couldn't resist pointing out.

"Everyone in the house knows he often works late at night. He told me she tried to kiss him. He wanted to be sure I knew what happened in case she should make up her own version and he wanted to save me from embarrassment in case the staff found out. He also didn't want Mom to know. She was having a hard enough time, as it was, trying to accept Kim as my wife."

Holland couldn't forget now how Gage tried to explain to her about Kim's antics. She felt ashamed she hadn't at least let him have his say. She turned her attention back to James when he continued about Jamie. The baby was safe according to the woman, but what about Jonathan?

"Did something happen to your brother in Mexico?"

"He got himself kidnapped. The woman said Jonathan laid low for a while to keep us off his trail before he showed up at a hotel in her town with Jamie in tow. She said he wanted to give the baby to her because she couldn't have kids of her own. Can you believe the gall of my louse of a brother? Apparently she was his girlfriend. He's been seeing her for over a year."

"Do you mean your family wasn't aware of this?"

"Not a clue. Jon usually hopped from place to place on his travels. We stopped asking where he was, as long as he checked in by phone, so Mom would know he was okay. The woman from Mexico wanted us to know she didn't know Jamie existed until my brother called her from his hotel and said he had a surprise for her."

Holland put a hand to her temple, as she tried to follow the seemingly endless shocking details behind Jamie's disappearance.

"He must have very deep feelings for this woman to want to give her a child."

James snorted into the phone.

"Well, he's a fool if he does. Those are the kinds of feelings that got me snowed under. Anyway, the woman thinks someone at the hotel must have found out my brother was worth a lot of money and decided to grab him for ransom."

"How much are they asking?"

"A million to begin with; and if we refuse they'll start sending us Jonathan's fingers and toes with an added price tag for each piece of him."

"Dear God, that's horrible," Holland gasped, appalled

"Serves him right."

"James, you can't mean that. What Jonathan did was wrong, I'll admit, but do you really want to see him be tortured?"

"I guess not. But right now I'm more worried about the baby. Those guys could get it into their heads to come after him. That's why Gage made arrangements with the woman to find someplace to hide and stay put until he can get to her. He's setting everything up right now. You know, getting the money, making arrangements for a private plane, and stuff like that. I really wanted to go with him, but I'd only slow things down with my broken leg."

"I'm sure this must be very frustrating for you. Hopefully everything will go well for Gage."

"Yeah, me too. Hey! I just had an idea. Gage is going to need help with Jamie. The baby knows you. Will you go with him to get my son?"

Holland was so taken aback by his suggestion that she couldn't immediately answer James.

"Are you still there?"

"Ye . . . yes. But I can't go, as much as I'd like to help rescue Jamie."

"Why not?"

"Well, for one thing, Gage will probably be gone before I could drive to your house."

"No need to drive. You can go by air."

"The closest airport is over two hours away and you don't have any near your town."

"I meant that you'll take a helicopter. Ours is often in the backyard because Gage uses it for business trips. I guess you never noticed it when you were here."

She couldn't help thinking how some people kept statues of gnomes or pink flamingos in their backyards. The Howards kept a helicopter in theirs.

"No, I didn't."

"I'll talk to Gage. He can go by and pick you up on his way. It'll save time."

Her quick intake of breath had her spluttering a refusal. "I . . . I can't."

"Why not? I thought you'd want to help."

"There's something Gage probably hasn't told you. He and I didn't part on very good terms when I left your house. I doubt if he'd be willing to have me tag along on this trip. I'm probably the last person he'd want to see right now."

"If that's true, then how come he hasn't stopped talking about you and how much he wished he would have taken your comments about Kim more seriously?"

Holland felt her pulse do a little flutter.

"Really? He said that?"

"Just about every day since you've been gone. Gage was devastated that you ended up being drugged and dumped in the tunnel. He blames himself for not taking better care of you."

"I've stopped blaming him for that. He shouldn't continue to hold himself responsible."

"Well he does. Gage doesn't know how to be anything but responsible. A lot of people probably think he's a mama's boy because he's always so concerned about our mother's welfare. I want to tell you something about my brother that I'm sure you don't know. He was five years old when his dad left. Mom worked at a minimum wage paying job. She told me while other children were playing he would be out looking for aluminum cans she could take to a recycling center for money. He never asked for anything for himself. They lived in a studio apartment and barely had enough to eat by the end of each month. Mom said every night when she tucked him into bed he'd tell her he would take care of her. He's kept that promise to this day."

Holland actually felt tears welling in her eyes picturing Gage at such a young age trying to look after his mother. She couldn't forget the day he told her he would like to be married, but he was too busy looking after his family. It seemed he'd spent his whole life putting everyone's needs before his own.

And she'd turned her back on him when he said he needed her.

She couldn't stop the regret that ripped through her knowing now how callous she'd been in ignoring his plea. James drew her attention back to him.

"It wasn't easy for Gage keeping what happened to the other nannies from you, but he had to so you'd take care of my son. It was a judgment call. He chose Jamie's safety over yours, but don't think it was easy for him. He agonized over that decision. I'm partly to blame because I turned on Gage every time he tried to talk to me about Kim. Please come back and help him bring Jamie home. Gage doesn't like to ask people for help. He thinks he has to be strong all the time. This is your chance to make up. He really does miss you."

"Well, we were starting to become friends."

"I'm telling you he wants you to be more than just a friend."

"Gage may not want me tagging along," she said, making one last feeble attempt to refuse.

"Sure he will. Trust me. I'll have him call you with the particulars as to where you can meet. Please Holland, won't you do this for Jamie?"

The whirl of the helicopter blades whipped the dust around Holland where she stood in a large empty field. Gage arranged to meet her after their brief phone conversation. He'd insisted on going alone at first, but she could hear James in the background arguing that Gage would need someone to take care of Jamie on the return trip.

Gage finally agreed, but made it clear it was only for Jamie's sake. Holland supposed she shouldn't have expected anything else, despite what James said about Gage wanting to see her. But she still made up her mind that she would make an attempt to apologize to him for her rude behavior the night she left his house. Whether or not he'd listen was another thing.

She didn't try to talk to Gage over the noise of the helicopter, which he piloted himself. They arrived at the airport a short time later and he was too busy seeing to the final preparations to give her his attention. The private plane he'd hired to take them to Mexico was much larger than she'd expected. He obviously wanted to make Jamie's flight home as comfortable as possible.

Holland wondered if Gage would be flying this aircraft, too. She watched and waited as he talked with the pilot before he finally settled into one of the plush seats for takeoff. She buckled her seatbelt and peered warily at him out of the corner of her eye. He stared straight ahead, but she knew he was very aware of her by the tension she detected in his body.

He wasn't the only one feeling tense. Holland knew a lot of it was due to the unfortunate situation with Jonathan and Jamie. But she also had a feeling she needed to clear the air with Gage about what had happened after he'd rescued her from the tunnel. She decided to wait until they reached cruising altitude. He surprised her by breaking the silence first.

New Beginnings
Olivia Claire High

"Would you like something to drink? Coffee? Tea? Water? A soda? Wine? Something to eat?" he asked in that same formal tone that he'd used on the phone.

"No thank you. What I would like is to talk to you about the day I left your house."

"Why bring that up?"

"Because I was wrong about you."

"Trying to salve your conscience now?"

"No, more like trying to tell you that I believe you did the right thing in deciding not to tell me about what happened to the other nannies."

"What makes you think I give a damn what your opinion is about my decisions?"

He pulled a laptop to him and stared at the screen, ignoring her. His silence grew until Holland began to think James said Gage missed her just so she'd agree to go on this trip.

"It seems you'd rather give me the silent treatment like the typical non communicating male rather than talk to me," she finally said, trying to bring his attention back to her again.

He looked up, but she almost wished he hadn't when he pinned her with a freezing glare.

"What do you want from me? The last time I tried to communicate you didn't like what I had to say. You left making me feel like the monster who'd put you in the tunnel. Satisfied?"

"I never wanted you to feel like that," she denied, suddenly filled with renewed remorse.

"Did you enjoy having me beg, Holland?"

"No! It makes me sick even now thinking about it. But please try to understand that I was still on edge from being drugged; and when you told me about the other nannies, I just lost it."

He shoved the laptop away. His expression was hard, almost fierce-looking now, and his voice held just enough steel to make her flinch.

"We both know the real reason you left is because you saw me in the kitchen with Kim, once again convincing yourself she and I were lovers. I don't need her, and I was wrong about saying I needed you. I told you before my money will get me any woman I want; so if this is your way of trying to worm your way back into my good graces you're wasting your time."

Was there nothing she could say or do that would gain her even a small bit of his forgiveness? Holland realized she didn't want it so much for herself, as she did for Gage. Bitterness could consume a person. No one knew that better than she did.

"I can see that no matter what I say nothing is going to be the right thing. I shouldn't have come. Why didn't you hire someone else, since you obviously can't stand the sight of me?"

"I wanted Jamie to see a familiar face. He's been through enough as it is."

"Is that the only reason you agreed to do as James asked?" she dared to inquire.

Gage shrugged.

"What other reason could there be?"

"To hurt me. I let James talk me into this because he said you told him you missed me."

"Don't flatter yourself. I was drunk at the time, as I recall."

"You got drunk because of me?"

"More gloating? The fun just keeps going on for you doesn't it, Holland?"

"Please don't keep saying such things."

"What's the matter, can't take a dose of your own kind of medicine?" he mocked.

His continued resentment was cutting through her like a knife. She couldn't let him go on believing she actually found any enjoyment in his humiliation. There had to be some way she could penetrate the hard shield he'd erected against her.

"Gage, I've never felt so alone like I did after I left you. I've had a constant ache inside of me that won't go away. Not even leaving Ray could compare because I didn't care about him by then. I can see you don't believe me, but I will always regret tossing your words back into your face when you said you needed me. I didn't try to contact you sooner because I was afraid this is how you'd react. I can't undo what I did. I can only say I'm sorry."

She waited for him to reply and felt her throat tighten when he remained quiet.

"I don't expect you to want me in your life, but please don't hate me," she whispered in one last desperate attempt to get through to him.

Seconds ticked by, each more agonizing than the last leaving her emotions in shreds.

"I don't hate you," he said at last in a ragged voice.

"You've sure been acting like you do."

"What did you expect? You're not the only one who's been hurting."

He scrubbed a hand down his face, much as he'd done that night. Holland saw how tired he looked now and silently chastised herself for putting her emotional needs first, when he had to be going through a tremendous strain considering what was happening with his family.

They all went to him whenever they had a problem, expecting him to make things right.

Holland could just imagine their voices droning on. Fix this, Gage. Make it better, Gage. What should I do, Gage? Help me, Gage. Do this. Do that. And she hadn't been much better.

"I should have told you about the other women," he continued. "But you know why I didn't. Unfortunately, my timing was lousy when I did reveal the truth. I was so concerned about Jamie that I forgot to protect you. I have to live with the fact that I'm partially responsible for your ordeal in the tunnel. Just so you know, I've had my share of tormented nights since then."

"It wasn't your fault. I accept that now. I didn't realize it until you mentioned it, but you're right about me being bothered more thinking you wanted to be with Kim. I couldn't bear that, Gage. I just couldn't."

"Jesus, Holland. You make me want to shake you. How many times do I have to tell you I've never been with Kim? I never wanted to be with her. Ever. You were wrong when you said I don't need anyone. I do get lonely to have a woman in my life, but she'd be the last female I'd choose for a partner. I wish to God you'd stop doubting my fidelity. I'm not Ray, damn it."

"I've told you he made me afraid to trust any man, but I know you're not like him."

"You left the cheating SOB and supposedly got him out of your system."

"I did. I have."

"No you haven't. He's still there between us."

She thought about that for a moment. "You're right. I've let the past mess up my future."

Holland left her seat and moved across the aisle to kneel in front of Gage. It was her turn to beg and not because she wanted to even the score. It was the only thing she could think to do.

"You may not want me now, but I know I'll go to my grave needing you. It's my fault that Kim's the winner here. She wouldn't want us to find happiness together, and she's getting her wish because I handled things badly. All I can do is beg you to give me another chance."

Gage scrutinized her expression; and she stared back, watching as the hard chill in his eyes slowly turned to a soft warmth easing the tension that had gripped them both. Holland saw him let down his defenses allowing the last barrier to crumble like a wall no longer able to stand.

"Come here," he said and hauled her onto his lap. "For the record, I did miss you. I hated knowing I'd lost someone I cared for, but ours was an argument I couldn't win."

"No thanks to me. How about a makeup kiss?"

"You'd better be sure, because I'm in no mood for games."

"Neither am I."

He cupped her face and whispered her name. Hunger burst through them the instant their lips touched. Holland dove her hands into his hair, as Gage wound his arms around her pulling her close. Every breath, every taste became a desperate attempt to grasp what they'd both thought they'd never have again. He ran his hands restlessly up and down her back using long fingers to caress and knead her quivering muscles.

Gage shifted her away and Holland started to protest until she realized he was only trying to make himself more comfortable. Their kissing definitely had caused a change in his body. She hid a smile when she heard him grunt and reach down between them to unlatch his seatbelt. They continued to torment each other until she looked over his shoulder toward the rear of the plane.

"Is that a bed I see back there?"

"Yes, it is, and I hope to God you aren't asking because you need a nap."

"I'm not sleepy," she said, sliding off his lap. "Let's go check it out, shall we?"

They took their time slowly undressing, each watching the other. Holland's boldness began to falter, as she stripped off the last of her clothing. Would Gage like what he saw? Did he prefer women who were on the thin side, she wondered? Because she was a bit curvier.

She didn't know what he thought of her body, but he definitely was a treat to her eyes. It'd been quite a while since she'd seen a naked man. Gage's body was magnificently made. Lean and muscular with powerful looking shoulders, narrow hips, washboard abs, and well defined biceps made him a sculptor's dream of perfection. Her eyes traveled from his chest down the length of his body to below his flat abdomen.

She stared wide eyed at the blatant evidence of his desire and felt her mouth go dry. No one could ever nickname Gage, Stubby. Holland felt a rush of heat shoot through her whole body before she scrambled into the bed where she quickly pulled the sheet up to her chin. A nervous little laugh escaped her.

"I'm sorry to act like a scared virgin, but I haven't done this in a long time. And you're . . ." She swallowed. "Well, you know, pretty well equipped."

Gage slid into bed with a great deal more finesse. He gave her a reassuring smile before rubbing the pad of his thumb over her lips.

"You don't have to be nervous, Holland. I won't hurt you. I just want to make love to you."

Holland voluntarily lost her virginity in college. Her partner had also been a virgin. The coupling was a clumsy and somewhat painful experience that she hadn't been in a hurry to repeat anytime soon. But she remembered being anxious to share Ray's bed. Surely being in love and given his experience their lovemaking would make all her girlish fantasies come true.

But the reality turned out to be much less exciting than her imagination. She thought their sex life was as good as it could be even though she usually felt unfulfilled. He seemed to be with her physically, but not emotionally. Holland recalled how Ray would lie back after they'd made love and ask her how it was, as though he expected her to hold up a sign rating his performance. She assumed in her naivety that was normal.

She was about to find out she'd assumed wrong.

Gage softened his raw passion with tenderness and reined in his own urgent need by patiently allowing her body to respond to him. His hands and lips roamed, stirring her to heights of desire she'd never known, making her tremble with a hunger as unexpected as it was exhilarating. Holland let out little gasps of pleasure rubbing her fingertips over his hard flesh.

Her body twisted beneath him silently urging him on until Gage took what she so urgently offered and gave her even more in return. She felt as though they were joining their souls as well as their bodies. Bright sunlight showed through the windows, but she was too blind to see. The plane's engines hummed, but she was deaf to any sound except their ragged breathing.

Her mind went blank, but somehow her body knew what it had to do. Gage became her world. Nothing else mattered except that she respond to him until her body arched and an urgent cry tore out of her leaving her gloriously spent. Gage followed with his own release groaning out her name like a dying man who'd just been given his last request.

Holland lay breathless and stunned realizing this is what she'd been missing with Ray. She may be thousands of miles up in the sky, but it was the result of Gage's love making that made her feel like she was soaring through the clouds.

"Thank you," she breathed through the little shivers that still rippled through her. "I didn't realize I could feel like this."

He rolled them onto their sides.

"Why not? You're a very passionate woman, Holland."

"I must have been storing it up because I had no idea making love could be so amazing. Ray was only interested in his own pleasure. I thought there was something wrong with me."

"Ray was a narcissistic fool. He was too ignorant to realize what he had with you. What we just experienced together was amazing for me, too. I think I started to become attracted to you the day you spilled the berry juice on my shirt and then proceeded to give me the third degree."

She wrinkled her nose.

"I wasn't very nice. I wanted to pay you back for being rude to me."

"Rude?" Gage snorted. "I acted like a pompous ass."

"Well, maybe a little pompous, but not quite an ass."

"I knew I was a goner when I kissed you in the woods. I hoped it was going to be the beginning of something mutually satisfying between us. But when you left my house I knew I'd destroyed whatever chance I'd had of any kind of relationship."

"You're a good man, Gage. Deep down I know that. I should have had more faith in you."

"Hmm, maybe I didn't do enough to entice you. Would you have stayed if I'd played the piano for you?" he asked in a teasing tone. "You know, something like, 'You Are My Sunshine'." Holland buried her face against his chest and laughed.

She looked at him, her eyes shining with amusement. "I'd love to hear you play anything. I would have phoned you sooner if I'd known we were going to end up in bed together."

"What made you change your mind and make the call?"

"My dad. He knew I was dying to know if you had any news about Jamie. I also confessed to him that I wondered how you were doing. It didn't take him long to realize I had feelings for you, but I didn't know how you felt about me. It helped when James said you missed me."

"Why do women always need to know how far they've turned the screws?"

Holland heard the subtle change in his earlier tone and hastened to defend her statement.

"That wasn't it. If he told me, you hated me I'd have to accept that I was the one who ruined any chance of a reconciliation between us. I did wish you'd told me about the other nannies, but who's to say Kim still wouldn't have found a way to drug me?"

"She was certainly determined. The real shock has been Jon's involvement."

"I can imagine." She touched the shadows beneath his eyes. "You haven't been sleeping."

"Not much."

"Do you think he was the one Kim was talking to that day in your office?"

"Probably, which means he could have fathered Jamie."

"Unless she lied. I noticed James still refers to himself as Jamie's dad."

"I intend to keep it that way. We're going to see the woman who says she's Jon's girlfriend. She has Jamie. You and the baby will return to my house in this plane as soon as you have him."

"What about you?"

"I'll be staying on to deal with Jonathan's kidnappers. If all goes well, they'll take the ransom money, hand over my brother, and we'll be on the next plane out of there."

"Wouldn't it be easier if I just waited for you?"

He shook his head.

"I want the baby back home as quickly as possible. This whole thing has been very stressful for my mother and James. It might be a good idea if you pack whatever you'll need for Jamie. I asked the people who stocked the plane to add some kind of bag you can use."

"Okay." She touched his chest. "This is probably going to sound like a very inappropriate request given the circumstances, but I wish we had time to make love again."

Gage sucked in a breath when her hand moved over his belly and crept slowly lower.

"We'll take time."

They were met by a heavily built Hispanic man holding a handwritten sign with Gage's name on it.

191

Holland expected someone more neatly dressed, but this man was clothed in faded jeans and a khaki shirt with a small patch sewn on one elbow. He introduced himself as Manuel. Holland stared in surprise when Gage answered in flawless Spanish.

He handed Gage a sealed envelope. Gage immediately tore it open and read the message. He said something to Manuel who nodded and led them to an open Jeep that looked as well-worn as the brown leather boots Manuel wore. So much for her assumption they'd be traveling in a nice, comfortable limo. She barely had time to crawl into the back, put her bags down, and buckle her seatbelt before they were speeding away from the airport.

Manuel wove through city traffic like a man driving an obstacle course with Satan hot on his tail. Holland wished she was wearing a crash helmet and body padding when they left the paved highway and ended up on a dirt road riddled with potholes. Was it her imagination, or did he drive over every single one?

They arrived at a small village four hours later. Manuel pulled the Jeep to a stop in a puff of flying dust and a screech of brakes. Several modest mobile homes were scattered in the area along with simple houses varying in different kinds of construction materials. Manuel parked halfway down the narrow lane in front of a small cinder block house painted bright turquoise with windows framed in peeling pink paint.

"That was a pretty rough trip. Are you okay?" Gage asked, as he helped Holland climb out.

"I think I left a kidney back there somewhere along the way."

He grimaced.

"I hear you."

"When did you learn to speak Spanish so well?"

"My step-father felt it was important that my brothers and I learn because we do a lot of business with Spanish speaking countries. He hired a private tutor for us when we were kids."

"Is this where we're meeting Jonathan's girlfriend?" she said pointing to the little house.

"Yes."

Gage grabbed the tote bag, while Holland took her purse before they followed Manuel over a walkway made from broken pieces of cement half buried in the dirt. She watched her footing, careful not to stumble. The scarred front door opened revealing a young woman in her early twenties. Holland thought she made a lovely picture with her creamy light coffee colored skin; large thickly lashed black eyes, and ebony hair that fell to her shoulders in shiny waves.

Holland could see why Jonathan would be attracted to her. Her hand trembled a bit when she waved them inside. She was obviously nervous despite her friendly smile. Gage greeted her in Spanish and introduced Holland and himself.

"I speak English, Mr. Langdon. My name is Charo Ramos. Please come in."

They followed her inside the dim interior where tiny shafts of sunlight filtered into the room through a couple of small windows. They sat on a couple of roughhewed wooden chairs. She gave them each a bottle of water before sitting down herself.

"I know you must be worried about the baby, but I assure you he is fine. I'll take you to him as soon as I've answered any questions you may have. This is my grandmother's house. Your nephew is a few houses away at my aunt's."

Gage nodded.

"Thank you. My family is grateful to you all for taking care of Jamie."

"Jonathan's been good to the people here, but we'd have kept the child safe in any case."

"I'm sure you would have. Is this where you met my brother?"

"No. I live with my parents in a large town. They make their living selling flowers. I work as a secretary in a health clinic. When I'm not working there I wheel one of our flower carts around town selling flowers to tourists. Jonathan was driving too fast one day and hit my cart."

Gage swore under his breath.

"I hope you weren't injured."

"He only knocked over the cart and scattered the flowers. He stopped right away to help me and insisted I take money for any damages. I was about to refuse when I fainted. Your brother thought he must have hurt me. But that's not why I passed out. I was ill only I didn't know how sick I was at the time. I hadn't been feeling well for quite a while and woke that morning feeling especially bad. I shouldn't have left the house, but I didn't want to worry my parents."

"Had you seen a doctor?"

"Not at that point, which is silly with me working around medical people. Jonathan took me to the clinic. I was eventually diagnosed with cancer of the uterus." She looked down at her neatly folded hands. "My surgery left me unable to bear children."

Holland felt the woman's pain, as though someone had plunged a knife into her. She wanted to offer sympathy, but couldn't find the words, so it was Gage who spoke.

"I'm very sorry."

"It was a difficult time for me. Jonathan helped to ease my sadness. He visited often, and we fell in love. He asked me to marry him. I told him he needed a woman who could give him babies. He said he already had a baby. Now you know why he brought your nephew to me."

"He must have been planning this for months. Did he bring Jamie to your parents' house?"

"No. He invited me to his hotel. He said he had a surprise for me. He was always buying me gifts, so I thought it must be something like that. I was shocked when he handed over Jamie."

"What did he say about Kim, the baby's mother?" Holland couldn't resist asking.

"He said the baby's mother died in childbirth. But he avoided looking at me when he said it, and seemed on edge when I tried to ask questions about her. I told him I couldn't keep the baby. He became very angry and slammed out of the room. Then he . . . he was kidnapped."

"Will you tell me why you waited so long to get in touch with my family?"

"Jonathan gave me a false last name. I'd have called sooner, but I swear I didn't learn the truth until I got the ransom note." Her voice was strained, as though she expected him to object.

"It's all right, Charo. I'm not blaming you," Gage told her in a soothing voice. "Can you tell me anything more about what happened after my brother left the hotel room?"

"I called the front desk when he didn't return after a couple of hours, but no one knew anything. I stayed in the room until morning hoping he'd return, but he didn't. I couldn't afford the hotel, so I took the baby to my parents' house. I brought Jamie here to hide him from the kidnappers after they sent my note. Did Manuel give you yours?"

Gage patted his shirt pocket. "Yes. I'm in your debt for taking such good care of the baby."

"Jamie's mother didn't die, did she?" Charo asked in a quiet voice.

"No."

She drew in an unsteady breath.

"I thought as much. So Jonathan really did lie to me."

"Yes. I'm sorry. He has a lot to answer for. God willing, I'll bring him back and deal with his subterfuge."

"The men who took Jonathan won't care what God thinks."

Gage cocked a brow.

"They just want your money," Charo explained in a voice wobbling with fear.

Chapter Thirteen

Holland followed Gage and Charo outside just as Manuel came out of a house across the street. She waited while Gage talked to him. She assumed it concerned her trip back and also probably something to do with the kidnappers. She couldn't stop feeling anxious to leave this place as soon as possible. She just wished Gage would be going with her. She walked beside Gage, as Charo led them to her aunt's house. Manuel waited by the Jeep.

"I can't believe Jonathan had an affair with Kim while romancing Charo at the same time," she whispered under her breath.

"He used to brag about how many women he slept with on his travels. If there's ever a play written about reproduction Jon would probably take the role of the sperm."

"Or the part of the anatomy that shoots out the goods."

Holland chuckled briefly at the image before her nerves took over again. Charo's comment about the kidnappers made her worry about Gage's safety. What would keep them from killing him and keeping Jonathan to hold out for even more money?

A skinny black dog ran up the street, chased by a young boy. She watched them hoping the diversion would pull her away from her dark thoughts. Charo stopped in front of a house built much like the one they'd left. They waited while she went inside.

"Is Jamie in there?" Holland asked Gage.

"Yes. Are you all right? You looked like you were a million miles away."

"I'm a little edgy about you being at the mercy of those kidnappers."

"I won't be alone. Manuel's arranged for a friend, Pablo to go with me. He'll be armed."

"Armed?" She shuddered. "Oh God."

"It's just a precaution. Try not to worry. I'll be finished before you know it. The meeting place is only a half hour away from here."

He gave her the name of the village. Holland tried to repeat it, but the word made her tongued tied. "I can't say it. I should have taken Spanish in school instead of French."

"You speak French?"

"No, I was so lousy the teacher asked me to leave. That's why I should have taken Spanish."

He smiled. "I'm glad you haven't lost your sense of humor."

"Don't let me fool you because I feel like I'm barely hanging on by a thread."

Charo stood in the doorway and motioned them inside. Holland felt her whole body sag with relief when she saw Jamie looking healthy and seemingly quite content.

"I can't get over how much he's grown since I last saw him."

New Beginnings
Olivia Claire High

Charo introduced them to the woman holding the baby as her aunt. She handed Jamie to Holland. It immediately became apparent she thought Holland was Jamie's mother. Holland didn't bother to correct the mistake. She hadn't realized how much she'd missed the baby, as she cuddled him enjoying having him in her arms again.

Gage smiled, and thanked Charo's aunt. Holland saw him hand an envelope to the older woman, which she supposed must be money. But she didn't take it until Charo said something to her.

They went outside and walked back to the Jeep. Charo ran into her grandmother's house to get her belongings, while Manuel got behind the wheel. Gage opened the door for Holland.

"He's not much on manners, but he'll get you back to the plane safely."

"I'm glad Charo is going with me. I'd hate to have him as my only companion, since he can't speak English and my Spanish is limited to enchilada and taco."

"You're forgetting the baby," Gage teased.

"Not to underestimate Jamie, but I don't think he speaks Spanish, either."

"I'll have to work with him when we get home."

Holland wondered how Gage could appear so calm when he was heading into a potentially dangerous situation. She was using humor to try and control her fears. But looking at him she saw that even if Gage was frightened, he wasn't showing it. She realized that was probably because ever since his step-father died, Gage was largely responsible for handling the family's problems. They expected him to be strong and he obviously didn't expect any less of himself.

Charo came out of the house as Gage gave Holland a lingering kiss. He made sure both women and the baby were settled in the back before he said something to Manuel who grunted.

"Mr. Langdon, please tell Jonathan that I accept his marriage proposal. His being kidnapped made me realize I don't want to live without him. Tell him we can adopt babies."

"I'll be sure and deliver your message and thank you again for keeping my nephew safe."

Holland gave him a beseeching look. "Please be careful."

"I will. I just got you back in my life and I intend to continue where we left off on the plane." She blushed and he gave her another lingering kiss before smiling and waving them off.

Holland kept waving until she could no longer see him and only then did she sit back.

"I see you two are in love," Charo said with approval shining in her dark eyes.

"What? Oh, no, no, we're just friends."

"I think for him it is more than that. He looks at you like a man ready to lap at cream."

Holland squirmed with discomfort thinking about the things Gage had done to her with his tongue when they'd made love on the plane. Her mind scrambled trying to change the subject.

"Um, what did Gage say to Manuel just before we left?"

"He reminded him that there is now a baby along and he should not drive so fast. I've ridden with Manuel before. I have a feeling your trip here was like having your bones being rattled."

"That about sums it up. But he does seem to be going a lot slower right now, so Gage must have gotten to him. I'll just be glad when Gage is finished with this filthy business."

"Will you be flying home with Jamie as soon as you get to the airport, Ms. Wallace?"

"Please call me Holland. Yes, that's what Gage wanted, but I was thinking since it's only a half hour away to the kidnappers, maybe I should wait. Gage could be ready to go by tonight."

Charo frowned at her.

"I don't understand what you mean. It'll take Mr. Langdon almost three hours one way to where he's meeting the kidnappers."

"Three hours!" Holland jerked against her seatbelt with a start. "Are you sure? What's the name of the place?"

Charo told her and although Holland hadn't been able to repeat it back to Gage, she did know it wasn't the name he'd given her.

"I think something may be wrong here. That's not the place Gage mentioned to me, and he specifically said it was only a half hour drive."

"Do you remember the name he gave you?"

"I couldn't pronounce it. Name some villages in the area. Maybe I'll recognize it."

Holland held up her hand for Charo to stop when she got to the third name.

"That's not in the same direction he's supposed to be going. You said the word was difficult to pronounce. Perhaps you misunderstood."

"I don't think so. But I'm going to call Gage to make sure." Holland dug in her purse.

"You may not be able to get a signal. The cell service is very poor in this area."

Holland checked her phone after a few seconds. "You're right. No signal. Please, can we go back? I'd like to try and catch Gage before he leaves."

Charo leaned forward to tap Manuel on the shoulder, but Holland grabbed her hand and hissed under her breath. "I'm not sure if we should trust him. What if he's in on this switch?"

"No one in my grandmother's village would betray a brother of Jonathan's."

"Well, it seems like somebody did."

"I trust Manuel with my life."

Manuel clearly wasn't happy when Charo told him to go back, but he quickly agreed when she explained what Holland told her. Holland knew she was going to have to rely on this young woman and her friends to help her. She listened to them talking, wishing she could understand what they were saying.

Charo turned to Holland after a few minutes.

"My aunt will not mind having the baby at her house again. I will be with you to explain why we came back. Manuel and I have decided to ask my Uncle Tomas and his son Andy to help us."

"This could turn out to be dangerous. Are you sure they'll want to get involved?"

"Jonathan helped them when my uncle had to have surgery on his shoulder last year. He not only paid the medical bills, but he made sure the family didn't go hungry."

Manuel drove them back to the village. Charo and Holland rushed into her aunt's house with Jamie while Manuel headed off to find out if Gage had left. Charo explained things to her aunt. Then they sat down and waited for Manuel to return.

"I'm still not sure we're doing the right thing to involve your family and friends. I bet they won't forgive me if any harm comes to them. I know I won't forgive myself if someone gets hurt, and I'm certain Gage wouldn't, either."

"People were willing to take the chance. Many others wanted to help Mr. Langdon get Jonathan. But he thought it might make the kidnappers feel too threatened."

Manuel came into the house and drew Charo into conversation. Holland sat and waited, eager to know what they were saying. Charo finally spoke to her after a few minutes.

"Manuel says Mr. Langdon is gone. We will go after him, but he says it would be best if you stay here. I agree with him."

Holland jumped to her feet.

"I can't stay here while you put yourselves in danger."

"It'll be more dangerous if you go because you don't speak the language; and also you will draw too much attention since you aren't one of us. I know it is difficult for you to stay, but it will be safer for us all if you do."

"Oh, but . . ."

Manuel tugged on her sleeve and Charo nodded at him.

"We have to go now. The others are ready to leave, and we don't want to allow the kidnappers any more time to do their mischief. I will try to get word to you if we don't return by nightfall."

Holland stepped back, knowing she had to accept defeat in this.

"I hate feeling so helpless. If only there was something I could do."

"There is . . . pray."

Gage glanced at the man beside him. He'd said very little. But this wasn't exactly a pleasant drive through the countryside. Gage felt sweat trickling down his back by the time they stopped.

He climbed out and stared at an old, rusting single wide trailer situated on the outskirts of this village. The battered van parked in front wasn't in much better condition. Pablo got out of his truck and stood next to Gage. The trailer door opened a moment later spilling out the sound of men laughing. Jonathan hurried down the steps and gave Gage a light punch on the shoulder.

"You made it. I told the guys you would. Did you see Jamie? Is he okay?"

"Yes and we'll talk about him later. But right now I'd like to know what's going on here."

"Come inside, and I'll explain. It's not as bad as you think," he called over his shoulder.

Three men sat at a table playing cards. Jonathan pointed to two older men. "This is Juan and Xavier, and this is Ramon," he said waving a hand toward a much younger man. "How's Charo? Did she miss me? Did she cry?"

"She's very concerned about you."

Jonathan pumped his fist in the air.

"Yes! I knew this kidnapping thing would get a rise out of her if I stayed away long enough. I also wanted to give her time to get used to Jamie."

Gage gave him an incredulous look. "Are you saying you faked your abduction just so Charo would worry about you?"

"Yeah. I needed to find out if she really loves me. It was Juan's idea to pretend I was kidnapped when I told him Charo wouldn't marry me even after I brought Jamie to her. And before you get all ticked off about me taking him you should know that he's my son. Kim and I fooled around before she hooked up with James. She got pregnant and started whining about me marrying her. No way was I going to do that, not when I love Charo. I tricked her into bagging James. He wanted her anyway."

Gage glanced at the men. "I'm surprised your people allowed you to do this."

"Oh, they're not from around here. I met them in a bar."

"I think it's safe to say you've reached a whole new level of stupidity," Gage said with growing frustration. "Where is Kim? She left the house with you."

"I don't know where she is. We did leave together, but only because it was the only way I could take Jamie without her alerting everyone. She kept bugging me about taking her away, so I told her we were going to Hawaii. But I had it all planned out to dump her at the airport. I waited until she went to the restroom and hopped a plane here."

"And you thought that would end things with her? Jonathan, think! She's married to our brother; and you took her child without her permission."

"She doesn't want Jamie, So what's the big deal?"

Gage fought to reign in his growing anger.

"The big deal is that she can accuse you of kidnapping the baby. She might even claim that you kidnapped her, so she can cause more trouble. Knowing Kim, she's going to do whatever she can to destroy you for dumping her."

"That's bull. I didn't kidnap her. She came willingly. She had the hots for me, so I used that to get her to cooperate."

"How did you manage to keep your affair a secret from the family?"

"We'd sneak around the house and find places to be together. Sometimes I returned from my trips without telling you, hide in the tunnels, and meet with Kim there."

"I see, and which one of you drugged James and Holland?"

"Hey, you can't lay that on me. I never messed with the drugging part. Kim took care of that. But I admit, I did carry Holland down to the tunnels. Kim said they'd be okay. She put James out plenty of times. Oh, and she did the other nannies, too."

"Where did Kim get the drugs?"

Jonathan sent him a sheepish look.

New Beginnings
Olivia Claire High

"I picked them up here in Mexico."

"So you planned this whole fiasco just to get Charo to marry you?"

"Not such a fiasco if it works, which I think it will now that she's so worried about me."

"Personally, I think if she had any sense she wouldn't have anything more to do with you for causing so much anxiety. But she's not the only female you've upset. Did you ever stop to think what all this would mean to our mother?"

"Oh yeah, Mom. Is she all right?"

"No she is not all right. How did you think she would react to being told her son left with her grandchild, drugged two people she cares a great deal about, and now believes got himself kidnapped? On top of that, Holland was frightened half out of her mind, and James very nearly didn't wake up from his drugging."

"Damn. I told that maniac Kim to be careful she didn't give him too much. Is he okay?"

"He is now, but it was a close call. What about Holland? She's probably going to have nightmares for months after what happened. My God, how could you condone the drugging?"

"It was Kim's idea. I didn't like it. But I had to go along with her to make sure I stayed in her good graces, so she'd have Jamie. I wanted to give Charo my baby, so she could be a mom."

"He's not your baby. Holland is taking him back home as we speak and you will not, I repeat, not say anything to James that you think you're the baby's biological father."

Jonathan jutted out his chin. "Well I am, dammit."

"I wouldn't be too sure about that if I were you."

"What do you mean? I told you I was with Kim before she hooked up with James."

"What makes you think she wasn't sleeping with him while she was doing you?"

"Because she said she loved me."

"I doubt if she knows the meaning of the word, unless we're talking about self-love. I'm sure she's very busy right now plotting out what kind of revenge she's planning for you."

"You really think she'll come after me?"

Gage rolled his eyes towards the ceiling. "Tell me you're not actually that naïve. Do you honestly think she won't? You used her for your own gain. She's going to want to settle that score, and knowing Kim, it won't be in a very nice way. In my opinion you deserve what you get considering how you tricked her."

"Since when are you in her corner? I told you, she never wanted the baby. I did her a favor by taking him away. I'm your brother. You should be on my side."

"I'm on Jamie's side. He can't stand up for himself, so I will. You and Kim are both in the wrong because you both deliberately hurt people for your own satisfaction."

"She never fit in with our family anyway. So what if I used her? It's not like she didn't enjoy being with me. She uses people, too. She drugged James so she could sleep with me."

"I certainly don't condone her behavior, but try to put yourself in Kim's shoes. She obviously believed you cared enough about her to have a future with her."

"The very idea makes me want to puke. I can't stand the woman."

"I don't imagine she's feeling very fond of you herself right now. You created a powerful enemy when you ran out on her, Jonathan."

"I was just playing a joke."

Gage became aware of how the three men had slowly maneuvered themselves until they were surrounding him and Pablo. They reminded him of snakes getting ready to strike.

"No. You were playing with people's lives and there's nothing funny about that."

Gage looked at the men.

"I think it's time I take my thoughtless and irresponsible brother home where he deserves to be punished for causing so much trouble."

The end of a pistol suddenly pressed against his temple.

"I must disagree with you."

Jonathan's head jerked toward the man. "What are you doing, Juan? Put that gun away."

"I'm afraid I cannot do that. You see, you have your ruse and I have mine."

Xavier searched them and took away Pablo's gun making Jonathan's eyes widen further.

"I thought you guys were becoming my friends, but I can see you did this for the money,"

Juan lowered the pistol and took a step back, but kept the gun aimed at Gage.

"What else? The hotel clerk told us you were rich, so we followed you into the bar thinking we'd lift your wallet. But when you started complaining about your girlfriend, it wasn't difficult to convince you we could help make her jealous by this phony kidnapping."

"I'm not giving you a dime after such a lousy trick."

Gage sent him a steely glare.

"Shut up."

"You should listen to your brother," Juan said, waving the gun towards Gage.

Jon stared at the gun and bit his lip. "You'll let us go once we give you the money. Right?"

Juan shook his head.

"Sadly for you I'm being paid too much not to let you go."

"What do you mean? Who's paying you to keep us here?"

Gage kept his expression under control, not wanting to expose the turmoil roaring through him.

"Who do you think, Jon?"

"I believe you're about to find out the meaning of the saying, *hell hath no fury like a woman scorned,* Juan said with a wicked grin.

Kim stood at the bank of windows in the living room of her family home. Her fingernails dug tiny crescent shapes into the soft palms of her hands. She held herself rigid with her jaw clenched. The scene offered a view of sloping emerald green lawns flowing down toward the edge of a forested area. The sun lay a shimmering blanket of gold over the water on the nearby pond just visible through the trees. It made for a serene setting, but did nothing to soothe the foul mood emanating from her body.

Her father, Winslow Orray entered the room. A short, stout man with thinning salt and pepper hair, he stood for a few seconds studying his daughter before clearing his throat.

Kim whirled to face him.

"Have you found Jonathan yet?"

"Yes. I've had him traced to a remote village in Mexico. The people I hired have him."

"Finally! I want him to pay for the way he humiliated and used me."

"He will. I'm sure you'd like to know that Gage has the ransom money. He's with Jonathan now."

"All the better for me. I want him to suffer, too."

Winslow raised his eyebrows and started to protest, but stopped when Kim's lips trembled.

"I didn't want to have to tell you, but Gage started harassing me to sleep with him."

"My God! Why didn't you tell me?"

"He threatened to hurt Jamie if I did. I'm just thankful he finally lost interest in me."

Winslow's nostrils flared.

"I won't forgive him for treating you like that. But speaking of Jamie, I know how you feel about the baby, and I understand considering how Jonathan handled things. But the child is my grandson and heir. I want him away from the Howards. You are my only child, and Jamie may well be my only grandchild. Do you have a problem with me bringing him here and raising him with the Orray name?"

"Actually, that's a very good idea because the Howards will hate it, but that won't be enough. I must have my revenge."

"I promise you shall, my darling."

Chapter Fourteen

"I'll pay you double what Winslow Orray and his daughter are offering if you'll let my brother and Pablo go," Gage said, his gaze never wavering from Juan.

"Pablo was never in danger of being kept."

"What about my brother? Will you let him walk away if I stay here in his place?"

Juan shook his head.

"I cannot. He's the main target."

Jonathan wiped the back of his hand across the layer of sweat covering his upper lip.

"This is all my doing. My brother hasn't done anything. Please let him go, Juan."

"Your family loyalty is very touching. Perhaps if you had thought about it sooner you wouldn't be in this predicament. Not that it matters to me. My colleagues and I will be paid handsomely thanks to your treachery with your sister-in-law."

Gage tried again.

"I'll triple what Orray is paying, and you can still keep me here while Jonathan goes for the extra money."

Xavier and Ramon looked at each other and motioned for Juan to step outside with them.

"It seems your latest offer has created some interest. Pablo goes with us. I'd advise you not to do anything to displease me or he will be the one to suffer for any foolishness on your part."

Jonathan faced Gage when the others left. "I can't let you do this. I'm the one Kim wants."

"Yes, and God only knows what she'll have these thugs do to you to satisfy her need to get even. That's why I'm trying to get you out of here. Hopefully they'll take me up on my offer."

"I never thought things would turn out like this. I'm really sorry, Gage."

"I hope you've learned a lesson on what happens when you lie to me."

Jonathan bobbed his head up and down.

"For sure, but I'm still worried about you staying."

"I'll be all right. I'm not the one Kim wants. Juan has no reason to harm me."

"Yeah, but what if . . ." he stopped when the men trooped back inside.

Gage faced Juan. "So, have you made your decision?"

Holland rushed outside when she heard voices. She skidded to a halt when she saw Jonathan among the group of people standing there. Her eyes darted anxiously about, but there wasn't any sign of Gage. She elbowed herself through the crowd and marched right up to him.

He stared at her in surprise.

"What are you doing here? I thought you went back home with Jamie."

"Where's Gage?" she asked, ignoring his statement.

"I don't know."

"What do you mean you don't know? He went to negotiate your release from the kidnappers."

"I, um, pretended to be kidnapped. I had no idea the guys I was with were hired by Kim's father and were taking me for real. I did it to make Charo worried enough to want to marry me."

"Are you insane?" Holland started to raise her hand to slap him, but ended up balling her fingers into fists. "I'll ask you again, why are you here and Gage isn't?"

"He offered the kidnappers more money and himself as collateral. They set me free, so I can get the extra cash. I have to wait to hear from them and find out where they've taken Gage."

"I can't believe you let your brother stay and put his life in danger for your stupid trick."

"I didn't want to, but it was the only way they would let me leave."

"You don't deserve a brother like Gage. Have you thought about who will be the one to clean up your messes if he dies?" she cried before running back into the house.

Charo found her there minutes later sitting in a chair rocking her body back and forth in silent misery. Holland turned a tear stained face toward her. "How can you love such a selfish, misguided man like that?"

"My grandmother once told me that love has many facets and that some are more attractive than others. I know Jonathan is sometimes immature. That childishness was part of his charm to me. Now I find myself being appalled at this side of him.

Granted, he had no idea he would be sacrificing Mr. Langdon's safety when he concocted this outrageous scheme to make me marry him. But his foolishness has altered my feelings for him."

"Maybe you should tell him," Holland said, wiping tears away with the back of her hand.

"I did and I'm not the only one. He's finding out now that the people here no longer hold him in such high regard. It's going to take more than money to gain back their allegiance."

"I'm more concerned with whether or not money will be able to pay for Gage's freedom."

A knock at the door prevented Charo from replying. Jonathan shuffled into the little room.

"I know I'm the last person you'd want to spend time with right now, Holland. But I need to take Jamie home and get the money for Gage. I was hoping you'd go with me."

"What will you do if his kidnappers decide not to cooperate?"

"What I should have done in the first place, offer myself instead. I'm the one Kim hates. I shouldn't have let Gage talk me into leaving. But he always . ." his voice trailed off.

"Takes care of his family," she finished, not bothering to hide the bitterness she felt.

"Yeah. Now it's my turn. I also need to set things straight with my mother and James."

"To say the least." She stood up. "All right, I'll go with you for Jamie's sake."

"I want you to know that I'm going to turn myself over to Kim's father as soon as I get back.

I'm sure that'll be enough to make him call off his men and release Gage." He looked at Charo.

"It would be better if you didn't come back here if you fail," she said in a cool tone.

"I figured that," he said giving her one last haunted look before walking out.

It felt like time was moving in slow motion, as they drove to the airport. Holland sat with Jamie in the back while Jonathan sat up front with Manuel. Charo stayed behind in case the kidnappers sent word about Gage. Jonathan seemed convinced no harm would come to him. But Holland feared Kim's ego would demand retribution for Gage spurning her sexual advances.

They drove in tense silence without anyone willing to talk until they reached the airport. Manuel glared at Jonathan, but surprised Holland by shaking her hand and saying something to her in Spanish. She raised a questioning brow to Jonathan.

"He's wishing you God speed and good luck," Jonathan translated.

"I would think that's something he'd be saying to you."

"I'd be burning in hell right now if he had his way. The whole village hates me now. I can't blame any of them after the way I screwed up."

"Are you expecting me to feel sorry for you?"

He looked down at his feet.

"I guess not."

"I'll go with you to see Mr. Orray to make sure you don't mess that up for Gage's sake."

"He'll be okay. He's worth too much to the kidnappers for them to hurt him."

Gage shifted and groaned, his sore body protesting the movement. Every muscle ached as though he'd been used as a punching bag, which now that he remembered was pretty much what had happened. Juan filmed the assault at Kim's insistence, saying his punishment was all for her benefit. Gage realized he'd underestimated her need for revenge when he told Jonathan not to worry about him. But being informed that Jonathan wasn't there had apparently set her off on a furious tantrum compelling her father to order Gage to be beaten in an effort to offer some appeasement to his ranting daughter.

Things started off in the beginning pretty civilized as abductions went. Jonathan was allowed to drive away with Pablo, vowing to return as soon as possible with the extra money.

Juan warned him they would be moving to another location, and he'd be in touch. Gage was ushered into the back of their windowless van where he shared the hard floor with Ramon and Xavier while Juan drove. It turned out to be a long, hot trip, and they were all sweating profusely by the time they arrived at their destination.

Gage was ordered out of the van as soon as they stopped, and that's when any attempt at civility ended. They hit him from behind, causing him to stagger. He fought back the best he could in his dazed state, but wasn't able to do much against three men. He'd been beaten, stripped of his clothes, and left lying naked in pitch darkness with his arms tied behind his back and his ankles bound together.

He tried to break free from the ropes, but sharp pains spiked through his body making him stop. Gage listened, but the only thing he heard was the sound of his own harsh breathing. Otherwise, his surroundings were as silent as a tomb. The comparison made him grit his teeth. His skin burned where he'd tugged at the coarse rope. All he'd accomplished was to cause himself more discomfort.

Right now it hurt just to breathe; and the pounding inside his head made him nauseous. He hated the idea of giving up any effort to save himself, but common sense dictated that he would have to wait. He didn't know what the kidnappers had in store for him and could only hope the promise of the ransom money would be enough to pay for his life.

It galled him that he had no other choice but to lie there like an inept slug awaiting his fate. The only thing he could be thankful for was how he'd made Holland go back to the plane.

Knowing that she and Jamie were safe was the one thing helping him keep his sanity through this madness.

Reminding himself that Jonathan was the key to his release didn't exactly fill Gage with confidence. Hopefully, others would be willing to come forth to aid him. He had to believe Charo could get the people in the village to help. Gage also had to take solace in the fact that if his brother was shrewd enough to trick Kim into believing he loved her for all those months, surely he had enough brains to successfully head up a rescue mission.

But Gage also couldn't overlook the fact that he personally wouldn't be in pain lying in this makeshift prison if his brother hadn't toyed with Kim's emotions in the first place. He rested his head wearily on the floor wishing he could slide out of this nightmare and into a more peaceful existence. He closed his eyes trying to block visions of the rage Kim must have felt when she'd discovered Jonathan had dumped her.

Nor could he forget the times he himself had brushed off her advances. No doubt she wanted to make him suffer for rejecting her. Gage remembered hearing through the haze of his beating Juan telling the others to make it look good for Mr. Orray's daughter.

Gage swallowed and tasted blood in his mouth.

God only knew what other punishment Kim would demand his captors inflict on him.

Chapter Fifteen

Holland sat by Jonathan listening while his brother and mother vented their anger after he'd confessed the folly of his plans to dupe Kim and give Jamie to Charo. She worried he'd slip and say the baby was his son, but thankfully he kept that a secret as they continued to chastise him.

She finally broke her silence after several minutes to remind them Jonathan had brought Jamie back home and now needed to concentrate on saving Gage. James insisted they call in the authorities, saying Jonathan couldn't be trusted not to mishandle something so important.

Jonathan protested and Holland interrupted long enough to inform James that the kidnappers might kill Gage if his family involved the police. But she immediately wished she hadn't been forced to be so blunt when Marguerite burst into tears.

His mother's reaction caused James to smother his temper long enough to help Jonathan make arrangements for the exorbitant ransom money and transportation back to Mexico. Both he and his mother expressed relief when Holland said she'd be going with Jonathan to face Kim and her father. Marguerite embraced Holland at the door imploring her to bring Gage safely home.

Winslow Orray's eyes raked over Jonathan in blatant disgust before turning to glare at Holland with equal distain.

"Who is this? Your whore of the moment?"

She barely stopped herself from saying if he thought she was a whore, what did that make Kim who'd not only slept with both Jonathan and James, but tried to get Gage into her bed, too?

"My name is Holland Wallace, Mr. Orray. I enjoyed being Jamie's nanny until . . . "

"A hooker with a heart?" he mocked, interrupting her.

"You shut up you old . . ." Jonathan began.

Now it was Holland's turn to cut in before the meeting deteriorated any further.

"I was Jamie's nanny, as I was saying until your daughter slipped me a hallucinogenic drug in my tea that made me ill."

"What lie is this?" Winslow demanded.

"It's no lie. I brought copies of the lab results that were taken after Kim drugged both Holland and James. My brother almost died," Jonathan said, leaning forward for emphasis.

"They could have taken the drugs themselves."

"All of the previous nannies were also drugged."

"Kim wouldn't do such a thing, and she certainly wouldn't have access to such drugs."

Jonathan sat back and inhaled a bracing breath. "I got the drugs when I was in Mexico."

"There you go then. That makes you the person responsible, and not Kim."

"It was her idea for me to get the drugs, and she did the research, so I would know exactly which ones to buy. She especially wanted to drug my brother, so she and I could sleep together."

A bright red hue crept up Winslow's neck slowly flooding his face. "You're lying, you despicable slime! You should be castrated for the criminal way you treated Kim."

"I tricked her into thinking I loved her. That would hardly be classified as a crime."

"What about Kim? She has a right to be compensated for the anguish she's gone through. She's so distraught I didn't tell her about this meeting."

"It's my fault, and I'm willing to take responsibility for my actions. I promise to let Kim do whatever she wants with me, but I want my brother's freedom in return."

"I'll tell you where Gage is, but they won't release him without the ransom money."

"I know. I have that money, plus triple what you're paying them to do your dirty work."

"You mean to tell me they're double dipping?"

"What did you expect?" Holland jeered. "We're not exactly talking good Samaritans here."

"Why would Gage offer them more money?"

"That was the only way they'd let me go."

"I didn't realize that. They told me you had escaped. Kim became hysterical when she heard. The only way I could calm her down was to say I'd have Gage beaten. She demanded someone must be made to suffer, and you were unavailable; so you see my dilemma."

Holland paled, while Jonathan became so angry he nearly jumped out of his chair.

"Are you saying you actually had those guys follow through with such a terrible thing?"

"I had to." Winslow took a handkerchief out of his pocket and wiped it across his sweating brow.

"I'm sorry."

"My brother's the one you should be apologizing to," Jonathan said glaring at Winslow with all the disgust the older man had shown him earlier. "You allowed three men to beat a helpless man. Who's the despicable slime now? My brother is an innocent victim, and yet it didn't stop you from letting Kim dictate that he be hurt."

"I had to do something for her after the way you used her."

"She used me just as much. I admit I'm no prize, but I never had to coax Kim into bed. She begged me for the sex." Winslow started to sputter a denial, but Jonathan stopped him. "Before you go on about your daughter being taken advantage of, just remember she was married to my brother. If that doesn't convince you that your precious daughter is a slut, you should know she tried every trick she could to get Gage to bed her, too. He refused, so her demanding that he be beaten wasn't to make up for losing me, but rather to punish him for ignoring her."

Winslow's face turned redder. "How dare you talk about my daughter like that. She said Gage tried to force himself on her."

"That's a lie." Jonathan's voice took on a dark edge now. "You can play the outraged father all you want, but you should know Kim told me about the different servants she lured into her bedroom here and any other guy capable enough to take her on. You'd fire them, but she'd end up doing the same thing with the new help. Being in denial and always trying to cover up for her won't change things. But I didn't come here to debate that with you."

Holland raised her brows. Not only had she just learned that Kim would sleep with just about any man, but she'd discovered that Jonathan possessed some moxie after all.

"You don't need me. I'll give you the money. That's all they want."

"You made my brother the sacrificial lamb. Now it's your turn."

"I refuse to go with you."

"You either walk out of here on your own power. Or I drag you out along with dragging your reputation through the mud by telling everything I know about Kim. Come to think of it, I might insist that you and Kim do some jail time. She ought to be real popular with the other inmates considering how pretty she is."

Gage realized he must have dozed off. He had no idea how much time had elapsed, but he was pleased to know the pounding in his head wasn't quite as bad. The pain in his ribs and back was also more manageable as long as he didn't move too much or breathe too deeply.

But now he had a new problem. Raging thirst. He tried to lick his cracked lips, but his tongue kept wanting to stick to the roof of his mouth. Had Juan already collected the ransom money without bothering to let him go? Had he been left here to die? What of Jonathan? Could they have tricked him into paying only to God forbid, kill his younger brother?

The sound of voices penetrated his unpleasant thoughts just when Gage began to think he was doomed to rot here. He watched beneath half-closed eyelids, as a door across the room flung open and Juan stood silhouetted against the light coming from behind him. Gage couldn't stop the groan that escaped him anticipating the possibility of more punishing treatment.

"Ah, so you are awake, my friend. Good. We have been a bit rough on you. I apologize for that. But it became an unfortunate necessity to keep things in my favor."

Gage watched warily as Xavier and Ramon entered. The last time he saw these men they'd tied him up leaving him unable to defend himself as they beat him. His body flinched when Xavier knelt down and began cutting the ropes.

Gage's muscles were so cramped he needed help getting to his feet and their support when he tried to walk. He saw that he'd been kept in an outbuilding. He stumbled along between his captors, squinting against the early morning light, as they led him toward a small house.

Xavier and Ramon took him into the kitchen where they lowered him onto a straight back wooden chair. Juan handed him a bottle of water. Gage's fingers were still numb making him almost drop the bottle in his eagerness to drink. Juan unscrewed the cap and held the bottle. Gage immediately started to drink in big gulps before Juan pulled the bottle away.

He held out his hand with a couple of tiny white pills in the palm.

"To ease your pain."

"No thanks," Gage said in a raspy sounding voice.

"So you do not trust me?"

"Your hospitality does leave something to be desired. Do I take this sudden concern for my welfare is because you've heard from my brother?"

"Yes. You'll be happy to know we're in the process of arranging a time and meeting place for your release. We will make you as comfortable as possible in the meantime."

He handed Gage the bottle again. Gage drank greedily as some of the water dribbled down his bare chest. He finished and wiped a hand across his mouth.

"What about Winslow Orray? Are you still working for him?"

"Perhaps it would be more accurate to say he's working for your brother. I underestimated Jonathan. He's bringing Orray here to make sure we get his money from his own hand. I would not have treated you in such a manner if it wasn't for Orray's daughter insisting on payback for your interference in getting your brother freed. She demanded that you be punished, bound, and left to suffer. You have a powerful enemy there. What did you do, kick her out of your bed?"

Gage shook his head.

"I never invited her in."

"Ah, well, that's explains it. I think a woman such as her would not take rejection lightly."

Gage realized he'd been right about Kim wanting to get even. He didn't know how Jon was able to convince Kim's father to cooperate, but right now he just wanted to get out of here.

Juan turned to Xavier.

"Help Mr. Langdon to the shower and give him his clothes."

Gage felt thankful that his strength had returned enough for him to walk on his own. He didn't want Xavier touching him, especially the way the man's dark eyes roamed over his body. Gage had a feeling Xavier wasn't just enjoying the handiwork of bruises, but seemed more interested in his nakedness.

He was led to a small bathroom with toilet, single sink, and a shower stall. Xavier opened a cupboard under the sink, took out a bar of soap, removed the wrapping, and held it out. Gage snatched it from him and stepped into the shower, closing the curtain with a snap. The water was tepid and it came from the showerhead in a sparse spray, but never had a shower felt so good. He didn't have a washcloth, so he used his hands to work up a lather and wash himself.

Gage turned off the water when he finished and pulled back the curtain. His gut clenched when he saw Xavier standing there leaning against the doorframe holding a towel. Gage scanned the room, but there wasn't any sign of another towel to dry the water dripping from his body.

"Where are my clothes?" Gage demanded, barely suppressing his fury.

Xavier's eyes traveled slowly over Gage before motioning him into the hallway where he walked to a bedroom. Gage saw his clothes thrown on a bed. He would have closed the door, but Xavier stood there holding it open. Gage felt his flesh crawl remembering that he'd been naked and utterly vulnerable to this man's every whim when he'd been unconscious. He gritted his teeth, turned his back, and began to pull the clothes on over his wet skin.

Juan called from the kitchen and was just setting a bowl on the table when Gage entered the room. "Sit. Eat. I promise you it isn't poisoned." He took a mouthful. "You see? It's safe."

Gage picked up his spoon. His stomach rumbled in response. The soup looked hardy with red beans, peppers, tomatoes, onions, and chunks of meat swimming in a thick broth. A plate of tortillas sat on the table. Gage watched as the men scooped up soup in their spoons while dipping torn pieces of the tortillas into their bowls. He'd never eaten soup for breakfast before, but it only took one taste for Gage to realize the soup's heat and spiciness didn't agree with his sore mouth. He ended up only eating one plain tortilla.

Juan finished his own meal and stood up beckoning for Gage to follow him. He led Gage back to the bedroom and pointed to the single bed.

"Sleep now. I'd advise against trying to escape," he warned when Gage's eyes strayed to the window. "I'll wake you when it's time to go."

Gage didn't argue. Not only was he exhausted, but he knew he wouldn't get far with his battered body even if he did manage to leave unnoticed. He lowered himself onto the bed.

"Fine. Just keep your watchdog Xavier away from me."

"So you have noticed his attraction to you. I admit to letting him look his fill."

Gage's fingers dug into the quilt, and he glared at Juan making the man laugh.

"You look at me with much hatred, but you really should be thanking me."

"For what?"

"For not allowing Xavier to use your body the way he craved."

Juan left the room then leaving Gage to grapple with that disturbing image.

Chapter Sixteen

Jonathan twisted in his seat and looked over his shoulder at Holland, while a silent Pablo kept his eyes on the road as he drove.

"Gage is going to kill me when he finds out I let you come. I should have listened to Manuel when he insisted I leave you back at the village."

"I had to come."

"Why? So you could have a front row seat in case I mess this up like I've done everything else?" he asked in a bitter voice.

"I would have gone crazy if you'd made me stay behind."

"What will you do if something goes wrong?"

"We have to believe everything is going to be all right. I know you're scared. I am, too. But remember we have Manuel and Pablo, plus several others from the village as our backup."

Winslow, sitting next to Holland, let out a loud snort.

"What do you have to be scared about? We've brought enough money to buy a small village; and I still say you didn't need me along."

Jonathan glowered at him.

"You're responsible for my brother being taken, which makes you responsible for making sure he's released."

231

"I'm responsible?" Winslow lifted his brows. "I noticed you're quick to shift blame, but you seem to be conveniently forgetting Gage wouldn't be in this predicament if you hadn't set up your own sham kidnapping."

Jon shot Holland a quick, tormented look. She turned her head away, knowing she wouldn't be able to find any words to defend him. How could she when she agreed with Winslow?

Pablo stopped a few minutes later and waited until Manuel and the others pulled up alongside them. Manuel got out, walked over to their car, and said something to Jonathan while pointing at Holland. She tapped Jonathan on the back.

"What did he say? Why are we stopping here?" She looked around at the emptiness surrounding them. "Is this where we're supposed to meet up with the kidnappers?"

"We're stopping because this is the point where I agreed to leave you. Manuel and the others refuse to go any further unless you stay behind."

"All right." Holland kept her voice even trying not to succumb to disappointment. "But please hurry. The longer Gage is kept with those men, the more I'm worried what they may be doing to him."

"How do you think it makes me feel?"

"I don't know, but however bad you're feeling I doubt if it can compare to what Gage has had to endure."

He started to say something, but stopped and motioned to Winslow to follow him, as he climbed out of the car. Holland knew Jonathan was very upset about Gage, but she also suspected part of his irritability had to do with the fact that he'd ruined his relationship with Charo and lost much of his good standing with the villagers. He enjoyed being a hero to them, but things changed once word got out that his kidnapping was fake.

He not only put his brother's life in jeopardy, but he'd also exposed Charo's people to potential danger by getting them involved in the rescue operation. The kidnappers had proven themselves to be unpredictable, and they were certainly an unwanted element in the simple lives of the villagers. There wasn't any guarantee that Juan and his money-hungry henchmen wouldn't decide to kidnap a villager in the future thinking Jonathan's family would pay a ransom.

Holland sat in the car while Jonathan and Manuel talked for a few more minutes. She watched as Winslow suddenly started yelling and shook his fist in Manuel's face. Manuel shoved him making Winslow stagger back a few steps. Manuel wasn't a patient man, but she'd want him on her side in a fight. It was about time Winslow Orray found out not everyone was willing to put up with his demands, no matter how much money he had.

Jonathan came back to the car.

"We're going now. I'll ride with Manuel and Winslow will be in one of the other cars. You stay here with Pablo. We'll be back as soon as we can. Pablo knows what to do if . . ." He sucked in a shaky breath. "Just don't give him a hard time if you have to leave here in a hurry.

Okay?"

A chill shimmied up Holland's spine at his grim words, but she gave him a determined look. "I won't leave without Gage."

"You may not have a choice."

"Stop saying that!"

"I'm just trying to prepare you if things don't go right."

"Well, man up and make sure they do; or you'll have me to deal with."

His mouth turned down at the corners.

"Join the club if you can find a spot."

He whirled away and climbed into the Jeep with Manuel.

Holland watched them drive away, and kept watching long after they were out of sight and the dust from their vehicles had evaporated into the warm air. She supposed she shouldn't be so hard on Jonathan. He was getting enough flak from everyone without her adding to the burden he carried, but it was difficult to forgive a man who'd turned a scratch into an open wound.

Her throat felt tight with suppressed anger thinking how the combination of Jonathan's idiocy, Kim's revenge, and the kidnappers' greed had mixed together into a recipe for a very toxic brew with Gage sitting in the middle of the pot. Holland couldn't help being afraid for him. He'd been at the mercy of his kidnappers long enough for them to do whatever they wanted.

They'd beaten him once. Would they do it again? She knew she'd upset Jonathan by voicing her fear about what else might be happening to

Gage, but she couldn't keep the fear she was feeling locked inside her.

Such tortured thoughts and the heat compelled her to shove open the door and climb out of the car. Pablo instantly followed. Holland knew he was doing his job by keeping an eye on her. She hoped he wasn't going to insist she get back in the vehicle, but he merely stood close by watching her. She looked up and shaded her eyes against the bright sun. What did she do with her dark glasses? She couldn't remember.

The midday heat felt hot on her bare skin. Tiny drops of perspiration pooled at her throat and trickled between her breasts. More sweat broke out on her face. She blotted her cheeks against the shoulder of her blouse letting the material wipe away some of the moisture. Pablo reached into the front seat and handed her a thermos motioning for her to drink. Holland smiled her thanks and took several short swigs. The water was warm, but at least it was wet. She handed the container back to him.

She wished they could communicate. She wondered what he was thinking. Was he annoyed that he'd been dragged into this drama? Holland wouldn't blame him if he did feel resentful that he and the people of his village had their peaceful way of life interrupted all because of Jonathan's foolish scheming.

Her entire body tightened thinking how Gage put himself in such peril just so his younger brother would be protected. She couldn't help admiring the dedication to his family, but when was it ever going to be their turn to stand on their own two feet and stop expecting him to sacrifice himself to make their world more comfortable? Holland silently prayed Gage was going to be all right. Meeting him had been a life altering experience for her. Their newfound intimacy on the airplane had proven that they were just beginning to explore the possible depths of how deep their relationship could go. Holland understood now that they'd each been lonely in their own way. Now they both had a chance to be happy.

But only if they could be together.

And Kim and her father were doing their damnedest to ruin any chance of that.

Gage sat in the van. Juan insisted he ride up front with him this time, rather than in the back with Xavier and Ramon as he had before. He'd supplied Gage with a fresh bottle of water and chattered to him as though they were a couple of guys out for a friendly drive. No doubt his plan was to give Jonathan the impression that he and his friends weren't so bad.

Gage knew otherwise, and he had the bruises to prove it. The van's shocks were nonexistent and every time the vehicle bounced over a rough spot it jarred his body causing pain to ripple through him. He remembered seeing a rather large bruise when he looked in the mirror after his shower. It covered the area over one kidney where he'd suffered some particularly hard kicks during his beating. He knew there was some damage done when he saw blood in his urine. He wouldn't be surprised if he had a couple of injured ribs.

The van lurched making Gage brace his hands against the dashboard in an effort to steady himself. The road reminded him of a washboard and Juan seemed to enjoy driving on it like a teenager trying to see how much speed he could get out of this poor excuse for a vehicle.

He flashed Gage a wide grin.

"Do not worry, my friend. Soon you will be united with your brother, I will have your money and we will both me happy. Yes?"

"Yeah, and maybe you ought to use some of that money to buy yourself a vehicle with decent shock absorbers."

Juan leaned his head back and roared with laughter. "I like you Mr. Langdon, and I think I am going to miss you."

"You'll pardon me if I don't share your sentiment."

Juan barked out another laugh and stomped his foot down harder on the accelerator making Gage swear under his breath.

Holland paced. She knew it probably wasn't such a good idea in the heat, but she couldn't seem to stay still. She glanced at Pablo from time to time, but his expression never changed. Whatever thoughts were going through his head certainly didn't show on his face. Did he have any idea how long it would take to bring Gage back here? She supposed not. Was he nervous? Even if he was he wasn't walking a rut into the dirt at their feet pacing like she'd been doing.

Holland thought she heard the sound of vehicles, just when she feared she wouldn't be able to stand the waiting for another minute before she ended up screaming out her frustration. Was it wishful thinking, or was someone really driving this way?

She strained her ears listening and heard the sound again, louder this time. Her head jerked toward Pablo and knew he'd heard something when he moved away from the car and stood staring in the direction where the others had driven away what seemed like ages ago. Holland moved closer to him and didn't realize what she was doing when her fingers dug into his arm.

They stood silently together watching and waiting as the vehicles drove closer. Holland shaded her eyes with her hand squinting into the sunlight willing herself to make out the people, hoping she'd spot Gage among them. Two cars pulled up and stopped. The door opened on one and Jonathan climbed out holding a bloody handkerchief to his nose. Winslow heaved himself out of the other car wincing as he touched fingers to one red and swollen eye.

Holland dragged her hand away from Pablo's arm. How did Jonathan and Winslow get hurt? Why wasn't Gage with them? Had the rescue attempt failed? Please God no, she shouted inside her head. She looked frantically toward the road again. Where was Gage? Her heart pounded so hard she could barely breathe. She hurried over to Jonathan, as he walked toward her.

"What happened? Didn't you get Gage? Did the kidnappers do that to you?"

He pulled the handkerchief away from his nose and pointed to Winslow.

"No. This was Manuel's way of letting us know what he thought of us. As to what happened to Gage, you can ask him yourself," he said, pointing over her shoulder.

Holland didn't wait. She spun around and began running, as adrenalin rushed through her making Manuel stop several yards away. She barely gave Gage a chance to climb out before rushing up to him. He grunted in pain when she hugged him and rained kisses over his face.

"Go easy, honey. I've a few sore spots."

She immediately pulled away. "How badly did they hurt you? Do you need a doctor? Let me see," she begged, reaching to unbutton his shirt.

"Later. Right now I just want to get the hell away from here."

Holland got her chance to see how badly Gage was injured when he changed into clean clothes on the flight home. Tears filled her eyes when she saw the results of what he'd endured at the hands of his captors.

Jonathan's eyes widened.

"Oh Jesus God, you look awful, Gage."

Winslow struggled to choke out his words.

"I told them not to hurt you too much."

Gage lifted his brows.

"Did you? My bruises say otherwise."

"I only suggested a couple of punches." He pointed to one particularly large bruised area. "I never expected anything like that."

"Oh come now, Winslow. Surely you were entertained, as you and Kim watched Juan film what you ordered those men to do to me?" Gage retorted in a sarcastic voice.

"She asked him to record your beating? My God. I honestly didn't know. I'm sorry," he mumbled. "I know it's too late now, but I truly regret my decision."

Jonathan bit his lip.

"I wouldn't have left you with the kidnappers if I'd known they were going to do this to you. I shouldn't have let you talk me into going. How can I make amends?"

"You can start by keeping yourself and Winslow the hell away from me right now."

Gage turned to Holland.

A tear slowly slid down her cheek, making the one tiny drop more poignant than a torrent of tears would have been.

"Come lie down with me," he said stretching out his hand to her in invitation.

He took her in his arms on the bed.

"I didn't expect you to be here, but I'm glad you are."

"I couldn't bring myself to go without you. Will the kidnappers hurt Charo's friends?"

"No. Manuel took care of them."

She caught her breath. "Oh! Well, thank God Jon saved you. Hopefully Kim will go away."

"I wouldn't bet on it."

"What do you mean? Are you expecting her to cause more trouble?"

"Kim still has a score to settle with Jon, and she may not be done with me."

Holland buried her face against his chest. No matter how much she wished it otherwise, Kim was still tied to Gage's family. She was the bad apple in the barrel and unless they could do something to pluck her out, she was going to continue to cause them to be subjected to her decay.

Chapter Seventeen

James knocked on his mother's door and limped inside when she called for him to enter. Marguerite smiled at him and closed the book she'd been reading.

"Where's Jamie?" she asked, waving him to a nearby chair.

"In the nursery with Colleen."

"I'm so thrilled to have him back."

"Me, too."

He cleared his throat.

"I need to talk to you and please hear me out before you offer an opinion."

"What is it?"

"I just got off the phone with Kim."

Marguerite's hands flexed on the book. "You said you never wanted to speak to her again."

"That's before I knew what really happened. She only slept with Jonathan willingly one time and that was because she was so upset when he told her I was having an affair with Carol, the kitchen girl. But then Jonathan threatened to tell me how he'd slept with Kim if she didn't drug me, so he could continue taking advantage of her."

"I see. Did she mention why it was necessary to also drug Holland and the other nannies?"

"Yes, she explained that. Jonathan insisted they use the nanny quarters when they, well you know," he mumbled, as hot color flowed into his cheeks. "He also didn't want them around in case they might discover what was going on."

"Did she explain why she tampered with Jamie's formula?"

"She did it to protect him."

"By making him ill?" Marguerite shook her head in disbelief. "That doesn't make sense."

"Kim had a feeling Jonathan was going to try and steal the baby the way he kept talking, so she thought she could keep Jamie here if Jonathan believed he was sickly. But when that didn't work and he took Jamie, the only thing Kim could think to do was go with Jonathan and try to get the baby away from him when Jon was distracted."

"But her plan backfired when Jonathan ended up distracting her instead and taking Jamie."

"Exactly. Mom, can't you see that Kim really does love the baby? Jon made her pretend otherwise. Everything that's happened is his fault."

"How convenient for her to have someone to blame."

His jaw clenched for a moment.

"I know you've never really cared for Kim and that makes me sad. I guess it's also what made me love her all the more because everyone here was so against her. I want to be with her, and she wants to be with me and Jamie. She asked me to come to her and bring him. And . . . and that's what I'm going to do."

Marguerite frowned. "You're taking the baby? When?"

"Today. Colleen's packing the things Jamie will need. I'll want her with me to take care of him. I'll have her return to you as soon as I can. Jacob is packing me a bag. I can send for the rest of my things later. I don't have the helicopter here and it's too far for me to drive with my leg, so Kim is sending a car. The driver's on his way here right now."

"I can see your mind is made up, but can't you at least wait until Jonathan and Gage return?"

"I'd rather not. I'm in no mood to deal with Jonathan right now. I'm happy Gage is safe, but if I wait for him he'll try to talk me out of going. I'll call him after I get settled."

"Where exactly are you meeting with Kim?"

"She's at her dad's house, but that'll just be temporary until we can get our own place."

Marguerite's eyes filled with anger. "How could you even think about going to Winslow after his involvement in what happened to Gage?"

"I'm going to see Kim, not her dad. She feels terrible about what he did. This is my chance to have Kim and Jamie to myself and for us to be a real family together. We couldn't make it work when she was here. You saw that for yourself. Please Mom, can't you be happy for me?"

"Not when I know in my heart that Kim is setting you up for her own dubious purpose."

James surged to his feet.

"I'm sorry you feel that way. But that's exactly why I have to leave because you're never going to give Kim the opportunity to prove her love for me and our baby."

Marguerite rose slowly from her chair.

"Please, just wait until Gage is here."

"I've waited long enough trying to gain the family's approval for my marriage. None of you are obviously ever going to accept what I want. This is my life, and I know what's best."

"Will you at least leave Jamie here until you and Kim move into your own home?"

"Absolutely not. I don't want my son anywhere near Jonathan."

"We just got Jamie back. Please don't take my grandson away from me again."

"I'm sorry things have to be like this, but it's the only way I can reunite him with Kim. That has to be my priority. I'll bring Jamie to visit you. Maybe someday you'll welcome Kim, too."

"Don't do this, please," she begged again. "It's a mistake."

"The only mistake I've made is believing our living here was the best thing for Kim and Jamie. Obviously I was wrong. Goodbye, Mother."

He walked to the door, jerked it open, and slammed it behind him.

Marguerite watched him leave and sank down onto her chair with a heavy foreboding feeling for her son and grandchild. She felt with every fiber of her being that her daughter-in-law was a dark, dangerous woman. But poor besotted James was so blinded by his feelings he didn't realize how he'd fallen prey to her seduction. The treacherous siren was luring her son into a trap, and Marguerite knew there was nothing she could do to save him.

Tears filled her eyes reminding her that she was also helpless to save her precious grandson from whatever lay in store for him.

"God, please protect them both," she prayed.

James sat back in the limousine's cushy leather seat and breathed a sigh of relief when Jamie finally stopped fussing and fell asleep in his car seat. He had to agree with Kim that the baby's crying did start to get on your nerves after a while. He saw that Colleen had nodded off. She didn't have the same knack as Holland when it came to dealing with his son. Kim would have to find someone more competent, especially if they were going to have more personal time together to patch up the rough spots in their marriage.

He rolled down the tinted glass window. Everything seemed to be covered in a soft muted gold as the sun began its slow descent. They'd been on the road for a couple of hours and still had a long drive ahead of them. He rolled the window back up and exhaled an impatient breath.

James knew he'd already be with Kim if he'd had the use of the helicopter, but ended up being forced to go by car, no thanks to his idiot brother. His pulse picked up as resentment began to build inside him when he thought of Jonathan and the dirty tricks he'd pulled. His fingers folded into fists with the need to settle things in what their mother probably would call a less gentlemanly way. Well, he wasn't feeling much like a gentleman toward his no good, conniving twin. The louse not only tried to ruin his marriage, but ended up stealing his son.

That was bad enough, but Jonathan had nearly gotten Gage killed trying to impress his girlfriend. James felt almost ill now remembering Holland's phone call telling him how the kidnappers had beaten his big brother. She urged him not to tell his mother the gruesome details.

As if he would. Why upset her more? He bit his lip thinking about the rest of the call. According to Holland, Winslow ordered Gage to be beaten, but only because Kim demanded it.

James shook his head. No. It just wasn't possible. It had to be a misunderstanding. Kim wouldn't have wanted something so awful to happen to Gage. Jonathan was the guilty one. The kidnappers were probably the sick kind of people who got their kicks out of hurting people. He bet they took it upon themselves to rough Gage up without any incentive from Kim or her dad.

James stretched his aching leg out in front of him. He shifted in the seat trying to get more comfortable. He'd taken a pain pill that morning, but now it'd worn off. They eased the pain, but they might as well be a sleeping pill the way they always made him so groggy; and God knows he'd had enough of feeling like a zombie.

But he wanted to be pain free when he showed up on his father-in-law's doorstep. He tugged the small prescription bottle out of his pocket, shook two pills onto his palm, and washed them down with water. Hopefully by taking his meds now he'd curb the pain, take a little nap if he needed to, and be in good shape when he saw Kim.

James knew it wasn't only his leg that caused him stress. All the drama with the family the last few months would be enough to wear on anyone's mind and body. The tension in the house was bad enough with the nanny drugging and Kim not being well after Jamie's birth. But worrying whether or not Gage would survive his kidnapping had nearly ripped them all apart.

He respected his older brother. Gage might sometimes be overly protective, but at least he genuinely cared about his family and unlike that snake Jonathan would never do anything to deliberately hurt them. James was almost sorry he didn't hang around to see how Gage was going to deal with their brother, if he hadn't already. But as much as he would have liked to witness his brother being reprimanded, he wanted to see Kim more. He had every confidence that Gage would handle the situation better than anyone else could.

James leaned his head back and yawned. Yeah, everything was going to be fine now. He might even be able to forgive Jonathan in time. But not yet. His main concern was getting back with Kim. Being invited to come and bring Jamie was a big step in the right direction for making things work out. He couldn't allow what his family thought about Kim to spoil this opportunity.

He wasn't happy the way he'd left things with his mother, but he had a right to live his own life. He loved Kim, and she loved him. A rush of heat shot through his body imagining how good it was going to feel making love to her again after so long. That brought a smile to his lips. He closed his eyes and listened to the soothing sound of the tires humming on the road.

His lips were still tilted in a grin when he slid into a deep sleep.

James slowly opened his eyes and found himself engulfed in pitch-black darkness. He must have fallen asleep. But not a very restful sleep considering he kept dreaming about people shouting his name and shaking him. He rubbed his eyes and pulled himself into a sitting position, feeling disoriented until he remembered he was on his way to see Kim. It took a few seconds to realize the car wasn't moving. They must have arrived and no one wanted to wake him.

"Damn, I shouldn't have taken two pills," he muttered, and groping for the door handle, stepped outside to the sound of crickets and the hoot of an owl.

He squinted into the darkness and using the moonlight, made out a thicket of gnarled oaks while the scent of forest plants floated on the breeze that ruffled his hair. He turned in a full circle. Where was the Orray mansion? The manicured grounds? The long gray driveway with its neat line of cedar trees? He'd envisioned Kim running down that driveway in her anxiousness to greet him. But the only thing greeting him right now was the eerie feeling that he must have awakened in the Twilight Zone.

Maybe he really was having a nightmare. Did the pills he'd taken mess with his brain? He didn't care for this bizarre turn of events, whatever the cause. Colleen was gone and there wasn't any sign of his son, either. His heart plummeted. Dear God, had the baby been kidnapped again?

He ran to the front of the car and yanked open the door on the driver's side. The driver lay unmoving, slumped down on the seat. James sucked in his breath, tore his cell phone out of his pocket, and nearly cried out in frustration when he realized it was useless.

He looked around in desperation. No Colleen. No Jamie. No cell service. And possibly a dead driver. He slumped back against the side of the car, shaking.

If this wasn't a nightmare, then what the hell was happening?

Chapter Eighteen

Gage walked across the room to accept Marguerite's embrace.

"Hello, Mother."

"Oh thank God you're home."

Her welcoming smile wavered when he stiffened ever so slightly as she hugged him. She stepped back, frowning.

"Something's wrong. Are you hurt?"

"I'm fine," he said and kissed her on one cheek.

"I don't believe you; and I'm sure you're trying to protect me, as usual." She raised a questioning brow at Jonathan. "What do you know about this?"

His face flushed as Gage sent him a warning glare.

"He's okay, Mom. You know Gage. He's tough as an old boot." He rubbed his hands together. "Any food going? I'm starving."

"I know you're trying to change the subject and I'll allow that for now. But you and I will be having a private chat later, young man. I've asked Carol to bring sandwiches and coffee."

Marguerite turned to Holland next and hugged her. "Thank you for all your help."

"I don't know how much help I was, but I couldn't stay away."

Gage eased himself down next to Holland on the sofa while Marguerite returned to her own chair. "This is a terrible way to welcome you home, but I'm worried about James and the baby."

Gage waved her protest aside.

"Your phone call said he left this afternoon."

"Yes, and I expected to hear from him by now. He's not answering his phone. I called the Orray house and asked to speak to Kim, but the person who answered said she wasn't taking any calls until further notice."

Jonathan snorted. "The two lovebirds are probably so busy having sex they don't have time to take any phone calls."

"That'll be enough out of you," Gage scolded.

"Just sayin'," he mumbled and flopped onto a chair.

Gage turned back to Marguerite. "You said a car was sent, and Colleen went with James."

"Yes. He was quite angry that he didn't have the helicopter at his disposal. I even called Colleen's cell, but she's not answering, either. That's not like her to ignore my calls."

"It's possible none of them are getting a signal, depending on what route the driver took."

"Oh. I never thought of that, but why wouldn't Kim take my call at the house?"

"Because she's a bitch," Jon blurted. "Sorry for the language, Mom. But you know she is."

Holland dragged her bottom lip between her teeth. The ongoing problems with Kim wasn't her business. She wasn't even Jamie's nanny now. But that didn't mean she stopped caring what happened

252

to the baby. This family had suffered enough and when she looked at the lines of worry on Marguerite's face and thought about what Gage endured, she decided to speak out.

"I don't know if this will make you feel any better about James taking Jamie away. But I had time to talk with Mr. Orray while Jonathan was busy. He told me he felt certain this would be his only chance at having a grandchild and heir. He wanted to bring Jamie to live in his house and have the opportunity to know the baby. He said Kim agreed."

"So he was handling the arrangements to get James to bring the baby there, while he was dealing with the kidnappers at the same time," Gage said.

"Apparently. I told him Jamie had suffered with feeding problems and suggested he give the baby more time to live here with all of you. He assured me his grandson would be well taken care of beginning with having Jamie brought to his home in comfortable style."

Marguerite nodded. "Yes. They sent a limousine."

"Maybe we could track them down if we knew what company he used," Jonathan said.

"I doubt if their policy would allow them to give us any information, even if we did." Gage pulled his phone out of his pocket. "Kim obviously isn't going to be any help if she isn't taking any phone calls. Winslow should be home by now. Let's see if we can get him to work with us."

"He might not cooperate, since he hates my guts right now," Jonathan pointed out.

"He'll cooperate because he owes me."

Holland thought about the ugly bruises Gage had hidden beneath his clothes. Yes, Winslow Orray certainly did owe Gage. But would the man be willing to make good on that debt?

Especially when he was so easily manipulated by a daughter whose only obligation was to herself.

Winslow looked at his daughter in exasperation. "Are you sure James left his house?"

"Yes. I already told you. That old bat Marguerite called here wanting to know if they'd arrived. It would have been fine if you'd let me handle this."

"I was trying to take over because you've been so upset over this business with Jonathan. I told you I would take care of everything."

"Oh, you took care of everything all right by running off to Mexico to save the very man who upset me in the first place. I'm surrounded by morons."

Winslow's mouth pinched into a disapproving line.

"Watch your mouth, young woman. I'm still your father, and as your parent I had to agree to go to Mexico to keep Jonathan from calling the police and having you arrested."

"Arrested for what?"

"Drugging their nannies and almost killing James."

She studied her fingernails.

"I don't know what you're talking about."

"Unfortunately, a lot of other people do." He ran fingers through his thinning hair. "The kidnapping got out of hand. I shouldn't have listened to you when you insisted Gage be beaten. He's a decent man and didn't deserve to be treated like that."

"Decent? Do you call it decent when I refused to have sex with him, and he locked me in my room for three days?"

"As much as it pains me to say this, I don't believe he did lock you in your room. You may as well know considering your past behavior here, I also don't believe he was the one who insisted on having sex with you. I'm sure it was more a case of you being the instigator."

"So much for parental support. I don't care what you believe because I know what really happened, and Gage deserved a couple bruises for how he treated me."

"More than a couple." Winslow shuddered. "My God, it still turns my stomach when I think of what those men did to him. He told me you had them film his beating. Is that true?"

"How else could I be sure they did the job? Don't forget you gave them the go ahead."

"Yes, to my everlasting regret. We can't take back what happened, but I did apologize to Gage, and I want you to do the same."

"Like that's going to happen." He stared at her until Kim raised her eyebrows.

"What?"

"One of these days you're going to ask too much of me, Kimberly. I can only hope that if and when that time comes we'll both be able to do the right thing."

"Is that a threat?"

"No. Just an opinion."

James couldn't stop shaking. He was scared and all he could do was stand there wondering what had happened. Had his mother been right urging him not to go? There had to be a reasonable explanation for his present predicament, but right now he couldn't think of one. He had to find Colleen and Jamie. He checked his phone again and felt like flinging it into the dark trees when there still wasn't any signal. He made himself look back inside the car to see if the keys were in the ignition. No luck there. In fact, the only luck he seemed to be having tonight was all bad.

Maybe the keys were in the driver's pocket, which meant he'd had to search the guy. That made him feel squeamish, but he forced himself to reach into the man's trousers and nearly jumped back when he heard a groan. So he wasn't dead after all. Well, at least that was something in his favor. He gave the driver's shoulder a little shake.

"Hey buddy, are you okay?"

James leaned in further to help when he realized the man was trying to sit up. He felt a trickle of fear go through him at the sight of a line of dried blood coming from the man's temple and streaking down one side of his cheek. Several drops dotted the front of his white shirt showing through the black suit coat.

"How did you get hurt? Can you talk?"

New Beginnings
Olivia Claire High

The driver moaned again and rested his head against the back of the seat.

"I'm very sorry about this Mr. Howard."

"Just tell me what the hell is going on. Where's my son and the woman who was with me?"

"She's not here?"

James gave an impatient shake of his head. "Would I be asking you, if she was?"

"She must have gone for help."

"Are you out of your mind? Why didn't you wake me up? What's your name? I'll have your job over this . . . this incompetence."

"My name is Lon Berger. The car started having engine trouble and ended up dying. I was barely able to pull off the road. I tried calling my company to send a tow truck, but I couldn't get a signal. I didn't have any luck with the car radio, either."

"My phone's having the same problem. You still haven't told me why you didn't wake me."

"We tried, but you wouldn't budge. The lady said you take pain pills that make you sleepy."

James felt a quick spurt of embarrassment. "Yeah, for my bad leg. So go on."

"I told her to stay here with you and the baby while I went for help. A deer jumped out at me. The impact of its body threw me down. I fell and hit my head on the road. I blacked out for a while. I came back to the car as soon as I woke up."

"Well that explains the blood, but why did you allow Colleen to leave? Lots of people hit their heads and still manage to walk."

"This isn't easy for me, sir. I'm not one to let anyone else do my job. I did try to go again, but my legs collapsed. The lady said I probably had a bad concussion and told me I'd better take it easy. I knew I couldn't leave us sitting here on this back road not knowing when anyone would ever come along, so I tried to walk again. But I was having trouble with my vision. Then I started vomiting."

"Okay, so you were out of it. I got that. But why did you let her leave?"

"She insisted she was going to keep walking until she could get a signal on her phone. I suppose she took your son with her since she wasn't sure when you'd come around, and I'm in no condition to take care of myself, let alone a baby. I remember telling her not to go. I must have blacked out again because the next thing I knew you were bending over me."

"I guess my body is overly susceptible to my pain pills. If I hadn't taken two you would have been able to rouse me, and Colleen wouldn't be out there on her own in this cursed darkness with my son. I've got to go after them. Do you have a flashlight?"

"There's a couple in the glove compartment." He leaned over and opened it. "One's gone. I guess she must have taken it." He took the remaining light and handed it to James.

"At least the weather isn't too cold or rainy. I haven't seen any other vehicles go by here. This obviously isn't a main road. What made you go this way?"

"I was taking a shortcut."

New Beginnings
Olivia Claire High

"Oh great. Why did you decide to do that for crying out loud?"

"Your wife insisted that I get you to her as quickly as possible."

"She did? "James felt good hearing that. It meant Kim was just as anxious to see him, as he was to be with her. "I see. Well, do you know how far it is to the nearest town?"

"About twelve miles."

"Jeez. So far? I sure hope either Colleen or I will be able to get a phone signal before then. She'll never be able to walk that many miles and I probably won't either with my darn leg, but I've got to try." James moved away from the car. "I'll send someone back, as soon as I can."

"Thank you. I'd advise you to stay on the pavement as best as you can, so you don't wander off into the woods and lose your way. I'd go with you, but I'm afraid I'll be more of a hindrance than any help. I'm awfully sorry about this. "

"Yeah, so am I. You mentioned a deer earlier. Do you think there are any other large game animals around here? You know, like maybe bears?"

"I wouldn't be surprised."

"Sweet Jesus, help me. Sweet Jesus, help me."

Colleen repeated the words like a mantra, as she walked, keeping to the middle of the road. The muscles in her arm burned with fatigue where she lugged Jamie in his carrier. The more she walked, the more she began to doubt the wisdom of coming out here on her own. Every shadow, every noise made her heart thump faster. The air was pleasantly cool, but sweat dewed her brow and dampened the hair at her temples.

She heard a sudden cracking sound like someone stepping on a dried branch. She stopped and held her breath. It came again, louder this time and much closer. Colleen swung the flashlight toward the sound and screamed as a large figure emerged out of the thick forest and lumbered toward her.

Chapter Nineteen

"Stop your caterwauling and get that light out of my face, woman," a man demanded in a deep, rumbling voice.

Colleen swung the flashlight away and breathed a sigh of relief.

"I...I thought you were a bear."

"If I were, I'd be long gone after the fuss you were making."

Jamie started to whimper. Colleen set his carrier down, thankful that she hadn't dropped him in her fright.

"It's all right, sweetheart," she said, and bent to soothe him.

"What in tarnation are you doing out here at this time of night – and with a child yet?"

"Our limousine broke down."

"Yeah, and my Rolls Royce is parked back in my garage," he drawled in sarcasm.

"No, seriously. I'm with my employer. This is his son. Something went wrong with the car, and the driver had to pull over. We couldn't get a signal on our phones. The driver was going for help when he fell and passed out. He hurt his head and . . . and needs a doctor. I . . . I was trying to get to a place where I could use my phone," she jabbered in quick jerky sentences.

"You mentioned an employer. Is he hurt, too?"

"No, sir. He's on medication, and it sometimes makes it difficult for him to stay awake."

"Medication, huh? You mean the kind you buy from a guy on a street corner?"

"Certainly not! If you're trying to imply that my employer is using illegal drugs you couldn't be more wrong. He's recovering from a badly broken leg. The pills are to ease his pain."

"Must be pretty potent stuff if you couldn't rouse him." He scratched his thick, bushy beard and pointed to Jamie's carrier. "All right, then; pick up that contraption and follow me."

"Follow you where?" Colleen said, as he turned away. "I . . . I don't know you, sir."

"We'll exchange birth certificates later. And stop calling me sir. You said you left an injured man in a car that won't run. It just so happens I do have a running vehicle, but it's parked back at my cabin."

"Oh. You live around here, then."

"Going on thirty years. Saw your light while I was checking my traps. Decided to investigate before you scare all the game away." He started to walk away, but Colleen still hesitated. He stopped and looked at her over his shoulder. "You coming or not?"

"I'm not sure," she said, standing there wringing her hands.

"Well, you might want to watch out for bears while you're thinking about it," he grumbled and turned to go.

Colleen gasped, bent to pick up Jamie's carrier, and tottered after the man before he could completely disappear into the woods.

Winslow stopped pacing, and slid into the chair behind his desk. He reached for his phone as soon as he realized who was calling.

"Gage, I was just getting ready to call you."

"Were you, now?"

"Yes. I don't blame you for not believing me, but right now, I think we should put our differences aside considering the situation with your brother and my grandson."

"Agreed."

"Have you had any news from James?"

"No and I take it you haven't, either."

"Not a word. I'm very worried, Gage."

"How do you think my mother feels? Are you aware that Kim refused to take her call?"

"I just found out. Please tell Marguerite I apologize for my daughter's insensitivity. I'm afraid she's so wrapped up in her fury at Jonathan she's wanting to punish your entire family."

"Including her infant son?" Gage asked, anger edging his words.

"I don't think Kim is thinking very clearly right now."

"Which should be enough to make you realize Jamie is better off here."

"I suppose you're right. But what about the emotional pain Jonathan has caused her? Are you simply going to allow him to pretend nothing happened?"

"No. He's agreed to come and see Kim. They're going to have to work things out between themselves. But I believe finding James and Jamie should be our priority right now."

"Definitely. I want you to know I'm personally doing everything I can to help. I just got off the phone with the company who provided the limousine. They haven't been able to reach the driver. His last contact was to tell them he was making a change to his route."

Winslow repeated the road information to Gage. "I'm not familiar with that area."

"Nor am I," Gage revealed.

"The person I spoke to assured me their man is very reliable. They're worried there may have been an accident. They've contacted the police in the general vicinity. Apparently some of the side roads are surrounded by deep woods, and it's difficult or impossible to get cell service. Please let me know if you hear anything and I'll do the same."

"All right," Gage said, ending the call.

"Would anyone like to join me for a moonlight drive?"

He explained his conversation and they all agreed it'd be best if Jonathan didn't go because of the tension between him and James. Gage also wanted someone to stay with Marguerite. That left Holland, and she gladly agreed to accompany Gage to search the back roads for the missing car. Luckily, Gage received a call from Winslow with the exact location before they left.

New Beginnings
Olivia Claire High

James leaned against the limousine talking to the tow truck driver who would be hauling the crippled car away. Lon was on his way to the hospital, while Colleen sat on a stool feeding Jamie a bottle. Her mysterious woodsman disappeared after finding James on the road and driving them to where they could get phone service.

James rushed to greet Gage and Holland when he saw them getting out of the car.

"Boy, am I ever glad to see you two."

"How is Jamie?" Holland asked.

"He's good." James pointed behind him. "Colleen's over there feeding him. This whole thing has been pretty rough on her. Would you mind talking to her? I'm sure she'd appreciate it."

"I'll go to her right now."

"Thanks." He turned back to Gage. "It sure is good to see you. I was really happy when I heard Jonathan didn't bungle your release from the kidnappers. You're okay, right? I mean, those guys didn't hurt you too much did they?"

"I suppose that would depend on what you mean by "too much", but as you can see I'm still upright and mobile."

"That's great. Um, I need to ask you about something Holland said when she called."

Gage crossed his arms over his chest and arched a brow. "Let's hope I have the answer you're looking for."

"She said Kim was responsible for you being beat up. I know that has to be a mistake. She's real sore at Jonathan, but not you. She'd never condone such a lousy thing."

"You seem very certain about that."

"Oh come on, Gage. You don't believe Kim wanted those guys to hurt you. I bet they . . ."

Gage sliced through his protest.

"She demanded they film my beating, so she could watch. Your wife's behavior goes way beyond vindictiveness. When are you going to accept that Kim is ill, James?"

"You're just saying that because none of you ever liked her."

"What's to like about a person who drugs others and deliberately tried to make her own child sick? The woman obviously has sadistic tendencies."

"No she doesn't," James quickly denied.

Gage clamped a hand on his brother's shoulder. "For the love of God she tried to kill you, man."

James jerked away.

"All that drugging business wasn't her fault. Jonathan forced her to do it. She explained everything to me and begged my forgiveness. Things are going to be better between us now. Kim just needs us to be together and away from our family for a while. That's why I'm going to take Jamie to her."

"No you are not. Do you really think I'd allow a defenseless child to end up being anywhere near such an unstable person?"

"Damn you, my wife is not unstable. Jamie's our son, and I'm taking him where he belongs. Stop trying to be my father and get off my back!" James yelled in hot anger.

Gage's eyes blazed with his own fury.

New Beginnings
Olivia Claire High

"Get off your back? Oh, that's rich, coming from someone who's been clinging to mine like a leech for years. No, I'm not your father; and I can only be thankful he didn't have to see how you and your brother have used me all these years to clean up the messes you two continue to make."

"I won't have you comparing me to that idiot Jonathan. I love Kim. I'm taking our son to her and there's nothing you can do about it."

"Watch me," Gage replied in a voice dripping with ice. "I'll drag you into court if it comes to that. How do you think things will go for you when a judge finds out your wife switched formulas to deliberately make your son ill? And let's not forget how she ran off with Jonathan before she drugged you into a coma."

James stumbled back.

"You'd do this to me?"

Gage shook his head.

"I'd do it for Jamie."

Kim stood in the kitchen, cup in hand watching as silver slivers of dawn inched their way between the shutters at the windows. She raised the cup to her mouth, drank a couple swallows of coffee, and dumped the rest down the sink. She set her cup aside and glanced at the clock on the wall. She'd been up all night waiting to hear news about James. Time to rouse her father and find out if they could have a conversation without him lecturing her.

She walked with determination from the room, the leather soles of her loafers clicking on the tile floor, echoing in the room like the sound of castanets. She hurried along the hallway and up the stairs to his bedroom, where she pounded on the door and waited. Her teeth clamped together in annoyance seconds before, she knocked harder until her fist began to hurt.

"It's Kim. You'd better be decent because I'm coming in."

She swung the door open and let her eyes go immediately to Winslow's king size bed. The heavy moss green comforter and large pillows lay undisturbed. The bed obviously hadn't been used. She knew her father sometimes dozed on the leather couch in his office if he found it necessary to work late.

She found him there sitting behind his desk with his head leaning back, eyes closed. Too bad for him, but she was about to disturb his nap. She slammed the door watching in satisfaction when his eyelids snapped up and his body jolted awake. Winslow gripped the edge of his desk to pull himself into a full sitting position. He looked at Kim before glancing out the window.

"Good lord, what are you doing up so early?"

"Why do you think? Have you heard anything from James yet?"

"No, but Gage called."

Kim rolled her eyes toward the ceiling.

"Of course. *Mr. Take Charge* to the rescue."

"It's too bad you feel that way because he's a good man to know in times of trouble."

"You might think differently if you had to live with him. Did he find out what happened?"

"Yes. I thought it would be best to let him know what I was doing here at our end. I called the limo company and got the route the driver was taking. They called the police in the area where they'd last had any contact from him. Then I called Gage."

"So what did he say for God's sake?" she demanded in a clipped voice.

"He drove to the area and found James. The limousine broke down. None of them could get a phone signal, so the driver started to go for help. But he fell and hurt himself."

"And you thought I was being sarcastic when I talked about being surrounded by morons."

He let that pass.

"A trapper living in the area took them to the nearest town where they were able to get word out. Gage said the driver had to be taken to a hospital, and the limo was towed to a nearby garage. The whole experience was upsetting and rather than wait for the company to send another limo, Gage took James, the baby, and the woman caring for Jamie home with him."

"So I'm back to where I started," she grumbled. "When do you expect James to come here?"

"I don't." Winslow got out of his chair and came around his desk.

"What do you mean you don't?"

"Gage felt it would be better if James and Jamie stayed at their house for now. I agreed."

"You agreed? You!" Kim shouted, fury building on her face. "What about all that noise you made about bringing Jamie here, making him your heir, giving him your name?"

"He's still going to be my heir, no matter where he lives. I'm gratified that you're showing this desire to be with your son, but I don't believe the best place for him is with you until you get your anger under control about Jonathan. You two need to work things out between you first."

"How do you expect me to do that when he stays away like the coward he is? I asked James to bring Jamie here because then I could threaten to do them some harm and force Jonathan out of his hidey hole."

Winslow shook his head in dismay.

"You want to hurt your husband and son?"

"I said I would threaten," she corrected. "Now thanks to you everything is all fouled up."

He watched Kim storm out of the room and sank back against the edge of his desk. So she'd been planning on using her husband and son to get to Jonathan. Winslow had begun to believe she wanted them here to build a better relationship.

But he'd been wrong . . . about a lot of things.

Kim stormed to her bedroom barely suppressing the scream building inside of her, as she slammed the door. Her body was literally vibrating with rage. She streaked across the room in a burst of energy, snatched up a vase filled with flowers, hurled it against a wall, and shattered the delicate china into dozens of tiny shards.

She sank down onto her bed. She'd lost another chance at getting Jonathan, besides revealing her plan how she'd hoped to lure him here. She hadn't meant to blurt that out, but she couldn't help herself considering how frustrated she felt with her father suddenly becoming so chummy with the Howards.

Her hands dug into the bedspread bunching the material between her fingers remembering how he'd promised to help her get her revenge. She was his daughter. His loyalty should be with her, instead of the people who she considered her enemies. She'd have to come up with another plan on her own and forget about getting any help from her parent. He'd gone too soft on her.

If she wanted something done right, she obviously had to do it herself.

Kim was pretty sure she could still manipulate wimpy James and handle Jonathan, too. But only if she got them away from Gage's influence. He was the tough one. If she could somehow get him out of the picture, she could probably have her own way with the brothers. But it'd be difficult to sever the strong influence Gage held over his family. Hadn't she tried hard enough to break that bond while she lived in their house? She'd never been able to entice Gage into sharing her bed. She hated him for that.

But her body still desired him.

And that made her hate him even more.

Chapter Twenty

Holland met Jonathan in the hallway while making her way to Gage's office.

"Hey, Holland. How's it going? You look happy."

"So do you."

"Yeah. I'm feeling pretty good. I just got off the phone with Charo. It's the best and longest talk we've had since my mega bout of stupidity. I think she's starting to forgive me."

"Do you expect you'll be getting back together?"

"I'm not sure yet, but I'm working on it. Of course, I won't be going anywhere for a while since my big brother put me on house arrest."

Holland heard the teasing note in his voice and was glad Jonathan wasn't being resentful toward Gage. She knew Gage had cut Jon off of any funds for the time being.

"Can you blame him?"

"God, no. I'm lucky he's still speaking to me after what I caused him to go through."

"Your brother is a good man."

"The best. But sometimes he's too good. He wouldn't have been hurt if he hadn't agreed to stay in my place. I just wish there was some way I could repay him for sacrificing himself."

"There is. Stay out of trouble. I'll see you later."

Holland tapped on the door to Gage's office and poked her head in when he called for her to enter. She started to back out when she saw he was on the phone, but he motioned for her to stay.

He pushed his chair back from his desk and patted his knee. Holland smiled and walked over to sit on his lap seconds before he ended his call.

"I could have come back later," she said, brushing her lips over his forehead.

"No need. I was just finishing up." He put one hand on her back and the other along her cheek.

"Now, how about a real kiss?"

He pulled her head down until their mouths met and clung, softly at first and then with more urgency as he took the kiss deeper. A humming sound escaped Holland while Gage growled low within his throat. Several seconds ticked by before he stopped.

"Let's go to my room and make love."

She raised her brows.

"Must I remind you that the doctor said you shouldn't overdo things for the next few days?"

"It's already been a few days, but if you're worried about me overexerting myself, then I'll just have to lie there and let you take charge."

The image of being the one in control of their lovemaking made excitement rush through her. Holland pressed her lips to his again. Gage wrapped his arms around her and returned the kiss until they were both breathing heavily. She forced herself to break away.

"I shouldn't have done that after telling you we need to curb our lust."

"You can lust after me anytime you want." He rubbed his thumb over her bottom lip. "You taste of strawberries."

"I just had a dish with your mother before I came in here."

"I appreciate you spending time with her. She needs the comfort of another woman right now, especially one who knows what she's been going through lately."

Holland toyed with the top button of Gage's shirt.

"James was supposed to join us for tea, but he sent word that he needed a nap. Your mother is worried that he's taking too many of his pain pills the doctor prescribed. He's been sleeping an awful lot lately."

"I know. I've been thinking the same thing. I'm going to have to talk to him about that, especially after what Colleen told me. She said he was sleeping so soundly after their car broke down that she was the one who ended up going for help after the driver fell. She didn't want to say anything, and I had to pry that bit of information out of her."

"She's very protective of all of you and wouldn't want to say anything disparaging that might cause a family conflict."

"We seem to manage quite well on our own when it comes to conflicts."

"All families have their differences."

"True, but my family does theirs on an epic scale."

New Beginnings
Olivia Claire High

"Well, your brothers seem to be getting along okay. At least neither one has tried to kill the other. I think James is suffering the most, though. Maybe that's why he takes the pills, so he can sleep and not have to be civil to Jonathan."

"I know there's a lot of hurt there. He's also still so hung up on Kim that I don't know what it's going to take for him to get over her."

"At least he brought Jamie back here instead of going to Kim as he planned."

"Only because I threatened to take him to court and reveal her involvement in the drugging."

Holland lifted her brows in surprise. "I'm sure that didn't go over very well. James is going to need time and a whole lot of convincing before he'll ever consider filing for divorce."

"Even if he did, I have a feeling it's going to take more than a piece of paper to make him move on with his life. He'll still have Jamie to consider. Kim may or may not want to have contact with the baby, but her father definitely does."

"Have you heard anything more from Winslow about having Jonathan go to hash things out with Kim?"

"He did call, but oddly enough he told me it'd be best if Jon didn't show up right now."

"Really? That's strange. All Kim could talk about was getting her revenge on Jonathan and daddy dearest seemed determined that his little girl would have her chance to get even. Why do you suppose she changed her mind?"

"I don't think she has. I have a feeling it's coming from Winslow."

"Maybe Winslow is trying to atone for what happened to you."

"Could be. He's apologized enough. Or it might just be a lack of communication with his daughter. He said he and Kim argued and she's been avoiding him. The woman's a hard one to have living under your roof, as you found out."

"Then maybe Winslow's lucky she's not speaking to him."

"There's a thought."

"Gage, I'm sorry to be so pessimistic, but I think you were right when you said we haven't heard the last of Kim. It's just not like her to walk away from a fight. I bet she's planning something terrible, knowing how much she hates us all."

"I've been thinking the same thing. I have a feeling she's ready to snap like a rubber band that's been stretched beyond its limit. But I can't convince James of that. The only thing I can do is keep her from getting back into this house."

Kim meant it when she told her father she wanted all the Howards to suffer. She'd been thinking a lot about how she could accomplish that. She tried before, but Gage kept stepping in and spoiling everything. Her father said he was a good man to know when you had a problem.

Why? Obviously because he was usually the first one in line to offer his help whenever there was trouble. He'd certainly proved that often enough where his family was concerned. In fact, they probably wouldn't last a week without his guidance.

If only she could think of a way to use their need of each other to her advantage.

She knew she'd have to create a problem so huge that she'd not only bring Gage to his knees, but crush James and Jonathan as well. The key was to find something that would devastate all of them. She mulled over the situation some more. On the other hand, perhaps the best way to hurt them wasn't so much in finding something, but rather in finding someone.

Kim felt a sudden surge of excitement shoot through her. Of course. That was it! Who was the one person all three brothers would sell their souls to protect? Marguerite. The pampered queen bee who everybody in the household tip toed around, so as not to upset her.

Kim blew out an unladylike snort.

"And they think I'm difficult," she muttered.

The problem was how to reach a woman who never left her house. Kim knew she couldn't go there, so she'd have to find someone inside to do her bidding. She could probably get James to inadvertently assist in some way, but she'd rather not have to rely on him completely.

She did a mental inventory of the people closest to Marguerite, immediately dismissing Jacob and Colleen. They were too devoted to the old lady. Most of the household help worked part time, coming in to help clean the endless hallways and rooms. Colleen did most of the cooking, but Kim knew she had the girl Carol to help in the kitchen on a regular basis.

New Beginnings
Olivia Claire High

Carol was young, and pretty, and anxious to get away from the tiny mountain community and experience life on her own. What would a girl like her do if she was suddenly to have enough money to quit her job? Kim knew Carol was the oldest of a houseful of younger siblings and a father who was often out of work. The girl was expected to work to help her family and that responsibility kept her shackled to her menial job.

Kim grinned in satisfaction, as a plan slowly formed inside her head. She spent the next half hour going over every detail until she was certain her plot would work.

"Time to dangle the carrot." She reached for her phone. "Now for step one."

James answered.

"Kim?"

She made her voice tremble.

"I tried not to call. But I can't turn my love for you off just because you never want to see me again."

"I never said that."

"Then talk to me. Tell me what's going on," she pleaded bringing forth a little sob.

"Please don't cry. I've been confused about some things, but not about loving you."

"Then why didn't you bring Jamie here like you promised? My dad said the limo broke down, but you went back to your house. I've been waiting to hear from you. Are you coming?"

He coughed, and cleared his throat.

278

New Beginnings
Olivia Claire High

"Gage, um, thought it would be best if Jamie stays here for a while longer. I decided I should be with the baby since you can't be."

"Oh James, when are you going to stop letting Gage run our lives? Jamie is our son, not his. It's bad enough he's keeping me from my baby, but now he won't even let me see my own husband. There must be some way we can see each other without your family knowing. It's been a long time since we've made love. I want you." she cooed, infusing desire into the words.

"Oh God, Kimmie baby, I want you, too."

"Are you sure?"

"Yes!"

"Then what are you going to do about it?"

Chapter Twenty-one

Gage lay on his back stretched out on a blanket, hands folded behind his head, legs crossed at the ankles, and with his eyes closed. Holland sat next to him putting the remains of their lunch into an ice chest. The sun felt pleasantly warm on her back. The clear, blue sky dazzled in its brilliance. Birds flittered among the trees filling the air with their sweet twittering songs.

She smiled at a chipmunk hovering by the base of a nearby tree, nose twitching, alert eyes studying her. She took one of the leftover oatmeal cookies, broke it into small pieces, and leaned toward the edge of the blanket where she and Gage had left their shoes. She scattered the crumbs over a patch of short grass and watched as the little rodent cautiously inched toward the offering and then quickly dashed forward, stuffed its tiny cheeks, and ran away, slender tail flicking.

"Bon appetite."

"Who are you talking to?" Gage asked, eyes still closed.

"A chipmunk. I gave him a cookie. I thought you were asleep."

"I am. I'm talking in my sleep."

Holland grinned. She loved seeing him so relaxed and in such a playful mood. It didn't happen often enough as far as she was concerned considering the constant demands on his time. Last night was a perfect example. She heard James arguing with him when she walked by the office. She hadn't stopped to listen, but she did hear Kim's name mentioned before she hurried by. Just the mention of the young woman's name made Holland insides coil in anger.

Kim may no longer live in the house, but her presence was still keenly felt. How could it not with James and Jamie being in residence? The situation continued to be an explosive one. Holland had a feeling they were all sitting on a powder keg just waiting for it to go off. She encouraged Gage to take a few hours off and come for a picnic today. The last thing she wanted to do was let images of Kim spoil the outing. She pushed all thoughts of the young woman away.

"I love this little clearing. It's so peaceful. Do you remember this is where we first kissed?"

"Yes I do; and we're about to do it again," Gage said and snatched her down on top of him.

He cupped her cheek keeping her mouth locked to his while his other hand rubbed over her back and buttocks. He nibbled on her lips, traced the shape of her mouth with his tongue before plunging inside to fully savor her sweetness. Long, pleasure filled minutes passed until Gage rolled Holland onto her back and sat up facing her.

"Lift your arms."

She blinked in confusion, her eyes beginning to glaze over with passion.

"What?"

"Lift your arms," he repeated. "I want to take your shirt off."

"Gage, surely you're not thinking of making love here."

"Oh yes, surely I am. Arms up, please."

Holland obeyed, and he pulled the shirt over her head, throwing it aside before removing his own shirt. Her breath quickened, as it always did at the sight of him like this. He used one hand to deftly unhook her bra and the other hand to flick open her jeans. He leaned forward dragging his lips down the slender cord at the side of her neck making her pulse jump.

She gasped. "We can't do this. What happens if someone should come here?"

"They'll see a couple of bare assed people making love," he grinned, yanking her pants down her legs and tossing them where their other clothes lay. He touched her panties. "I'd never get any work done if I thought about these tiny scraps of silk you wear."

She saw the growing gleam of desire in his eyes "You're determined to do this, aren't you?"

"Yes I am."

"Well, the least I can do is help," Holland laughed and lifted her hips.

"That's the ticket," he said and slid the panties off before shoving out of his jeans and underwear.

His hands skimmed over her breasts and down her stomach. She jerked against him, clutching his shoulders feeling the hard muscles rippling there. He took her mouth in another searing kiss while his hands roamed over her, rousing them both to fever pitch. Holland moved beneath him forgetting her earlier inhibitions, silently encouraging him to ease the unbearable tension enveloping her body.

"You're never going to have another man be with you like this. Do you understand?" he urged in a voice as demanding as his body.

Holland nodded, staggered by the sudden fierceness of his tone.

"Say it, Holland. I need to hear you say the words."

"I love you, Gage," she breathed out a jittery gasp. "Only you."

He felt intoxicated by her unexpected vow of love. He realized to finally gain her unconditional love meant more to him than all of his worldly possessions.

"God help us both because I love you, too," he groaned.

Blood roared in his ears, as he gripped her hips and surged forward answering her desperate plea. He felt her body let go and quickly lose control until he found his own release.

Holland awoke, blinked, and smiled when she realized where she was. The warmth from the sun and the exertion of their lovemaking made them drowsy. She saw Gage lying next to her still gloriously naked, one arm stretched up over his head and the other hand resting on his thigh. A lock of hair had flopped over his forehead making him look almost boyish. Beams of sunlight poured over his body highlighting every part of him. She couldn't help thinking once again how Gage really was a very impressive specimen of manhood.

A sudden wave of emotion washed over her and the temptation to touch his bare flesh became too strong to deny. Holland lightly danced her fingertips down his chest and over his flat abdomen, before circling his navel with the pad of her thumb. He opened one eye and grabbed her wrist just as she was getting ready to explore lower.

"You keep doing that and you're going to have yourself a handful," he said, opening the other eye to look at her.

"Promises, promises."

She squealed with laughter when he rolled on top of her, pinned her with his weight, and captured her lips with his mouth. He touched her gently now, slowly stirring them both to renewed passion. She put her arms around his waist, hugging him close. He looked at her.

"You are so beautiful," he said in a voice that sounded almost reverent.

"I feel beautiful when we make love. Make love to me again, Gage. Make me fly."

"Lucky for us both, I have my pilot's license," he said, pressing his hardened body into her.

And proceeded to make them both soar.

Later, she lay in his arms with her head resting on his chest.

"Gage?"

"Hmm?"

"What did you mean when you told me you loved me and then said, God help us?"

New Beginnings
Olivia Claire High

"I don't know what the future will hold considering I come with a lot of excess baggage, as you know."

"Who can really predict their future? We've come this far, and we'll just have to take whatever else there is one day at a time."

He didn't answer. Holland raised her head up, so she could look at his face.

"Why have you suddenly gone so quiet?"

"I think James is trying to bring Kim back into our lives."

Holland almost groaned out loud realizing all the complications that could come of that.

"God help us," she breathed, copying his words.

James drove on a little further before taking another anxious glance in the rearview mirror. Good, he wasn't being followed. Not that he expected to be, but he wasn't taking any chances. Everyone kept flapping their gums about how much he was sleeping and that he needed to get out of the house more. Well, thanks to them he had his excuse to go without any awkward questions being asked.

He'd told his mother he felt like going for a drive. What he didn't tell her was that he planned to meet Kim. He wasn't about to make the same mistake he did last time when he left to go to her. Give people too much information and they'll end up using it against you.

He wished he didn't have to leave Jamie back home, but there was no way he could explain taking the baby out with him. Kim said she'd figure out a way to get the baby later. James had little doubt she would think of something. Kim really was smart.

Right now the most important thing was being with her without letting anyone know, especially Gage. James tightened his hands on the steering wheel. Kim was right about Gage always trying to run their lives and James felt like kicking himself for allowing his brother to get away with it. He was tired of being treated like a child. He was a grownup. It was about time he stopped asking Gage for permission when he wanted to do something. Last night was a perfect example. He tried to get Gage to understand that he had every right to be with Kim, but he may as well be talking to a wall. *Looking after* one's family was one thing, but dictating their every move was something else.

The decision to go see Kim today felt empowering making him feel more like he was being his own man. Kim had a big hand in that. She set everything up for them. He was driving now to meet her in a small inn she found. It was only an hour from his house. She told him she chose the place rather than have him drive all the way to her dad's. The inn was tucked away where prying eyes wouldn't find them, but close enough in case he had to go back home for an emergency. She gave him her room number and the fake name she registered under.

Excitement coursed through James at the thought of making love with Kim again even though he felt a little nervous. She was a demanding lover, but on the plus side he never went away wanting. He felt a tightening in his groin remembering the wild times they'd had in bed. She sounded so eager to be with him when they talked on the phone this morning it made him quiver in anticipation.

He shook his head to clear his vision of making love and concentrate on following Kim's directions to the inn. A half hour later he turned off the main road, took a couple turns, and found the narrow lane leading to the place. James pulled up and parked. He thought his heart was going to jump right out of his chest when Kim came running to him just as he'd envisioned her doing when he tried to go to her dad's house.

"You're here. I've been watching for you."

She took him by the hand. "Come on, my room is this way. I have a bottle of champagne cooling in an ice bucket, but first we need to heat up the sheets. I bought a black silk teddy for the occasion, and I want you to take it off of me . . . with your teeth."

The thought of having his mouth all over her body almost made him swallow his tongue.

James collapsed onto the pillow, wincing a bit at the fresh claw marks Kim's nails left on his back. He was sweating and panting and fighting to catch his breath. Kim had drained every ounce of energy he possessed, but she was already recovered enough to be out of bed opening their champagne. He managed to rouse himself and lean on an elbow when she handed him a glass. She clicked her glass against his with a soft clink.

"To us," she said in a toast.

He nodded. "To us."

She sat on the edge of the bed while he devoured her nakedness with his eyes.

"Having a good time?" she cooed.

"Oh yeah. I'd pour this champagne all over you and lick it off if I had the strength."

"There's nothing I'd like better because I'm certainly not through with you yet."

"You're going to kill me, but what a way to go."

Kim laughed.

"Don't worry. I can always revive you."

She refilled their glasses and set the bottle on the floor near the bed.

"Tell me how you got out of the house without Gage catching you."

"He wasn't there. Mom said he and Holland went on a picnic."

"Oh they did, did they? He gets to go out with his girlfriend, but wants to deny you a chance to be with your wife. It's just one more reason why I think he's being so unfair to you."

James drained his glass and set it aside feeling fresh anger toward Gage. "He's being unfair to you, too. I never thought of challenging him about his relationship with Holland. That's a good point. They've become pretty inseparable. She's living in our house again."

"How convenient for them," Kim sneered. "Doesn't it bother your mother to know they're probably sleeping together under her roof?"

"You'd think it would, but she really likes Holland." Kim stiffened and he reached over, took a hold of her hand, and pressed it against his bare chest. "I know it's upsetting for you considering you're my wife and Holland's just a . . . "

"Convenient lay for my brother?" she finished.

"He's never had a woman in his bedroom as far as I know. This is a first for Gage."

"Bully for him," she said through clenched teeth. "Oh, never mind. Let's not let Gage spoil our time together. I want you to know I don't have any hard feelings toward Marguerite. She's clearly not happy keeping herself locked inside her house all the time. I feel sorry for her."

"That's really decent of you, sweetheart."

"Does she still suffer from those awful migraines?" Kim asked, easing her hand away.

"Yeah, unfortunately."

"I know of something that might help her. I'd like to tell you about it if you trust me."

"Of course I trust you. I know you wouldn't do anything to deliberately hurt anyone."

"Your trust means everything to me after Jonathan forced me into doing all that drugging business. Anyway, back to your mother's headaches. My dad's cook told me about this herb she uses for her headaches. She swears by it."

"I appreciate you wanting to help, but my mom has a thing about taking medicine."

"But this isn't the kind of medicine she means. It's all natural and perfectly safe. The cook gets it from an herbalist. It comes in a powder, so you can sprinkle it on food or in drinks. I'd be happy to get some for your mother."

"I still bet she won't try it, even if it is as safe as you say."

"You'll just have to find someone to put it in her food or drinks without telling her."

"Which would mean me and there's no way I could hang around the kitchen sprinkling some powder on Mom's food without someone getting suspicious."

"You're probably right." Kim bit her lip pretending to think. "I know. What if you had someone who works in the kitchen do it for you?"

"Like who? I sure can't ask Colleen. She tells my mom everything."

"How about Carol?"

"Carol?" James shook his head. "She's too loyal to Colleen."

"I'm not so sure about that. I got the impression she didn't always like having to jump every time Colleen snapped her fingers. But the poor girl needs the job. She's helping support her parents and siblings because her father doesn't bring in much money."

"Really? I never knew that. But it still doesn't mean she'll help me."

"I'm sure she will if you pay her extra. It'd have to be a secret, of course."

James rubbed a hand over his jaw. "I don't know."

"Think of how the money would help Carol's family, and the good you'd be doing your mother. Gage never lets you do anything for your mom because he wants all the credit for taking care of her. This is your chance to prove you can help your mother, too."

Kim leaned forward to press her breasts against his chest.

"Okay, I'll do it," James gasped before pulling her into his arms.

He closed his eyes to kiss her and missed seeing Kim's triumphant smile.

Chapter Twenty-two

Kim walked with James to his car. She gave him a lingering kiss.

"It's going to feel like forever before I get to see you again, but I need time to drive home and get the herb."

He hugged her to him. "I wish I could go with you."

"I know, but it's best that we aren't seen together yet. My dad might call your family and stir things up again. Just remember, we're doing this to help your mother, so be very careful Gage doesn't interfere."

"I hope I can do this without him finding out."

"Well, things would definitely be a lot easier if you didn't have him there in the house."

"I don't want anything bad to happen to him again, but I wish he'd go away for a while."

Kim couldn't believe he was making this so easy for her. "What a brilliant idea you have."

James pulled back a little and frowned at her in confusion.

"What did I say?"

"Gage could take a vacation. The longer the better. Hopefully someplace pretty far away and remote, like an island somewhere."

"Gage never takes vacations."

New Beginnings
Olivia Claire High

"He might if your mother suggested it to him. You talk to her in private. Remind her how hard he works for you all and rarely thinks of himself. Tell her he deserves the rest after his kidnapping ordeal. Try to convince your mother to have the trip all planned and reservations made before she talks to Gage; and make sure you convince her not to let him refuse."

"Yeah. He'd be less apt to turn her down because he doesn't like to disappoint her."

She nodded in approval.

"Exactly. That's why you have to be sure she doesn't reveal to Gage that it's your idea. You might even hint that he take Holland with him, as a kind of romantic getaway. Just be careful that you don't push too hard. We wouldn't want her to get suspicious and realize you're trying to get him out of the house."

"You're probably right. Thanks for the tips."

Kim ran a fingertip down his cheek, over his mouth, and down his chest.

"There's just one more little thing I need to tell you before you go. People react differently to the herb. Marguerite may or may not have tummy problems and possibly a headache or two at first. But that's just because her body is getting used to the herb. The main thing is she has to keep taking it so it can have a chance to do any good."

"How come you didn't tell me about that before?"

She heard the slight edge of accusation in his voice and pressed her body intimately against him.

"Well, I was a rather busy doing other things."

She felt a shudder go through him and knew she was in control once again. Kim allowed James to give her a long, hard kiss before he finally climbed into his car. She smiled and blew him kisses, but her smile faded as soon as he drove out of sight.

"What a schmuck."

She hurried back to her room, threw the few things she'd brought with her into a tote bag, and ran out to her car. She had to drive home and get the powder. Luckily, she'd anticipated his cooperation and already had the herb stashed in her bedroom. She spent quite a bit of time going over her plan with James stressing more than once that no one should know of her involvement.

She would have preferred to do this herself, but since she couldn't go near the house she had to rely on James. She hoped he wouldn't blow the conversation with Marguerite in getting Gage to leave. The man wasn't easily manipulated. James balked at first when she told him how much money to offer Carol every week. He thought it was too much, but she convinced him it had to be enough to keep the girl's willingness to continue assisting him for as long as she was needed.

He worried Carol might get greedy and demand more money or she'd tell his mother what was going on. Kim had that covered. All he needed to say to keep the girl in line was that he knew her dad was collecting disability checks for fake injuries he supposedly received on his job.

She'd learned a lot about the goings-on in the Howard household when she lived there just by being quiet and pretending she didn't really care about anything. She knew they all hated her. Well, she hated them right back. Feeling the way she did gave her all the more pleasure, when she knew she was masterminding something to hurt them.

Gage had been beaten, thanks to her, and all she had to do was shun James to make him suffer. She was still working on a way to have Jonathan pay for what he'd done to her. But knowing their precious mother was going to start being very ill had to be enough for now.

Gage and Holland walked into Marguerite's sitting room. He brushed his lips over his mother's cheek while Holland gave her a hug.

"You asked to see us, Mother?"

"Yes." She pointed to a couple of chairs. "Please sit down."

"Is anything wrong?" Holland asked.

Marguerite shook her head.

"No. As a matter of fact things are quite right for a change around here. Jonathan has been a model of good behavior. Jamie is thriving and James has stopped talking about going back to Kim. Which leaves you two."

Gage frowned.

"What about us?"

"I want you to go on a vacation . . . together."

"Mother, you know I . . ."

"Please do not interrupt. I'm sending you to Lanai in the Hawaiian Islands."

"I know where Lanai is," he grumbled.

Holland had to turn her head away to hide her grin when she saw Marguerite's scolding look that only a mother can give her offspring. Gage's expression reminded her of a little boy who'd just had his hand slapped.

Marguerite cleared her throat and sat up straighter in her chair. Holland couldn't help noticing how the older woman seemed to be filled with determination making her almost beam with this newfound sense of purpose.

"Now then. You two are going away, and I won't take no for an answer. I've already made the arrangements. A dear friend of Jamison's has a beach house on Lanai. I called him, and he was more than happy to offer it to you rent free. He rarely uses it, so there's no problem with you not having the place to yourselves for a month."

"A month! Absolutely not," Gage protested. "I appreciate you wanting to do this for us Mother, but there is no way that I can be gone that long. I have too many responsibilities here."

"You know I've always admired your ability to handle those responsibilities, but things aren't going to suddenly fall apart if you take a few weeks off. I know you'll still be able to stay in touch considering the electronics of today. But I do hope you will keep the work to a minimum. That would rather defeat my purpose in getting you away."

"Couldn't you have at least chosen someplace closer?"

"I would have sent you to another planet if I could."

New Beginnings
Olivia Claire High

Holland stifled a giggle when Gage sputtered another protest. Marguerite turned to her.

"I know I've no parental rights over you to include you in my plans, but I do hope you'll agree to accompany Gage. It'll be a lovely romantic getaway for you both. The house is in north Lanai on the most secluded beach. I chose the location because it's off the beaten path, so you should have plenty of privacy."

Holland gave her a helpless look before turning to Gage. She didn't want to be caught in the middle of an argument between mother and son, but she'd be lying if she said she didn't want to go. The idea of being alone with Gage for a month in a remote beach house was too tempting.

He leaned forward in his chair with his arms resting on his thighs. "Don't you think you're taking unfair advantage of Holland asking that she do this without getting her permission first?"

Holland wagged a finger at him.

"Oh no you don't. You're not going to use me as an excuse to wiggle out of this. Going to the Hawaiian Islands is one of the things on my Bucket List."

She gave Marguerite a big smile.

"I'd love to go. Thank you for thinking of me."

Gage sat back in his chair again and scowled at her.

"You're not being very helpful."

"Does that mean you find the idea of spending a month alone with me repugnant?"

"Of course not."

He looked from one to the other and sighed.

"Two women against one man in an argument is never a fair exchange. I know when I'm outnumbered. All right, I'll go, but only for one week."

"One month," Marguerite and Holland chimed in together.

"Two weeks," Gage countered.

"One month and I'll hear no more about you trying to convince me to agree to anything less," his mother insisted. "You might want to start doing whatever it is you need to do to get ready because you leave in two days."

Gage literally bolted out of his chair.

"Two days! That's not possible. I need more time."

"Well, you don't have more time, so I suggest you get started arranging things."

He raked a hand through his hair. "Mother . . ." he stopped, and huffed out a long breath, clearly exasperated.

Marguerite stood up and walked over to him.

"As much as I know how difficult it is for you to take this time away I also know that you deserve it. It will give me an enormous sense of pleasure thinking of you lying on a beach away from the family's business concerns and the burden of overseeing this household."

"I don't think of it as a burden."

She reached up and framed his face between her hands.

"I know you don't, and I love you for that, but it's time for you to play hooky. Go; and don't worry about me if that's another one of your concerns. Your brothers are here to look after me."

Marguerite stood at her bathroom sink and rinsed out her mouth. Oh how she hated to vomit. She always ended up doing it out of her nose, as well as her mouth. She sniffed, and almost gagged. The sense of sickness hung in the air. She'd have to do something about that, especially if Colleen came in here to clean. One whiff, and she'd know someone had been sick. The woman had a nose like a bloodhound.

Marguerite didn't want her running to Jonathan or James blabbing about their mother being ill. Knowing them, the first thing they'd do is call Gage, and he'd probably get on the first plane home. Well, she wasn't having that.

This was obviously another one of her cursed migraines. The unusual thing was how frequently she'd been having them lately. Also troubling was the annoying tingling in her hands and feet she'd been experiencing, making her feel as though her extremities were asleep. A severe stomach cramp suddenly gripped her making Marguerite grab the edge of the counter.

"Oh dear, I must have gotten a hold of some kind of nasty bug," she groaned, staggering out of the bathroom and collapsing onto her bed.

Kim silently sneered at James, as he lay sleeping after their latest round of sex. He was such an unimaginative bed partner she had to do her best acting not to succumb to boredom, but she knew she had to continue her role until she could get to Jonathan. Her need to see him in pain, preferably writhing in agony had become an obsession. She couldn't wait to savor that experience of hearing him screaming and begging her for mercy. But that would have to wait. Right now she had to be content with the knowledge that Marguerite wasn't feeling well according to James.

Kim told him to have Carol use more of the powder assuring him it would help when he mentioned giving up the herb idea. He hinted that maybe he should call Gage. She quickly discouraged that reminding him of their original plan to get his brother out of the house. She further convinced him by using the fact that their mother would be very upset if James became responsible for causing his brother to cut his much needed and so deserved vacation short.

Her thoughts wandered to Gage. Now there was a man that could turn her on just by looking at him. One of the few perks of living in that monstrous house was observing Gage's daily routine in the gym. She knew he worked out just before dawn every morning and she would sneak to watch him. Even now her mouth went dry remembering the sight of him clad only in a pair of swim trunks while he did his reps with the weights and ran on the treadmill until his body gleamed with sweat.

Next he would dive into the swimming pool and swim his laps, powerful arms knifing through the water like blades of steel. But she knew the best part came last when he kicked off his trunks and walked naked to the shower. Her heart would practically burst out of her chest at the sight of all that bare highly toned flesh. She'd seen both of his brothers naked, and Gage's body was far more superior to theirs.

It still galled her that she'd never been able to entice him into her bed. But he obviously didn't have a problem having Holland share his. What did he see in the woman? Kim knew she herself was younger, slimmer and in her own mind, much prettier. James said they were staying in a beach house on Lanai. How could Gage want to be intimate with that nobody nanny? Well, there was no accounting for a person's taste, she supposed.

But Kim smiled now recalling how she'd drugged Holland and had her dumped in the tunnel. She'd wanted to do something more to hurt her, but there hadn't been time. There was some satisfaction when Holland quit the nanny job and refused to talk to Gage. But that didn't last when Holland came back to the house with Jonathan when he returned to get the money to free Gage.

Jonathan. Memories of his betrayal flooded her mind. The coward never apologized to her like he promised her father he would. She thought it'd be enough payback when his mother's health continued to deteriorate, but it wasn't. Kim knew the only way she could ever get real gratification was to personally inflict physical pain on Jonathan.

But first she had to find a way to get him in her clutches.

Chapter Twenty-three

Jonathan felt so excited he wanted to dance a jig. Charo has agreed to come visit him. He'd been working on that, knowing he couldn't go back to her yet. It didn't hurt that she already knew and liked Gage. He used that angle telling her how Gage especially wanted to have her as their guest in appreciation for her help in Mexico.

Gage hadn't said that because he didn't know Jonathan was busy setting things up. But Jon had little doubt his big brother would agree. He liked Charo. It'd be a lot better if she had agreed to stay in their house, but she said she wouldn't be comfortable there, so he scouted around and found an inn within reasonable driving distance.

Jonathan couldn't blame her nervousness about being around James, considering how his brother felt about him trying to give Jamie to Charo. She was better off not even meeting him yet. That might not be a problem considering how his brother had suddenly started to be away from the house quite a bit lately.

The buzz among the servants was that he'd been seen hanging around Carol, the kitchen worker. Jonathan hoped they were right. It was about time James discovered there were other women in the world who were a lot better for him than Kim. Carol didn't come from a wealthy background, but that didn't matter right now. The main thing was to have his brother get free from Kim's hooks.

James had stopped talking about bringing Kim back, as far as Jon knew. Just thinking about that hellcat put a bad taste in his mouth. Jonathan didn't have any regrets about not apologizing to Kim for duping her. Why should he, when she was the one responsible for drugging everyone who got in her way? Gage warned him to be careful because Kim was still seeking retaliation. Jonathan shrugged. So she was gunning for him. He wasn't worried. He could handle her.

He switched his mind back to thinking about Charo. Now there was a sweet woman. It warmed his heart just picturing how great it was going to be to see her again. It wouldn't be much longer, thanks to the power behind his family's money in getting her here. But it had taken quite a bit of persuasion on his part to get her to agree to come.

Besides using Gage to gain her cooperation, Jonathan assured Charo that his mother was very anxious to thank her personally for keeping her grandson safe and helping to rescue Gage. That's when he pulled out his trump card explaining his mother couldn't leave the house, which made it necessary for Charo to come here.

He was on his way to break the news to his mother about Charo's pending visit. He didn't anticipate any rejection there. But something else bothered him about his mother. Jonathan pulled his brows together in a deep frown, thinking about her.

He hadn't been able to discuss Charo coming until he'd worked out all the details. Now that he thought about it, he hadn't been able to say much of anything to his mother because she was spending so much time in her bedroom lately and not encouraging anyone to bother her.

He'd questioned Colleen about that, and all she could say was that his mother was having more migraines than usual. He hadn't missed her worried look. This woman knew his mother better than any of them. If she was concerned then something more must be going on. Jonathan reminded himself he did suggest they should call a doctor. But Colleen told him Marguerite had refused saying there wasn't anything a doctor could do that they hadn't tried before.

He was also told his mother insisted that none of them should call Gage. She was determined that his vacation not be interrupted. Jonathan understood her feelings on that. His big brother never took vacations. The only times he went away was for business reasons. He rarely took the time to relax even when he was home. Jonathan decided their mother was right not to disturb his brother when he remembered that Holland was with Gage. It was about time he had a woman in his life. Jonathan knew he sure wouldn't want to be interrupted if he found himself on an island with his sweet Charo.

Thoughts of being with her again made him forget about everything else . . . including his mother's health.

New Beginnings
Olivia Claire High

Gage and Holland were jogging barefoot on the beach in their bathing suits. They'd started doing it their second day after arriving on the island. They developed a little ritual since then, including their jog, a swim, and then breakfast back at the house.

The morning air was cool on their skin, but the exercise soon warmed them up. Holland knew Gage held back his speed, so she could comfortably keep up with him. They'd been here for three weeks and every day felt like they'd stolen a piece of heaven. She had to give Gage credit for trying to follow his mother's advice and not be too involved with business concerns.

Holland had a feeling it was much more difficult for him not to be in contact with his family. But other than letting her know they had arrived safely, Marguerite told Gage she would ignore any calls or text messages from him unless it was an emergency. She also warned him that she would instruct the rest of the household not to interfere with her wishes.

Not that it was easy to get in contact with anyone considering the cell phone service was weak away from Lanai City, and the only way Gage could connect to the internet was to go to one of the big resort hotels. The owner told them when he had the house built he deliberately chose an area where he wouldn't have his vacations interrupted with problems from the outside world. Holland smiled to herself. She wouldn't be a bit surprised if Marguerite wasn't aware of the difficulty in communications when she chose this place.

So thanks to that good lady, they'd been left on their own to enjoy the island.

And each other.

The owner of the house left a Jeep at their disposal, and they'd used it not only to go into town to buy food and other necessities, but also to explore the red-dirt island, once known for growing pineapples. The entire area of the island was 140.54 square miles and with a population of just under 3200 people, it wasn't what one would call a busy metropolis, which was just fine.

Lanai didn't get as much rain as Holland expected and it was fairly cool in Lanai City, so she usually took a light sweater when they went there. She enjoyed the little 1920's era town. It was small and quaint and the locals were very friendly. Holland felt a sense of serenity here, and she hoped Gage was experiencing the same sensation.

God knows the man had earned this opportunity to set aside the never ending responsibilities of his life back home and wake up without having someone or something drag him into some kind of problem. Holland relished each hour they spent together and secretly enjoyed the illusion that they'd never have to leave. But it was becoming more difficult to block out the fact that their time in her little dream world was rapidly drawing to a close. She had to learn to live in the moment and be thankful for the beauty of their brief life here.

They finished their run and took a quick swim before heading back to the house to prepare breakfast. Gage stood at the stove tending to the scrambled eggs, while Holland cut up some fresh fruit. She knew this sweet intimacy between them as they share these simple chores would be one of the lasting memories she'd take with her when they did finally have to leave the island.

She glanced at Gage. The sun had streaked golden highlights through his hair and bronzed his skin to a healthy glow. She had a good view of his body clad only in navy blue swim trunks slung low on his lean hips. They wore very few clothes while in the house and sometimes didn't bother wearing anything at all, at his insistence.

Heat simmered through her when she recalled how Gage had said the less clothes, the faster they could get at each other. He decided they should make love in every room in the big house as many times as possible. This morning was a perfect example. Her blush deepened and her heart rate picked up as she recalled how he came up behind her in the pantry while she was getting a canister of coffee. One minute he was standing behind her nibbling on her earlobe and the next thing she knew she'd been hoisted up on the counter moaning while he shoved himself between her quivering thighs.

He turned from the stove, frying pan in hand, and began to scoop the eggs onto the plates they'd set out earlier. Holland walked to the sink, turned on the tap, and held her hands under the cold water hoping to cool down her raging hormones. All Gage needed to do was give her one of his smoldering looks and she'd probably drag him to the floor and leap on top of him.

"Your eggs are getting cold," he said from behind her.

Holland did her best to school her expression into a bland mask before turning to face him.

"I needed to rinse the sticky fruit juice off my hands."

"The pineapple is delicious as usual. I'm going to miss it when we leave here."

"You can buy pineapples in the Mainland, you know."

"Yes, but you know very well they won't taste as good as the fresh ones we get here."

She sat down and took a bite of eggs while searching for something else to say rather than talk about going back.

"The eggs taste delicious, too. What seasoning did you put in them?"

"Just something I discovered in the pantry." His mouth lifted in a sly smile. "That's not the only tantalizing surprise I found in there."

Holland didn't miss the twinkle in his eyes and felt her face burn with heat once again.

She tossed her napkin at him. "You ambushed me, you beast."

Gage laughed and tossed it back. They ate in silence until he got up to refill their coffee cups. "I was thinking of doing some snorkeling after we clean things up here. How does that sound to you?"

"It sounds good, but I need to get a couple of girly things in town. Why don't you go ahead and I'll join you later?"

"You sure you don't mind?"

"Not at all. In fact, you can go right now. I'll wash up."

Gage drained his coffee and leaned over to give her a kiss.

"Will you be going to our usual spot?" she wanted to know.

"Yes. Don't take too long with your shopping. I might get lonely."

"I'll hurry. Save me a place in the water."

"Will do," he said and ambled from the room.

Holland bustled around the kitchen before heading to the bedroom to dress. She felt a little sneaky, but the real reason she wanted to go to town alone was to make some phone calls. Even though she told her family she wouldn't be in touch for a whole month, it bothered her that she wasn't at least checking up on her uncle and aunt.

Holland did stop by before the trip to let them know where she was going and when she'd return. She knew she couldn't be gone an entire month without keeping her relatives informed. It didn't take long for her aunt to wheedle out the information that Holland's traveling companion would be Gage. May immediately started humming the wedding march, much to Holland's discomfort.

There hadn't been any talk about marriage between her and Gage, despite how close they had become. Holland knew she would be lying if she didn't confess to having her fantasies about being his wife. Gage was the epitome of the perfect male for her.

But did he think she was the ideal mate for him?

Holland parked the Jeep in front of the store she planned to use, but decided to make her calls before shopping. She phoned her parents first and found out everything was fine with them and the rest of the family. She actually had to brace herself before she called her uncle and aunt knowing they would probably hit her with a barrage of embarrassing questions.

May answered. "Holly? I thought you said you wouldn't be calling for a month. I have it on my calendar that you aren't due back for another week. Are you home?"

"I'm still on Lanai. I wanted to be sure you and Uncle Leo were okay."

"Oh we're fine, honey, which is more than can be said about Mrs. Howard from what I hear," she replied, wasting no time before sharing the local gossip.

Holland pressed the phone more fully against her ear. "What do you mean?"

"Word is she's looking real peaky and those young sons of hers haven't called a doctor."

"Marguerite sometimes suffers from migraines."

"Well, it must be a doozy because she's taken to her bed, and folks working there can hear her moaning day and night."

Holland knew her aunt liked to add her own embellishments to gossip, but what if she was right? What if Gage's mother really was seriously ill? Surely Colleen would have contacted a doctor if things were that bad, but she may not want to take on that kind of responsibility. She was just an employee, no matter how devoted she was to Marguerite.

May broke into her troubled thoughts.

"I know the two younger boys have never been very responsible, but I have to say it sure has shocked us here that her oldest son stays away while his mother could be dying. Of course, it's none of my business."

"No one has told Gage that his mother is ill," Holland said feeling the need to defend him.

"How is that possible? Hasn't he talked to her himself?"

"No, and I'm not going to take the time to explain that right now. Aunt May, I need to know exactly what's going on without any added conjecture. Who told you that Marguerite is so ill?"

"That woman who works for her."

"Colleen?"

"Yes, that's the one. She came by a couple of days ago. Said she thought she'd see how I was doing since she knew you were away. I thought it was kind of odd because we don't really know each other that well, but I invited her to stay for a cup of tea. That's when she told me about Mrs. Howard."

This had to be Colleen's way of trying to let Gage know how bad things were without disobeying Marguerite. She must have thought Holland kept in touch with her aunt. Holland knew the woman was careful to guard the family's private life, which meant Colleen must feel pretty desperate to share something so personal with someone she barely knew.

"Thank you for the information, Aunt May. I have to go now. Gage, um, is waiting."

"I'm not one to tell people how to run their affairs, but if it were me there on that island with him, I'd sure encourage that man not to waste another day before coming home."

Chapter Twenty-four

Holland's heart went out to Gage when she saw his stricken expression the moment she told him his mother was very ill. They literally threw their belongings into suitcases and raced to town, where Gage could get a signal on his phone to make the travel arrangements. He barely spoke on the trip home and seeing his struggle, she didn't waste her time trying to soothe the situation by offering meaningless platitudes.

Colleen met them at the front door. One look at the woman's face, and Holland gave up any hope that her aunt had exaggerated the seriousness of Marguerite's condition.

"Thank God you've come."

"Where's my mother?"

"In her bedroom, sir."

Gage rushed down the hall with Holland close on his heels. Marguerite turned her head on the pillow when they burst through the door.

"What are you doing here?" she asked in a hoarse voice. "You still have a week left of your vacation. I've been keeping count. Or am I wrong?" She put a hand to her head. "These headaches make it hard to think."

Gage got down on his knees by the side of the bed and took her hand in his, while Holland hovered in the background feeling appalled at how utterly ill Marguerite looked.

"Mother, how could you not let me know you've been so sick?"

"I didn't want to spoil your vacation. Who called you? I'm very angry with them."

"Never mind that. You need help."

He rose to his feet and motioned Holland to the bed.

"Stay with her while I go call the doctor."

Holland nodded and took his place by the side of the bed. Marguerite gave her a weak smile.

"Did you have a good time, dear?"

"Yes, it was wonderful."

She brushed a stray lock of hair off the older woman's forehead.

"Is there anything I can do for you?"

"I've just got a hold of a nasty bug, or perhaps it's more accurate to say it's got a hold of me," she said, trying to joke. She pointed to the carafe and glass sitting on the nightstand. "Would you mind pouring me some water? I seem to have developed a terrible thirst lately."

Holland did as she was asked, helped Marguerite to sit up enough to drink, and guided her back down onto her pillow when she signaled she'd had enough.

"I'm so sorry you had to cut your vacation short."

"Please don't concern yourself about that."

"Did you manage to keep my son away from work long enough to take advantage of the island?"

New Beginnings
Olivia Claire High

"Yes, he was a good boy. I think you need to rest," Holland said when she realized Marguerite was becoming short of breath.

She pulled a chair close to the bed and sat waiting for Gage. His mother had slipped into a restless sleep by the time he returned. He motioned for Holland to join him in the hallway. She tiptoed from the room, quietly closing the door behind her.

"I'm really worried about your mother. Something is obviously terribly wrong with her."

"So obvious that even a child would know she needed medical attention." His grim expression matched his grim words. "I've called the doctor and he's on his way. Come with me."

"Where are we going?"

"To the office. I've asked Jonathan and Colleen to meet me there. I want to find out what's been going on with my mother before the doctor gets here."

"What about James? Isn't he going to be in on this?"

"He's not here. Apparently he's been spending quite a bit of time away from the house since we've been gone."

Jonathan and Colleen both stood up when they entered the room. Gage pointed to their chairs. Colleen quickly sank down and folded her hands tightly in her lap. But Jonathan smiled.

"Nice looking tan you have there. Looks like being away agreed with you."

Gage appeared calm enough, but Holland recognized that tight lipped look. He was angry and why shouldn't he be? Jonathan was acting as though

315

nothing was amiss while their mother lay in her sickbed suffering from God knows what.

Holland took the chair next to Colleen and on an impulse reached over to give the woman's hands a comforting squeeze. Gage waited until Jonathan sat down before leaning against the desk with his hands pressed on either side of him. He turned his attention to his brother first.

"Mind telling me why you didn't let me know Mother was so ill?"

"You know darn well she told us not to, and she refused to let us call the doctor. I figured it was just a Godzilla size headache."

"Colleen says it's lasted over two weeks. Are you aware of that?"

Jonathan blinked.

"No. Gee. Poor Mom. She never said it was that bad whenever I went to see her and even when I did she didn't want me to stay too long, so I left her alone. Anyway, I've been kind of busy."

"Is that so?"

Jonathan leaned forward with excitement like a child anxious to share a new toy he'd just received. "I've been trying to get Charo to come and visit and she finally agreed. I needed to make all the arrangements before she could back out. I knew you wouldn't mind me inviting her considering how she helped you. I'm supposed to pick her up at the airport tomorrow."

Gage looked at Colleen.

"Did you know about this?"

"No, sir. Oh my, I'll need to prepare a room for her right away."

She turned to Jonathan.

"You'll have to let me know what kind of food she prefers. I might have to do some shopping."

Holland couldn't believe it.

"You're bringing Charo here, while your mother is so ill?"

"Well, she wasn't that sick when I started working on things. She said she was looking forward to meeting Charo when I mentioned it to her."

He gave Colleen his attention. "You don't have to worry about getting anything ready. I've made reservations for Charo to stay in an inn. It's close enough where I can easily bring her to meet Mom when she's feeling better. There was no way I could have her stay here and have James glaring at her all the time."

Gage opened his mouth to reply, but someone chose that moment to knock at the door.

"Yes?"

Jacob opened it.

"The doctor is here to see your mother, sir."

"Thank you. Show him to her room. Colleen, please go with him. I'll be there in a few minutes."

"Yes, sir."

Holland watched the servants leave and stood up. "Would you mind if I go with them? I have a feeling Marguerite is going to be upset seeing the doctor. I may be able to help calm her."

Gage straightened away from his desk. "I'd appreciate it."

She barely had time to close the door when she heard Gage release the anger he'd held in check.

She knew a storm had been building behind his quiet demeanor, and that Jonathan had unleased a thunderous tempest upon himself. She'd barely managed to hold her tongue and not say more to Jonathan for the glaring neglect of their mother's worsening condition. No wonder Gage was often so exasperated with his younger siblings. Their individual self-absorption would try anyone's patience.

Three days later Holland was in the same chair in the office watching Gage, as he sat at his desk with his head bowed and his hands pressed into his hair. Her heart ached for him when he raised his head, and she saw the agony in his eyes.

"All those tests with specialists studying the results, and still no one can find out what's wrong with my mother. She's getting sicker and sicker; and I can't do a damn thing to stop it."

Holland got up, walked around to stand behind his chair, and began to knead his temples with her fingertips moving in small circles.

"You're doing everything you can."

"Well, it's obviously not enough."

He tore out of his chair to pace the room.

"I shouldn't have gone away. I would have been able to get her help sooner if I'd been here. Instead, what was I doing? Lying on the beach with you getting a tan. God!"

Holland didn't take his words personally. Not when she felt the same way. If only she had thought to call her aunt before waiting so long. She felt almost ashamed to think of how much she'd been enjoying herself while Marguerite was here suffering.

"I must have been out of my mind to trust my brothers to take care of her. I wish I could slap some sense into their empty heads every time I think of them being here in the house watching her deteriorate, and still not do anything about it."

"I understand how you feel, but you know your mother refused to let anyone call a doctor."

Gage spun to face her.

"We both know why, don't we? If she agreed to see a doctor, then even my simpleminded brothers would have known something was wrong. My initial instincts were right about not agreeing to be gone a whole month. I will never forgive myself if my mother ends up dying because of my irresponsibility."

"You weren't being irresponsible. You were just doing something your mother wanted very much for you. I was there in that room with you when she laid out her plans, remember?"

"Yes, and I also remember you thinking it'd be wonderful if you had a chance to cross Hawaii off your Bucket List. Happy now?"

That stung. But the man was suffering terrible emotional pain. Not because of something either of them had done, but because Marguerite happened to become ill while they were away. None of them had any control over that. Regretting the trip wasn't going to change things.

"I will always be happy remembering the time we spent together. It didn't have to be Hawaii. You make every day special for me just by walking into

a room where I happen to be. I love your mother. I
know your heart will be broken if something
happens to her, but my heart will be broken, too."

She started to leave, but Gage reached out and
pulled her into his arms.

"I'm sorry, Holland. My God. I sounded as
immature as one of my brothers."

She wrapped her arms around his waist and
pressed her face into his chest.

"You're upset."

"Don't make excuses for my behavior. I should
have my tongue ripped out for saying such a
despicable thing to you."

They were both being eaten up by distress.
They stood in silence trying to give and receive
comfort from each other. Gage's phone rang. He
reached over the desk to pick it up with one hand
while continuing to hold onto Holland. He looked at
the caller ID and scowled.

"It's Jonathan. He's been calling ever since
Charo arrived, wanting to bring her to the house."
He answered. "Stop being such a pest."

"I know you don't want me bothering you, but
I've been telling Charo about Mom's illness and she
says she needs to talk to you."

"You know now isn't a good time. I told you
before I would visit with her later."

"I told Charo that, but she thinks she might
know what's wrong with Mom."

"You mean from something she learned at the
clinic where she worked? Come on, Jon. I've had
specialists working on this and they haven't been
able to diagnose our mother's condition. What

makes you think Charo could do what educated medical people haven't been able to?"

"She said Mom's symptoms sound like the ones that the people in her grandmother's village suffered a couple years ago. But she needs to see Mom to be sure it's the same thing. Mom's not getting any better. What's it going to hurt if Charo sees her?"

Gage swiped a hand around the back of his neck.

"All right. Bring her, then."

Charo let herself be led to Marguerite's bedroom after exchanging brief reunion greetings with Gage and Holland. She went immediately to the bed where Marguerite lay sleeping. She carefully picked up each hand and began to examine the older woman's fingernails.

"Jonathan says your mother has been suffering with headaches, vomiting, tingling in her hands and feet, stomach cramps, shortness of breath, and a hoarse voice," she spoke quietly keeping her voice low, as she rattled off the myriad of symptoms.

"She's also complained of being very thirsty. Why are you looking at her fingernails?"

"Are her nails usually so dried and cracked with these brown strips?"

"No. What do you think all this means?"

"I wasn't sure I was right when Jonathan told me about your mother, but now that I see her fingernails, I'm almost certain what is causing her to be so ill. It is the same thing that happened in my grandmother's village. The sickness came from their wells. The groundwater had been contaminated."

"We aren't on a well here."

"There can be other ways for this to happen. I learned a great deal while I was taking care of my grandmother. The condition is difficult to diagnose because it mirrors so many other illnesses. Doctors often miss it."

Gage folded his arms over his chest. "That's very interesting Charo, but what exactly is the condition you think my mother is suffering from?"

She moved away from the bed and let her eyes take in the anxious faces before settling her troubled gaze on Gage.

"I'm so sorry to have to tell you this, Mr. Langdon, but I believe your mother is suffering from arsenic poisoning."

Chapter Twenty-five

Silence filled the room. The kind of stillness that resonates inside the head louder than any noise could ever do. The implication of what Charo's words might mean hung in the air like an oppressive wave of heat that suffocates the brain, robbing it of coherent thought. This household had already experienced the shock of what hallucinogenic drugs could do to the human body. Now they must contend with the horror of a new threat.

Gage was the first to recover from Charo's disturbing revelation. He turned his head slowly, like a man coming out of a stupor. He stared at his brother, a painful question flashing in his eyes. Jonathan flinched and jerked back. All color drained out of his face. He held his hands out in front of him more in supplication than any defensive move.

"Oh God, no! Don't look at me like that, Gage. I know I let Kim use drugs on people here, but I swear on my life that I knew nothing about this arsenic poisoning."

Tears began to fill his eyes.

"I would never, ever condone something like this happening to Mom."

Marguerite's sudden moaning caused all eyes to turn to her. "Wa . . . water, please."

Holland hurried to the nightstand without thinking of anything for the moment except to help in any way possible. She poured the water, supported Marguerite's head as she'd done before, and held the glass to her lips before settling her back onto the pillow again.

"You said there can be other ways for this to happen other than through water. Do you have any idea how the arsenic could have gotten into my mother's system?" Gage asked Charo.

"Arsenic is a natural compound that occurs in the soil. Does she do any gardening?"

"Now and then in the house gardens, but not much. What else?"

His voice was clipped, waiting for answers he dreaded to hear, but needed to know.

"A person can ingest it through their food or drink."

"All our food is prepared in the kitchen and no one else has been ill."

"Yeah, but we don't all eat and drink the same thing," Jonathan offered in a quiet voice.

"True. Tell me, Charo. Wouldn't my mother have tasted any difference in her food?"

"There wouldn't be any flavor or odor."

"So obviously we're going to have to find out how she's been exposed to the arsenic. Will my mother have any lasting effects once she stops ingesting it?"

"That would depend on how much she's had and the potency, but her symptoms indicate she's been receiving quite a bit. Bad things could happen."

"How bad?"

"I'm not a doctor."

Gage looked at her, his jaw set in a hard line, his expression chiseled from stone.

"Just tell me what you found out from the people in your grandmother's village."

"Prognosis vary, but she could have heart and liver problems and possibly some degree of nerve damage. But that's for the most severe cases. The important thing is to get her treatment as soon as possible. You'll need to consult a toxicologist and perhaps an herbalist. But nothing will help until you find out how she's getting the arsenic. That is the key. You must start there."

"Then we'll begin searching for resources in that field right away." He looked at Holland. "I know you'll want to help, so I'm going to ask you to start personally preparing every ounce of food and drink that goes into my mother's mouth. No one, and I mean absolutely no one else is to go near anything my mother ingests. I'm also asking you to shop for whatever food you buy for her and keep it locked up where no one else has access."

"You know I want to help, but Colleen is going to be hurt if I do what you ask. She wouldn't be involved in something as horrendous as this."

"I can't worry about hurt feelings right now. She's not the only one working in the kitchen, and she can't keep her eyes on the others every second."

This reminded Holland of the time when she had to keep watch over Jamie's bottles when she suspected Kim was tampering with them. But Kim wasn't here. Who, she wondered, wanted to make

Marguerite so ill. And why? What had they hoped to gain from such cruelty?

James fumbled with the key and almost dropped it trying to fit the small metal piece into the lock. The owners of the inn obviously didn't believe in keycards. He hadn't had any trouble all the other times, but his hands hadn't been shaking then, either. His nerves had him twitching like a mouse ready to be pounced on by a cat.

The key finally slid into the slot. He shoved the door open, rushed inside, and leaned against it. Tiny beads of sweat dotted his forehead. He forced his legs to carry him to the bed where he collapsed onto his back. He couldn't even bring himself to move when Kim came out of the bathroom.

She stopped and frowned at him.

"What are you doing back? Did you forget something?"

"No."

"What's the matter?"

"Everything."

She came to sit on the bed next to him.

"Things can't be all that bad. Why don't you tell me what's bothering you?"

James struggled into a sitting position.

"Gage's back, my mother is dying, and Jon is here."

Kim stared at him dumbstruck, her brain working furiously trying to decide which statement to question first.

"One thing at a time, lover. I thought you said Gage was going to be gone for a month."

New Beginnings
Olivia Claire High

"He was, but someone called and told him about Mom, and he came back a week early." James knuckled his fists into his eyes. "God, she's really sick. I had no idea she was so bad. I've been keeping my phone off, and not checking my messages like you suggested. But I looked a little bit ago and saw that Gage has been trying to get a hold of me. There's even a text from Holland."

"I suggested you keep your phone off, so we could enjoy our time together without your family hounding you."

He scrambled off the bed, and stood in front of her.

"I know, but I should have kept in better touch. Carol told me when I gave her the last batch of the herbal powder that Mom wasn't doing well. I still think it has something to do with that stuff because she started feeling bad not long after I let Carol use it. I'm going to tell her to stop."

"That's fine, but you mustn't blame yourself. I told you the herb is harmless. If your mother is dying as you say, it certainly isn't from the herb. I think what we have here is an unfortunate consequence." Kim patted the bed, anxious to get to the part of his statements that meant the most to her. "Now come sit down and tell me what you meant about Jonathan."

James slumped down next to her.

"He's staying right here in the inn, or at least his girlfriend is. I saw them in the parking lot."

Excitement leaped in her chest, and she dug her fingers into his thigh.

"Did they see you?"

327

"No. I ducked behind some bushes."

He rubbed the sweat off his forehead with the back of his hand. "I can't believe they'd show up here considering all the other places he could have chosen. It's sheer bad luck, or maybe an ill omen. We'd better find another place to meet."

"Why? We were here first. The girlfriend is probably only here for a visit and won't be staying all that long,"

No way was she going to let Jonathan slip away again. He'd be coming back if the girlfriend was here. A thrill trembled through her. To think she'd been trying to find a way to get to Jon and now to have him literally show up on her doorstep was almost too easy. She might even have a go at the girlfriend. Kim dragged her attention back to James when he spoke again.

"Yeah, but he might make it difficult for us."

It was all she could do not to roll her eyes. What a pair the Howard twins were. Jonathan the liar, and James the coward. She had to keep James in line before he did something stupid and spoil everything. Time to remind him who was in control.

"Don't give in so easily to your brother. Have you forgotten how he used us both, and then ran off to Mexico to be with that woman?"

"No, and I'm still sore at him for all the trouble he caused, but his girlfriend was real helpful in taking care of Jamie and rescuing Gage."

"Actually, your brother used her too, when you think about it."

"Yeah, he's a real prince."

Kim crawled onto his lap and put her hands around his neck. He wrapped his arms around her waist and pressed his face into her breasts seeking comfort.

"You said you two have been avoiding each other when you're home, which means you still haven't confronted him for what he did. Don't you ever feel the need to have it out with him?"

James raised his head and looked at her.

"Yeah, I guess."

"Well, I know I do. I've never received an apology from Jonathan. Not one word or gesture of remorse for the terrible things he forced me to do."

She worked up a few tears.

"Look what he did to our relationship. He used me and made me so ashamed I couldn't bring myself to be with my husband, or even touch my own child. And don't forget he tried to give our son away to some stranger."

She made herself force more tears out until they dribbled down her cheeks.

"I don't like to see you cry, sweetheart."

"You have no idea how many tears I've shed because of what he put me through. I often wake up in the night crying. I need to confront Jonathan and have him validate my feelings. I need closure. It's the only way I'm ever going to find any peace. Will you help me end this torment once and for all? Please, darling, please," she begged.

"You know I'd like to, but how?"

"Bring your brother here to me, and I'll take care of the rest."

Gage drove, donning his dark glasses against the bright sun spilling into his vehicle. He didn't like the idea of leaving the house, but there were business meetings he'd been putting off that required his presence. He wanted to leave the helicopter at home in case of an emergency. It did ease some of his concerns knowing Holland was staying at the house keeping watch over his mother. He invited Charo to stay, but she refused saying she didn't want Colleen to have an added guest to worry about. It did enter his mind that she may still be weighing her feelings for Jonathan, so Gage made himself be content when she agreed to visit his mother each day.

What a difference those two women were compared to Kim. His lips tightened thinking about that piranha and her rampage with the drugs and now what had happened with his mother.

Thank God she was already showing improvement thanks to Charo's sharp eye and knowledge of the arsenic poisoning. Poisoned! God, he still couldn't believe it. He'd read all he could find about the effects arsenic had on the body and felt sick realizing what his mother had been going through and had yet to face.

He could only pray they'd caught it in time before any serious permanent damage was done. The fact that his mother's symptoms started to gradually lessen as soon as Holland began preparing and guarding his mother's food and drink was pretty significant evidence that was how the arsenic got into her system.

New Beginnings

Olivia Claire High

He thought Colleen was going to have a heart attack when he told her why Holland would be taking over his mother's menus until further notice. The poor woman started sobbing, and he'd ended up having to have someone help her to her room to lie down. His first inclination was to fire everyone else who had anything at all to do with kitchen work until he realized he might have to end up terminating the entire staff, since they all had access. It didn't seem fair that everyone be made to pay for one person's treachery. It also wouldn't help him to find the culprit.

He told the doctor his mother had been exposed to the arsenic from the fertilizer she used working in the indoor gardens. But Gage knew he must find the person who was responsible for his mother's poisoning. She could have died if it hadn't been for Charo. There was no way he was going to put this near tragedy to rest until he got to the bottom of things.

One good thing about driving was that he was getting some quiet time to mull over important issues. He went back to thinking about the people who mainly worked in the kitchen. That would be his starting point. Gage admitted that for a few sickening moments he'd actually thought Jon might be in on the diabolical scheme, but his brother's reaction was enough to convince him otherwise. What about James? He'd suddenly become an enigma. According to what Jonathan told him, James started taking off as soon as Gage left for his vacation. He would disappear for two to three days at a time, come home for a couple days, and leave again. He never told anyone where he was going and refused to answer any calls or messages. Gage could attest to that after he'd tried several times to get a response from James without success.

Another thing adding to the puzzle was when he did finally come home, he reminded Gage of a man walking over hot coals. He acted jumpy, evasive, and ready to run. The same sick feeling that had invaded his gut when he suspected Jonathan of being responsible for their mother's condition returned making Gage think the unthinkable once again. This was the first opportunity since he'd returned from Lanai that he had a chance to really concentrate on his brother's odd behavior.

Their mother's illness had taken top priority, but now he had time to focus on James. It wasn't so much that he thought his brother had done the actual poisoning, but Gage had a feeling James was holding something back. The more he thought about it the more he also thought it might have something to do with why James kept leaving the house.

He told Gage he was just driving around staying at different places taking mini vacations when Gage questioned him about his periodic disappearances.

Every instinct he possessed told Gage his brother wasn't alone on these little trips. Those instincts were now giving him a pretty good idea who was sharing the getaways with James. Could James have been sucked in once again by his conniving wife?

Gage tapped his fingers on the steering wheel wondering what he could do if he was right.

How did one get rid of a parasite when you couldn't convince the host he was being used?

Chapter Twenty-six

Holland smiled at Marguerite. "Would you like a little more soup?"

"Not right now, dear. But it was delicious. I can't tell you how wonderful it is to eat something and not have it taste like I've chewed on steel wool."

Holland remembered Charo telling her that people suffering from arsenic poisoning often had a metallic taste in their mouths.

"Well, that could have been caused by some of the medicines the doctor was trying for you."

"Or the arsenic," Marguerite said in a quiet voice. "You see, I had the taste before the doctor started treating me."

The shock of hearing her talk about the arsenic almost made Holland drop the soup bowl she was setting on a tray. Gage thought it'd be best to wait until his mother was fully recovered before they told her why she'd been so ill. Holland knew he would have kept the frightening news from his mother entirely if he could.

"Arsenic? My goodness. Whatever gave you that idea?"

"I was awake when Charo told you about the poisoning. I heard everything she said. I know that's why you've been preparing my meals. You think someone working in the kitchen is responsible. Colleen would slit her wrists before she'd do anything to hurt me; or allow anyone else to so much as harm a hair on my head."

"I agree with you, but Gage wanted me to prepare your meals as a precaution."

"I've lived in this house for all these years and was happy for the most part, even when the day came and I lost my courage to go outside. I won't say there haven't been days when the walls do seem to be closing in on me. I fight that by having more rooms built. But I felt safe in my own way. Then all that drugging with you and the other nannies happened; and now me."

"We're going to find out who did this to you."

"The walls may be made of stone, but they're useless in keeping out the evil that's come here. I think the house has become cursed. I always knew I was going to die here, but I never thought it'd be by someone else's hand."

"Then leave, Marguerite," Holland said on a sudden inspiration. "Gage and I will help you."

"You know that's not possible considering how I am."

"There are ways. Don't stay and let any more evil get to you. You can fight this."

Marguerite shook her head.

"I'm too old and too tired. What will be, will be."

Kim looked at the slender gold watch spanning her wrist. Not much longer now. She almost rubbed her hands together in anticipation. Everything was going according to her plan. That is as long as James didn't chicken out. She ground her teeth together. It was like pumping blood into a dead man trying to talk him into taking any kind of risk.

James did manage to follow her instructions so far according to his last text message. He came to Charo's room at the inn, introduced himself, and thanked her for taking care of his son in Mexico. He invited her out to lunch to show that he didn't bear her any ill will. Kim chose the restaurant and with her careful attention to detail, found a place in an area without cell phone reception.

That was a vital part to her plot because she didn't want Jonathan and his girlfriend being able to call anyone. Another important part of her scheme was to make sure James told Charo he came to see her without his brother's knowledge, and this would be their secret for now. It also helped that Gage was out of town on an overnight business trip. Kim didn't want him interfering. All it would take was one word from big brother, and that milksop James would probably fold. The next phase would be up to Jonathan himself. He would come to the inn to pick up Charo, and take her to his house as he'd been doing.

Only she would be the one waiting in his girlfriend's room.

This time Kim did rub her hands together.

Jonathan met Holland coming in the front door, as he was going out. "Hey, Hol. Been visiting your aunt and uncle?"

"Yes. Is your mother still napping?"

336

"She's just waking up. Colleen's with her. I'm on my way to get Charo. Do you need me to pick up anything?"

"Nothing that I can think of. What about Jamie? Is James with him?"

He shook his head.

"Nope. Brother is off on another one of his mysterious getaways."

"You don't approve?"

"Personally, I don't care what he does, as long as we stay out of each other's way. But it'd be nice for our mother's sake if he hung around here a little more."

"You used to be gone for weeks at a time from what I heard."

"A person has to travel if they hope to find the pot of gold at the end of the rainbow, and I found mine in Mexico when I met Charo. Besides, Gage was always here when I was away."

"True." She gave him a wishful look. "I'm glad he'll be back tomorrow."

"I bet you'll especially miss him tonight," he grinned. "Maybe you can borrow one of Jamie's teddy bears to sleep with."

"Shut up, Jonathan," she grumbled and pushed by him.

Laughter spilled out of him, as he climbed into his Jaguar, spun it in a U-turn, and sped down the driveway. God, he felt good. His mother was on the mend, he had money in his pocket again, and Charo was here. He could feel her melting a little bit more toward him every day.

Driving through town, he spotted some buckets of fresh flowers for sale standing outside the door of Holland's uncle's minimart. He pulled over, scooped up an armful, and walked into the store. Hopefully this offering would bring him another step closer to winning Charo over.

"Hello Mr. Tyler. Could you wrap them in some kind of paper?" he said handing the huge bouquet across the counter.

"A man buys that many flowers is either in trouble with his lady, or he's fixin' to propose."

Jonathan grinned.

"Only time will tell."

He paid, climbed back in his car, and roared away. He arrived at the inn, hurried to her room, and knocked on the door. He looked around. Luckily no cops had spied him tearing down the road. The last thing he needed was another speeding ticket.

Jonathan realized Charo must be hiding behind the door when it swung open, and he didn't see her. He smiled at her little game, stepped inside, and came face to face with his worst nightmare.

"Flowers for me? How nice. But you needn't have bothered. You're all I want, lover."

Jonathan dropped the flowers and staggered back.

His luck had just run out.

Gage walked into his hotel suite and tossed the keycard onto the table in the entry. He rolled his shoulders and loosened his tie. Business meetings all day, through dinner, and during drinks afterward never used to bother him, but there were too many issues going on at home right now for him not to resent being here.

One of those issues was concerning James. It was time he sat that young man down and asked him some pointed questions. Gage just hoped he didn't already know the answers. He walked over to the bar and poured himself a nightcap. He needed to shower and go over some notes before his breakfast meeting in the morning. But not before he called home.

Holland answered on the first ring.

"I was just getting ready to call you," she said.

He smiled.

"Miss me?"

"More than you know."

His smile instantly faded at her serious tone.

"Is my mother all right?"

"Yes and no. She's physically better now that we've got rid of the arsenic. But she's talking about dying here in the house."

"Damn it. It sounds like she's going into one of her depressions again."

"Small wonder with all that's happened. Now Jonathan's gone and James is also MIA."

"Are you sure Jon isn't with Charo?"

"I'm sure because she's here."

"I think you'd better start at the beginning and tell me everything," Gage said before slumping onto a sofa, his drink forgotten for the moment.

"I'll do my best."

Holland took a deep breath.

"James showed up at Charo's room at the inn and begged her to go to lunch with him. You know, to bury the hatchet kind of thing. She agreed. They came out of the restaurant after they finished eating and his car had a flat tire. He took her to a place higher up in the mountains where there wasn't any cell reception."

"Sounds familiar."

"Very. Anyway, James was having a difficult time trying to change the flat, so the guy who owns the restaurant finally did it for him."

"I'm not surprised. I doubt if James has ever changed a tire in his life."

"They were gone way longer than Charo expected because of the tire. She tried to hurry James, but he kept talking, and although she doesn't really know him she thought he acted nervous. She called Jon as soon as she could and told him to wait for her at the inn."

"Did she tell him she was with James?"

"No. He asked her not to. Jonathan didn't answer, so she left him a message. James dropped her off at the inn and left in a big hurry when he saw Jon's car parked there."

"I'm not liking the sound of this."

"Brace yourself, it gets worse. Charo went to her room expecting to find Jonathan. He wasn't there, but somebody had been. The place looked like a tornado had gone through. I know this for a fact because I went to the inn and drove her back here."

Gage's brow creased in a frown.

"Are you saying Charo was robbed?"

"Nothing was missing as far as she could tell, but there was evidence of some serious scuffling. Chairs overturned, a lamp knocked on the floor, and flowers everywhere."

"Flowers?"

"That's right. Jon must have got them for Charo. I know he bought them because they came from my uncle's store. I recognized the butcher paper he uses to wrap things in. I talked to Uncle Leo to be sure, and he verified that Jonathan was there earlier buying the flowers."

"Did anyone at the inn notice or hear anything out of the ordinary?"

"Yes, which is a darn good thing or we wouldn't know what happened. A guest saw two men taking a man fitting Jonathan's description to a van. She thought Jon may be drunk because the men appeared to be practically dragging him. I hate to tell you this, but I found out Kim and James have been staying at the same inn."

Gage swore.

"So that's where he's been going. No doubt he kept Charo away because he knew Jon was walking into a set-up. He may have let the air out of his tire to further stall her."

"Charo wondered that too because James did leave her in the restaurant at one point saying he needed to use the bathroom."

"Has anyone heard from James since lunch?"

"Not a peep. But here's another major bombshell for you. Carol just told Colleen James had her sprinkling a powdered herb on Marguerite's food. It was supposed to stop her migraines. He told

Carol to do it in secret because his mom didn't like taking any kind of medicine. She started doing it right when Marguerite began feeling ill. James had her stop the day we got back."

Gage went rigid for a moment.

"Mother of God."

"You can say that again. I'm still reeling from that bit of information. Carol insists James really thought he was being helpful. The only reason she finally mentioned this to Colleen was because she just heard about the arsenic. Now the poor kid is in a panic. I was surprised she kept the secret for so long, but Colleen said James paid Carol to keep her silence. That doesn't sound like something he'd do."

"Not without someone putting the idea in his head."

Gage got to his feet.

"I'll be leaving here right away. In the meantime, I want you to call the police and report Jon missing."

"I already have."

Chapter Twenty-seven

Gage tossed items he'd unpacked into his suitcase while calling the front desk to let them know he'd be checking out a day early and to have a valet bring his car. He grabbed the case and a garment bag before heading to the elevator. He stepped out into the lobby and set his luggage down before whipping his phone out of his pocket

"Hello?"

"Where is your daughter, Winslow?" Gage demanded, skipping any friendly greeting.

"Gage. I thought we'd put that business about your beating behind us."

"This isn't about me. Kim's taken Jonathan. I also have reason to believe she was involved in my mother's arsenic poisoning."

Winslow drew in a startled breath.

"Your mother was poisoned? My God! Is she all right?"

"It's too soon to tell at this point, but the doctors are optimistic that there won't be any long lasting effects. That's another reason I want to talk to your daughter."

"Wait just a damn minute. You're throwing a lot of serious accusations around. You're saying Kim is responsible for poisoning your mother. How is that possible when you haven't allowed her to come into your home?"

Gage gripped the phone.

"I've just been informed she had inside help."

"Well then, maybe that's the person to talk to."

"I intend to; but I still need to know where Kim is."

"Because you believe she's involved in Jonathan's disappearance? Well, I'd like to know how you think my petite daughter would be able to overpower your brother."

"A witness saw two men dragging him away from the inn where Kim's been staying."

"She's been staying at an inn? I had no idea. All I know is she's been coming and going two and three days at a time. Now you say she has Jonathan – are they meeting at this inn?"

"She's been there with James. I told you, Jonathan isn't with her voluntarily."

"You mentioned two men. That doesn't mean Kim was involved."

"A girl who cleans rooms at the inn saw your daughter get into the van with Jon and the two men. We both know how she feels about Jon, and we also both know what she's capable of doing. Where is she?"

"I wish I knew. Don't you think I'd tell you after what you just said about Marguerite? I'll question the staff and call a few of her friends. It's the best I can do."

Gage walked outside when he saw the valet drive up in his car.

"Let's hope that'll be good enough."

New Beginnings
Olivia Claire High

Jonathan sat tied to a chair with his arms pulled painfully behind him and his ankles secured to the chair legs. That would have been plenty enough to hold him, but whoever had tied him up obviously wanted to make him feel like a trussed up chicken. Ropes wound around his waist and chest and over his lap cinched so tight they cut into his clothing.

He shook his head trying to clear his brain. He tugged at the ropes that bound him, but they didn't budge. This must be how Gage felt during his ordeal. Now it looked like it was his turn. A hard ball of fear felt like a weight in his gut.

How did he end up like this? He shook his head again and remembered. The blood in his veins turned to ice. Kim!

He walked into Charo's room and saw Kim staring at him like a deadly cobra ready to strike. The next thing he knew the flowers he was carrying were knocked from his hands, and he ended up on the floor trying to defend himself against a couple of big bruisers who grabbed him.

He fought the best he could. But it was two against one, and the other men were much stronger. They'd held him down while that madwoman Kim jabbed a needle in his arm. He didn't know what she'd used, but almost immediately it began to fog his brain and weaken his limbs. His body shutdown until he couldn't even keep his eyes open.

Leave it to her, the drug happy fiend, to use a chemical to render him useless. Talk about not fighting fair. He should have known she wouldn't just sit down and hash things out like normal people do when they're at odds. He supposed he should have gone to her dad's and let her vent when he got back from Mexico after rescuing Gage.

But he never got around to making a phone call to Kim. Actually, he'd kind of thought at the time that his big brother was going to deal with her. He certainly had the right considering how she ordered him to be beaten. But then Gage went away and their mom got sick, so the timing just wasn't right. Thank God Charo wasn't in her room when Kim and her goon squad arrived. At least he didn't think she'd been there. His heart did an uneasy jump. He would never forgive himself if anything happened to Charo.

He had to get out of here and go find her.

He looked frantically around and realized he was sitting in the middle of what looked like an old barn. It probably hadn't been used in a long time from the look of things. The place smelled of dust and dried animal dung. Some of the boards in the walls were split and rotted through in some areas. The floor was littered with rodent and bird droppings. His eyes traveled upward to sagging beams draped with dozens of spider webs and a roof riddled with holes.

He may be alone now, but knowing Kim she'd be back. No doubt her ploy was to leave him here for a while, so his anxiety level would make him beg for mercy. Well, he wasn't about to give her the satisfaction. He'd find a way out of here by God, and then his not so dear sister-in-law was going to find out she'd messed with the wrong brother.

New Beginnings
Olivia Claire High

James huddled in his car feeling sick to his stomach and very much afraid he'd made a terrible mistake in helping Kim meet up with Jonathan. He'd received a message from Carol telling him his brother was missing and how a witness saw him being dragged from the inn. That was bad enough, but he almost lost his lunch when Carol mentioned what Kim told him was a healthy herb had turned out to be arsenic.

Dear God in heaven, he'd almost poisoned his mother to death! He gripped the steering wheel and pressed his forehead against his hands. Tears filled his eyes when he thought of how Kim had used his love for her to blind him to her wicked schemes. She'd seduced him with her body, fogged his brain with her wiles, and turned him into a monster.

No! His mind cried, as he raised his head and slammed his hands against the dashboard. She alone was the monster here. She'd turned her vengeance for Jonathan into a loathsome vendetta against his entire family. His fingers squeezed hard on the dash until pain shot up his arms and all the way to his shoulders.

Everything he'd done had been out of love for her, and everything Kim demanded was all because she was so filled with hatred. She'd plotted and connived until she tricked him into helping her perpetrate her evil plans to bring down not just Jonathan, but his entire family. Jonathan deserved whatever happened to him. But even though James acknowledged this, he personally couldn't take part in any more schemes to punish his brother. And he most certainly couldn't forgive Kim for deliberately trying to make his mother suffer.

James sat up very straight. Kim wasn't the only one who thirsted for revenge now. No one, not even a wife he once adored was going to get away with trying to kill his mother. How would she feel if someone used her? A sudden look of cunning came into his eyes.

It was time to find out.

Kim heard her phone chime and snatched it out of her pocket. Her mouth curled with distain when she saw it was James calling. Her first inclination was to ignore him, especially since she was getting ready to begin dealing with Jonathan. Now that was something to really look forward to. She wasn't in the mood to listen to James. But she reminded herself he still might be of some use if it came down to her having to explain Jonathan's disappearance.

"What do you want, James? Jonathan and I are busy. You went to all the trouble to get me together with him. What is so important that you have to interrupt us before we're finished?"

"So he's okay, then?"

"Of course he's okay."

"Thank God!" he blurted. "I helped you see Jonathan because you said you just wanted to talk to him."

"That's right, which is why I don't have time for this conversation with you."

"Well, you'd better take time."

Kim's brows lifted in surprise. She wasn't used to James sounding so threatening.

New Beginnings
Olivia Claire High

"Why don't you tell me what's on your mind?"

"A witness at the inn saw two men drag Jon out of Charo's room and stuff him into a van."

"They're lying," she said after a moment's hesitation.

"I don't think so. The woman used her phone to take pictures of the whole thing, including the van and its plates. And that's not the only damning evidence against you," he said, continuing to build on his story. "The girl who cleans the rooms saw you coming out of Charo's room. She knows what you both look like, so there can be no mistake that you're involved. Who were those men with Jonathan and what did they do to my brother?"

James could hear her sudden intake of breath and knew he'd struck a nerve.

"All right. I didn't want to worry you, but Jon had to use the bathroom right after he arrived at the inn. He tripped on the bathmat and hit his head on the edge of the bathtub. He knocked himself unconscious. I was so scared I ran out of the room to go for help when two men staying here happened to pull up in their van right then. I asked them to help me get Jon to the hospital. I would have called you, but I thought I'd better wait and see how badly Jonathan was hurt."

James pressed the bridge of his nose between his thumb and forefinger. What an incredible storyteller she was. The lies slipped off her tongue like an ice cream cone melting on a hot day.

"So you and Jon are at the hospital right now?" he inquired, as innocently as he could.

Wait for it . . .

"Well, no. I was following the men in their van when they pulled over. Jonathan awoke and insisted they stop, so he could get in my car when they explained what happened to him. I wanted to drive him to the hospital myself. But he told me he felt fine and since we'd waited this long to have our talk he didn't want to do it in such a public place."

"Okay, so you're not at the hospital. Just exactly where are you and Jon?"

"I'd rather not say until we've had a chance to be on our own for a while."

"I'm afraid you don't have a choice, Kim."

"Who says?" she demanded.

"The authorities. You see, they think you killed Jonathan."

"What?!"

"It's true. The police have been to our house questioning everyone. I'm sure you can guess it didn't take the cops long to understand how you feel about Jon. They don't have a very good image of you right now considering that no one in the house can stand you. I was your only ally, Kim and you blew that. Give up this vendetta you've got going. You can't win. Bring my brother safely back."

"No! No! No!" she screamed into the phone. "Jonathan's never paid for what he did to me. Now it's finally my chance to make him suffer."

James knew he was losing his edge and would have to use something else to pressure her.

"You think he hasn't suffered enough knowing he was responsible for having Gage beaten?

New Beginnings
Olivia Claire High

You made my entire family pay for whatever our sins were against you when you nearly killed my mother," he choked out.

"You're wasting your time if you think you can put the blame on me for your mother's illness. I think you're forgetting I wasn't anywhere near her when she got sick."

"Only because you knew you didn't have to be with me foolishly falling in with your diabolical plans. I found out the so-called natural herb you tricked me into giving her was in actuality arsenic. The police will want to question you about that."

"Why? You and Carol are the ones who gave it to her," Kim reminded him in a cold voice.

He felt bile rise in his throat. "So you admit it was arsenic."

"I'm not admitting anything."

"I'll tell the police you were the source."

"You can't prove that."

"My family already has thanks to your dad. He found some of the herb at your house after Gage called and told him about my mother," James said and prayed she really did have a stash there. "You're also forgetting that you were in Charo's room when you took Jon. You have too many strikes against you. Don't compound it by hurting him. Either tell me where Jon is, or bring him to the inn and I'll meet you there."

Sweat broke out on his brow and his heart was pounding so hard it felt like it would burst from his chest. She hadn't hung up, but she wasn't talking, either.

"What do you say, Kim? Do I get my brother back?"

He could hear her practically hyperventilating and pushed home his final argument.

"Or do you go to prison?"

Jonathan breathed deeply drawing air into his lungs and did his best to ignore the pain caused by the ropes digging into him. They'd been tight before, but now the cords were practically cutting off his circulation. He knew it was because he'd been scooting the chair across the floor trying to reach what looked to be the largest weak spot in the wall.

He planned to heave himself against the area and hope the weight of his body would make the decaying boards break away. Maybe someone would see him if he could get outside. He also hoped falling through the wall might loosen his ropes and enable him to wiggle out of the chair.

Jonathan admitted as plans went this was pretty pitiful, but it was the best he could come up with right now. He knew he had to hurry before Kim and her gruesome twosome returned. He was hurting, but considering how much she hated him he had a feeling he was going to be hurting a whole lot more before she was finished extracting her revenge.

The thought of that made his throat clog with fear. His body was awash in sweat. Rivulets ran down his face, burning his eyes, and dripping off his chin. He continued to scoot toward his goal determined not to give up even while he cringed as the ropes pulled tighter, and the chair legs scraped over the uneven floor.

He stopped when he heard the unmistakable sound of an engine. Was it Kim returning? He'd vowed earlier that he wouldn't give her the satisfaction of begging for mercy. But sitting here completely vulnerable and remembering how Gage's body looked after his beating, Jon began to tremble as apprehension rose to a new terrifying level.

He held his breath when Kim entered the barn through a side door. His eyes followed her as she ambled over to him glaring with so much hatred he now understood what people meant when they said *if looks could kill he'd be dead.* Adrenaline pumped through his veins. He watched, horrified as her hand came from behind her back to reveal a thick leather strap.

Whack!

The strap struck against his cheek with a surprising force he wouldn't have expected from someone so small. He gasped as pain turned his face to fire. Whack! The leather flew through the air and exploded against his other cheek clipping the corner of his mouth and splitting his bottom lip. Two hits from a woman, and he was quivering like jelly. Was this just a preliminary to what she had in store for him next? Jonathan started to scream out an apology for what he'd done to her hoping Kim wouldn't continue to hurt him. Or heaven forbid, turn her brutal friends on him.

His head jerked toward the sound of male voices. Two men came through the door. One carried a knife in his hand. Jonathan lowered his chin to his chest and began to weep.

Chapter Twenty-eight

Kim raised the strap in the air again.

"Enough!" James shouted, and raced across the room to wrench the heavy strip of leather from her hands. "I agreed I'd let you have two hits, but that's all."

She twisted her mouth into an ugly sneer before she backed away, and James turned to the man standing silently by his side.

"Jacob, please cut my brother free."

"Yes, sir," he said, and immediately began slicing through the ropes with the knife he'd carried into the building.

Jonathan couldn't stop crying.

James grabbed Kim by the shoulder when she started to walk away.

"Take a good long look. You've turned my brother into a broken down sniveling mess. He's bruised and bleeding. Is that what you wanted? Are you done now?" James said, firing the questions at her in rapid order. "Have you finally had your revenge?"

"Not even close, but I suppose it'll have to do, since it's the only way I can keep you from turning me over to the cops. He'd be a lot more bloodied if I had my way."

"My God, you really are a vindictive monster. And to think I loved you."

"Well, there's no accounting for taste, is there? I actually thought I wanted to be with Jon."

What she didn't reveal was how disgusted she was by Jonathan's cowardly behavior, and how shocked she was by this new, unexpected toughness in James. Kim stood there staring dispassionately at Jonathan, as each rope was cut and fell away from his body. A cruel glow lit up her eyes when he collapsed to his knees and had to be helped outside to the car. James motioned for her to get into the front seat while Jacob got in the back with Jonathan and offered him a bottle of water along with a handkerchief to hold against his split lip.

"Is.. . Charo . . . all right?" Jonathan asked in a halting voice.

"She's fine. Holland took her to the house."

Kim sniffed. "One big happy family."

"Which you wouldn't know anything about," James said before addressing Jonathan again. "How are you doing?"

"Okay I guess, if you don't count the fact that my face is throbbing, and the rest of my body feels like I've been run over by a train."

"You'll feel better once we get you home and some proper treatment."

Kim shot him a sharp look.

"What do you mean? You said you'd take me back to the inn."

"I lied. That's something you should understand."

"What do you hope to gain by taking me to your house?"

"You have some people you need to do some apologizing to."

"You never said anything about that when I agreed to tell you where Jonathan was. You tricked me," she accused, working into her usual fury.

"That's rich coming from somcone who wouldn't know the truth if it was rammed down your throat. You insisted on having Jonathan's apology. Now it's your turn to reciprocate."

"Like hell. I'll jump out of this car first before I go back to that crazy maze of a house."

"Be my guest. The door's unlocked," James said without easing up on the accelerator.

Her brows lifted.

"Well, well, it seems my spineless husband has finally found some backbone." She clapped her hands a couple of times. "I can't wait to see your second act."

"I'm glad to hear it because you're going to have a front row seat."

Kim sat at the bar perched on a barstool, as the family stared at her. She saw that they'd even brought Jamie to join the group. Her eyes shifted to where Gage and Holland sat with their chairs close to each other. Those two were obviously more involved than she realized if Gage was allowing her to sit in on this family summit conference, or whatever the devil they were all up to. James said he brought her here to apologize. It appeared he expected her to do it in front of an audience.

Well, no way was she about to grovel to any of these people. Kim leaned back on the stool, resting her elbows on the edge of the bar. She pretended to yawn. Several more seconds elapsed without anyone speaking. All those eyes staring at her and the continued silence was making her feel tense. She sat up straight again and glared back.

"What is this little gathering supposed to be? Shoot out at OK Corral? Last meeting for the condemned? Should I phone my lawyer? Call out the cavalry?" she rattled off in an effort to let them know she wasn't intimidated by having to face them on her own.

Gage stood and walked over to stand behind his mother's chair drawing Kim's eyes to them.

"Look at the people here, Kim. We all share something in common because of you."

"What? That you aren't going to be on my Christmas gift list this year?" she drawled, as her eyes swept over them all with searing contempt.

"A sharp tongue to match your sharp wit, but neither will be able to help you now. Perhaps a quick inventory might freshen your memory as to why I've assembled us together."

He touched his mother's shoulders.

"Poisoned at your request."

He pointed to James and Holland.

"Drugged by you."

His hand reached out to include Jonathan and then himself.

"Beaten to satisfy your thirst for revenge."

He walked over and returned a toy Jamie dropped.

"Your son made ill because you switched formulas. And let's not forget the nannies and how you spiked their tea."

He walked to stand in front of her making her shrink back.

"Get away from me."

"You've been a busy girl, Kim."

"So what do you want from me? An apology? Fine. All right, I'm sorry. Satisfied?"

"I don't know about the others, but I feel as though I've just been told to go to hell. Your apology didn't sound sincere because you don't mean it. I actually hadn't expected any real remorse on your part, but I wanted to give you the opportunity to prove otherwise."

She slid off the barstool.

"Then I guess we're done with this little party. I'll be going back to my dad's now."

Gage wrapped his fingers around her arm, as she started to saunter away. He applied just enough pressure to let her know he wasn't going to let her go. She looked down at his fingers before raising her eyes to give him a cold stare.

"Get your hands off me," she ground out through clenched teeth, as she tried to jerk free. "I told you I'm leaving. I don't want to be around any of you for another second. You make me sick. I hate this place. I've always hated it, and when I left I never intended to come back."

"You will be leaving, but you won't be going to your father's house."

"I'll go anywhere I damn well please."

"Not this time. Listen carefully to what I'm about to say to you, Kim. You're going to have to make a decision, or it will be made for you. Either you agree to go to a mental health facility and stay there until the medical people deem you stable enough to be released, or you . . . "

"I'm not going to any nuthouse," she burst in anger. "So you can all just forget that idea."

"You didn't let me finish. The alternative is that you will be arrested, and most likely be sent to prison."

"Dream on. James tried to pull that on me. There's no way my dad will let that happen."

The door opened drawing everyone's attention, as Winslow stood there staring at Kim. He gave the appearance of a man who'd been defeated in a painful personal battle. Kim tugged at Gage's hand again, and this time he let her go. She ran over to her father.

"Daddy! Thank God you've come," she made herself cry and wrapped her arms around his neck. "These people are trying to crucify me. Please get me out of here and take me home with you."

He reached up and pulled her arms down.

"Not this time."

Holland snuggled against Gage's side in his bed that night thinking about the ugly scene they'd gone through with Kim. If ever anyone doubted the woman needed psychiatric help, they would have only needed to witness her behavior. This ended up being especially true for her father. She went completely out of her head, when Winslow agreed she needed counseling and he wouldn't be taking her home with him.

She started pounding on his chest with her fists while hurling one curse after another berating him for being a worthless father. He rocked backward, struggling to defend himself while obviously not wanting to hurt her. Gage yanked her away just in time to keep her from clawing her nails down Winslow's face.

Remembering Winslow's horrified expression made Holland shudder now.

"Are you cold?" Gage said, pulling her closer to share his naked warmth.

"I'm not cold. Something is bothering me. I'm sure you'd rather not talk about it, but I won't be able to sleep until we do. I'm sorry," she said when he breathed out a resigned sigh.

Gage pulled them both up to lean against the headboard before snapping on the bedside lamp. "All right, court's in session."

"I can't help feeling sorry for Winslow the way Kim turned on him. The expression on his face reminded me of someone who'd just been pushed off a cliff by someone you love. I shudder to think what damage she'd have done to the poor man if you hadn't stepped in and stopped her."

"That poor man, as you seem to think of him is partly to blame for his daughter's behavior. He never denied her anything. The more she demanded, the more he gave. He continued to make excuses for her every time she did something wrong. Rather than accept the fact that he helped create the monster she'd become, he continued to feed her vicious appetite. Winslow should have gotten her into counseling years ago, but he turned a blind eye."

"I'm not condoning his misguided parenting and certainly not what he allowed to happen to you. I'm just saying I feel sad for him that his only child turned out to show so little love and appreciation after all he'd done for her. He did what he thought was best, Gage."

"Best for him? Or best for her?" He shrugged. "It doesn't matter. All I care about is that she's out of this house. That's the best news my family has had in a long time concerning Kim."

"I can understand, and I feel the same way. I have another question. Why didn't you report Winslow's part in your kidnapping? I would have thought you'd want some kind of payback."

"Technically neither Jonathan nor I were kidnapped."

Holland let out an indignant sniff. "You most certainly were."

"Not really. Think about it. Jon faked his abduction, and I volunteered to stay in his place."

"Oh. I never thought of it like that."

"Neither did Winslow. I agreed not to report what happed to the authorities if he stayed quiet about Jon's involvement in Kim's drugging activities."

"What about your mother's arsenic poisoning? Surely you want Kim punished for that."

Gage's fingers tightened on her shoulder for a moment.

"Same situation. I would have exposed James and Carol's roles in Kim's scheme, however innocent."

"Always the protector," she said and started to kiss him, but stopped when he cursed.

"I just had an ugly revelation."

"About what?"

He grimaced.

"Myself. You called me a protector."

"Well, you are."

"Because I'm trying to do everything I can to cover for my brothers' screw-ups? Jesus, I'm no better than Winslow."

Holland heard the disgust in his voice and moved, so she could face Gage.

"You are not like Winslow," she denied indignantly. "He spent years allowing Kim to have her own way even when she hurt people, whereas you've been endeavoring to guide both your brothers into becoming more responsible. It's not your fault they've taken so long to mature."

He flicked a finger down her cheek.

"My little cheerleader."

"Well, it's true; and your patience is finally paying off. James said he's filing for divorce and will request full custody of Jamie. He told me he rues the day he didn't listen to you sooner when you warned him about Kim. I've seen a big change in him just in the last few hours. I think you know Jonathan really is sick with guilt for the way you suffered on his behalf."

"I'm sure he expected me to say everything is okay and I forgive him, but I can't let him off so easily. His involvement with Kim started her rampage with some very serious consequences.

He needs to deal with that. He must learn to think first what will happen in the long term before he jumps into any kind of situation to bring him what he wants."

Holland nodded. "And that we can't always have what we want. Surely things will be better now that Kim's gone."

"It's going to take time. Was that all you needed to say?"

"That's it. Thank you for being so patient with me. Shall we try to go to sleep now?"

"Not just yet. I planned to wait until morning to discuss something with you, but as long as we're talking I'd like to get it said now. I should have dealt with the situation a long time ago."

She pursed her lips.

"That sounds ominous."

"That depends on how you look at it. I'm going to get Mother out of this house for good."

"How? I told you she plans on dying here."

"She can't if it's not here. I tried to get her away once before. I won't give up this time."

"How can the house be gone?"

"How does any structure cease to exist?"

"Are you saying you're actually going to tear down your home?"

"Stone by stone; and with my bare hands if I need to."

Holland let out a shocked breath.

"You can't be serious."

"Do I sound like I'm joking?"

"No, but shouldn't your family have a say in such a drastic decision?"

"This place ceased to be a home years ago when my mother kept begging me to add more rooms. It hasn't helped matters with all the trauma Kim has caused. She may be gone, but you can't change the terrible things she did here. I don't want my mother living in a place with those kinds of memories. The more anxiety she suffers, the less chance she has of being cured."

"What about your brothers?"

"It's time they leave the nest and start building a future on their own. I'm not a despot, Holland. I did discuss it with them, and they want her away from here as much as I do."

"But completely destroying it seems like a big waste. Why don't you just sell the house?"

"Who'd want to buy a place like this? Even if I did get a buyer, the fact that the house still stands might lure my mother back to relive all the rotten things that's happened here."

"Which brings me back to my question of how are you going to get her to leave?"

"She'll be put under a doctor's care, and as much as I'm sick of people being drugged, she'll have to be sedated. I want her out of this house and away from this area entirely."

"I suppose you're right. Do you have a place in mind where you want her to live?"

"Yes. The owner agreed to sell me the house on Lanai. He says he hardly ever uses it and was only too happy to have my mother live there."

"I hate to be pessimistic, but do you think she'll suddenly get over her agoraphobia?"

"It won't be sudden, and it won't be easy. Her panic attacks will have to be dealt with using medication, behavior therapy, and anything else the people I'm consulting can suggest. I made a halfhearted attempt years ago, but I didn't follow through. I'm not going to give up this time. I want her to have a normal life. That's why I have to get her completely away from here."

"It's going to be a huge adjustment, but living on Lanai will be good. It's so peaceful."

"I'm glad you agree. I'll send Colleen, but I'd like you to go with them."

"Me? Oh Gage, I want to help, but I'm not sure if I . . . "

"Please."

Holland didn't like to hear him begging her. He gave so much of himself and asked so little in return. But would she be the right person to help his mother overcome years of isolation?

Chapter Twenty-nine

Thanks to James and Carol, Gage's original plan to tear down his house never came to fruition. She mentioned how many people in the area, including herself who would be out of a job. That's when James on a sudden burst of genius, as far as Holland was concerned came up with the idea to turn the house into a mental health facility. That way all the people employed for cooking, cleaning, yard, and maintenance work would still be employed. Jacob was put in charge of overseeing that part of the staff, much as he'd been doing for the last several years.

James also came up with the idea to name the clinic after his father. Thus, the Jamison Howard Rehabilitation Center became a reality. Holland wondered if it helped Marguerite knowing it would now be a place of refuse for people with mental illness, rather than the prison it had become for her. The fact that the facility was named for her late husband did please her.

Gage ended up being the one in charge of seeing the old home be altered to fit codes, permits obtained, and regulations followed before it could be open to accept patients. While they had the people already available to do the upkeep, he had the task of interviewing and hiring the medical staff and setting up a board of directors. He'd worked on the project for months while carrying out his other business responsibilities.

Thinking of the facility made Holland's thoughts wander to Kim. According to Winslow, his daughter may never be released because of her increasing instability. Holland knew he was hurting, but she was happy to have Kim out of her life. She knew Gage's family felt the same – certainly no one more than James and Jonathan.

James divorced Kim and moved to another town where Gage put him in charge of managing one of the family's smaller business concerns. Carol went with him to help care for Jamie, but Holland wouldn't be surprised if there ended up being wedding bells in their future.

Charo accepted Jonathan back into her life, and they'd married. He took over a Howard business in Mexico where he and Charo now lived with their newly adopted baby girl. Gage felt Jon still needed to do penance for providing Kim with drugs, so Jonathan now spent several hours a month helping people in a free rehab drug clinic.

Holland knew Gage took a big risk putting his brothers in charge of these businesses, but she could see that vote of confidence had definitely helped them grow up. Gage had been visiting those sites on a monthly basis teaching his brothers how to handle their management responsibilities, but she knew he eventually hoped to pare the trips down to a few times a year.

Gage wanted happiness for his family, especially his mother. But Marguerite had suffered more than any of them in the transition. Holland wanted to give up several times after witnessing the tormented woman fighting her inner demons. The crying, the depression, and the panic attacks looked like they were draining the life out of her.

Colleen was more used to this behavior than Holland, but there were days that even she became exhausted trying to deal with her employer's phobia. Just living in a house with so many windows that brought the outside in was sheer torture for Marguerite. She would beg them to draw the drapes and insist that she had to stay in her darkened bedroom.

Part of the treatment was to take things one day at a time, so Holland and Colleen along with the people Gage hired as consultants, steeled themselves and continued to work with their patient. Holland hated to think of Marguerite that way, but in reality that's what she was. Her agoraphobia was an illness and it had stolen too many years from the fragile woman's life.

Holland would never tell Gage because she didn't want to lay that burden on him, but there were many times she'd come close to calling it quits and telling him to get someone else to help Marguerite. Then she'd remember how he told her he wouldn't give up like he had before. She knew he did this because he loved his mother, and he wanted what was best for her.

Holland was almost ashamed to admit that she resented him for putting her in this position. Easy for him to say he wouldn't give up. He wasn't here when his mother had one of her panic attacks.

New Beginnings
Olivia Claire High

Where was he when she lay awake at night in his mother's room worrying that the woman might try to kill herself? She wasn't a medical person. She'd never been around anyone who suffered from this condition. Why had she agreed to help Gage?

The answer always came to her loud and clear. She came, and she stayed, because she loved the man so much that she'd probably live here forever holding his mother's hand if it would please him. She also reminded herself that Gage had dealt with his mother's illness for years without complaint. He visited as often as he could, and that helped Holland's resolve to stay on.

But then he'd leave, and once again Holland wondered how she would endure staying and watching his mother suffer without having Gage here to lean on. Holland didn't have any idea how much she would miss Gage when she agreed to take on the challenge of coming to Lanai to live with his mother.

She despaired of seeing a happy ending to the situation until that breakthrough moment, when Marguerite opened the door and voluntarily took her first step outside the house. The first walk on the beach, trembling, as she clung to Holland and Colleen, as they encouraged her to go just a little further each day. The first ride in a car. That first trip into town to shop for food and seeing strangers going about their lives.

All these firsts were counted like golden coins being tossed into a chest to be admired like anyone would appreciate any other treasure. Holland savored each moment when Marguerite would invite her to go for a walk. Granted, Gage's mother may never have the courage to venture off the island, but at least she wasn't relegated to being inside a house with painted foliage on the walls and iron bars on the windows. Instead, she had real outside air to breathe and actual flora and fauna to see and touch in their natural surroundings.

Finally, one day after they'd been on the island for several months, Marguerite turned to Holland and told her she should go and visit her family. Holland almost cried, realizing this meant Marguerite was saying in her own way she would accept her life here without having to cling to Holland every day.

Gage met her at the airport, where he'd whisked her off to the condo he'd bought far away from his former home. Holland walked into the apartment and saw there wasn't much furniture. He explained the condo was a temporary residence because he thought the woman he married would want to help him pick out the house and furnishings to fit her own tastes.

And would she like to be that woman?

They'd married in her parents' backyard with all her family and Gage's in attendance, with the exception of Marguerite. Holland wouldn't ask that of her, and neither would Gage. It was enough that she got to see the ceremony thanks to the ingenious world of electronics.

Epilogue

Holland leaned down to where Gage was lying on a lounger and nipped him gently on one bare shoulder. He opened his eyes and looked at her.

"Ouch, that hurt. Do it again."

She laughed.

"Maybe later. Time to get up. Your mom and Colleen will be back any minute. They went to town. Marguerite wanted to get some fresh fruit for lunch."

"It's music to my ears when you talk about my mother going into town."

Holland sat down on the edge of the lounger.

"She's come a long way this last year."

He pulled her down, so she could lie next to him.

"It's been quite a year at that."

"Much better than this time last year, that's for sure," she said, snuggling against him.

Holland was still in awe every time she saw how different Marguerite was now compared to when she'd first met her. She still had to be carefully monitored for any sudden panic attacks. But the medication did help; and the fact that her depression was under such better control had changed her outlook in so many positive ways.

She'd even begun to take part in some of the social activities on the island.

Holland's mouth tilted in a smile when she heard Gage's soft snore. She knew how tired he was after months of having so many people and work related issues demanding much of his time. Not to mention the frequent flying trips he'd made here to visit.

They'd arrived late last night, and he rose early this morning to jog. They planned to arrive sooner, but a last minute business concern necessitated delaying their departure. Shaken out of her reverie by the sound of a car driving up, Holland gave Gage a gentle nudge. He lifted his eyelids and gave her a sleepy grin.

"Hello. Fancy seeing you here," he mumbled.

"I happened to be in the neighborhood. Sorry to wake you again, but your mother is back, and I know she'll want us to share lunch with her."

"We also need to remind her that this is supposed to be our belated honeymoon."

"You needn't worry about that. She told me this morning she made arrangements for us to stay at another beach house, so we'll have our private time. She's going to reveal her plan at lunch. Try to act surprised when she tells you."

Gage stood up and held a hand over his mouth to cover a yawn. Holland watched as a ray of sunlight suddenly glistened off his wedding band. She smiled, thinking of her own wedding ring and those symbols of the love and commitment they'd made to each other.

"I am surprised. I thought she'd be upset if we didn't stay here with her."

"Your mother may have been a widow for a long time, but she still believes in romance."

Marguerite chose that moment to call to them in a cheerful voice.

"Lunch is ready. Come inside, you two lovebirds."

He smiled.

"This is the new beginning and new life that I wanted for her."

"I know, and speaking of new beginnings and new life, what would you say about us starting a new life ourselves. . . as in making a baby?"

Gage grinned. "I can't think of anything I'd rather do."

He swung her up into his arms and started singing, '*You Are My Sunshine*', as he carried her into the house.

Other Books by
Olivia Claire High

The Crystal Angel

The Rose Cottage

Dreams~ Shadows of the Night

A Stranger's Eyes

The Wolf Deception

Kari's Destiny

The Black Feather